GREEN WITH ENVY

Lisa L Whitmore

CONTENTS

This book is dedicated to the ones who left; you are a survivor, not a victim. And to the ones who stay, may the Lord provide you the strength to find your voice and know you are not alone.

MOVING IN

Charleston ... who would have thought such a place was the fresh start I needed. Standing on King Street, looking up at the recently restored building that bestowed my newest home, the torturous heat of July mirrored the hell I had left in South Bend, Indiana.

Carrying the bags of groceries into the tiny kitchen, Kayla, my roommate, could be heard in the opposite room, shuffling through empty boxes. Standing on my tiptoes, I placed the staples away in our empty cabinets. We had only arrived a few days earlier and were working at an attempt to put our lives together in our tiny apartment. An empty cardboard box colliding with the others in the hallway filled the quietness of our apartment. Hollering to me, "Amber we should get out of this apartment," she suggested, the sound of tape ripping through the thin walls, "This move has been a hell of a lot of work," the squealing of mattress springs hollered, as she threw herself down on her bed. Kayla always had a flare for the dramatic, "Ugh, Amber! Hello?" impatience in her voice from my lack of response, "What do you think? You up for it?"

Finding a box of kitchen utensils, pulling the draw open, the clang of silver sounded as I tossed them in, in no particular order. Until I could get to the store for some organizing tools, this would have to do. Blowing my recently cut brunette hair from my eyes, "Maybe," I reluctantly replied. My head was reeling with such a big move in a short amount of time, but it held a promise of a new life, new beginnings, a necessary change of pace. With graduation from Notre Dame and a degree in Journalism under my belt, it wasn't long before I landed the job at *Lowcountry Magazine*, a small but respected local publishing. The job was entry-level with room for growth; a good starting point that I was looking forward to.

Though we have only been here a few days, Charleston is a place for refocus and somewhere for me to clear my head; to overcome the torment South Bend left me with. While Kayla was excited about the journey of us being roomies together, not everyone was thrilled with such an excursion. My parents, god help them, were not supportive of such a move. I'm not sure why they even cared; they never really supported anything I have ever done in my life.

Kayla Marks was probably the only one who stayed around and supported me through every facet of life. A pretty, petite woman, with blonde hair and blue eyes, she had been my rock of support through more than most would stick around for. After being accepted at the College of Charleston for her Master's Degree in Art Education, she begged me to come along. She actually found the opening at the magazine and practically stood over me until I applied. It didn't take long to find out I was hired, but my uncertainty left me to question if leaving South Bend was the right answer. Convincing me was hard, but given my last few traumatic months, moving away would be the best thing. At the moment, I still didn't know if it was the right answer. South Bend was the Devil's stomping ground in my book, the Devil playing his card each minute at my insecurities.

She entered the kitchen and plopping down in the chair, not looking up from her phone, "Umm, hello? Are you even listening?" I quickly realized I had left her question hanging in the air, "So, are we going to hit the town or what?" she queried, still not looking up from whatever distraction she was viewing, "It's Wednesday and we haven't done anything since we arrived." Finally glancing up and looking around the room at the still sealed boxes, she retorted in frustration, "Ugh, all we have done is unpack!" rolling her head back in disgust, "I'm sick of looking at brown cardboard," her attention returning to scrolling through her phone.

Throwing the cooking utensils in the crock, caving at her request, "I guess...where to?" Knowing Kayla, she had already concocted a plan for the evening. It would most likely involve a night on the town into the wee hours of the morning, daylight. Grabbing the counter, I thought back to the last time I had gone out and couldn't remember when. You would think with recently graduating college, it would have been a call for celebration but South Bend controlled that timeline. Squeezing my fingers into the granite fold of the counter, I swallowed my anxiety, allowing the light of this to be a step in the right direction to shine through.

"Well...I ran into our new neighbor, Keith...really hot by the way," *here we go.* Kayla had a knack for finding a hot guy and sorting out plans before confiding in anyone else, "and he said there is this awesome new nightclub called *ENVY*, that just opened about a month ago." Placing her phone on the table, her blue eyes reflecting excitement in my direction, "He suggested we check it out. It's just a few blocks up the road," her voice slightly higher pitched than a moment ago.

Tension grew in my shoulders at the thought of an evening out, "Sounds good," I said doing my best to hide the anxiety growing in the pit of my stomach. Something must have registered across my face, as Kayla was quick on her feet, her hand on my shoulder.

The tension slowly eased under her touch, "Hey! If you don't want to, we don't have to. I just thought," she returned quietly.

Turning to face her, doing my best to relax, "It's been so long Kayla," I started, as a lonely tear ran down my cheek.

Brushing what little hair remained off my shoulder, she said quietly, "Hey, I didn't mean to upset you! I just thought..."

"No," I interrupted her quickly, "This has just been a little overwhelming is all," wiping the tear away, "We can go. It will do me some good," as I turned back towards the boxes, even trying to convince myself this was something that I needed. The first step in escaping hell is to lock what was there away. Staying coward in my apartment was only going to allow the embers to continue to glow.

"You know letting loose may be what you need to step forward, Amber," Kayla remarked as her hand left my shoulder to return to her phone. Her words struck a chord, sending a harmonic note that chimed the truth. There was so much stress and anxiety built up, music had a way to dig into one's soul and allow the torment of restraint to unwind. The idea wasn't a bad one and my inner self finally caved, "Let me throw something on," I said reluctantly, leaving the half-emptied box in the kitchen, walking in the direction of my room. "Yes," Kayla exclaimed with an extended s-sound, as she stood and hustled off to her room to get ready.

Entering the tiny room, the smell of new paint was still evident on the walls. Boxes were lined along the opposite wall, carefully stacked to not block the window to the outside world; an easy escape route if needed.

Our apartment was recently remodeled, although some parts could still use some updating. It wasn't the greatest looking, but it held appeal. Walking over to the double paned window, the view reflected the park across the intersection of Calhoun and King. The bustling street below, evident of tourist season, satisfied my love of people watching. The waning hours of July evident as the shadows of neighboring buildings curtained the brick across the way.

Pushing away from the windowsill, turning back towards the room, a heavy sigh escaped me as my eyes scanned the room of boxes. Walking to the boxes by my closet, I rummaged through finally settling on a black lace top that was classy enough to wear anywhere. Finding my skinny jeans and a pair of black heels to accompany my top, I made my way to my mirror and began tousling my shorter brunette strands around, trying to find the right part. Just a few weeks ago, I had the longest locks of hair around, but fresh starts call for new looks. Settling on something that looked decent, I coated it with hairspray, trying to keep it still. Finishing the look with my black pearls and matching earrings, I admired my final appearance in the mirror, still unsure if a night out was the answer. Quashing the anxiety down, on a quick heel, I headed out to meet Kayla in the living room.

Upon entering, Kayla was already seated on the couch, her nose back to her phone. Reaching the end table, the clank of my keys caught her attention as her eyes lifted to do a once over, "Girl, you look great! You sure about this?"

"Yes, now can we go before I change my mind?" a slight whine escaping but still doing my best to keep my anxiety at bay. I'm not sure why I felt so anxious about going out, but when hell has reigned for so long, it's hard to escape. "If I didn't know you better, I'd say you were thinking of getting lucky?" Kayla winked at me.

"KAYLA MARKS!" I snapped, "Don't even!" perhaps a bit too harshly, knowing full well that finding someone, or even looking, was the last thing on my mind. My heart pounded at the minor panic attack of even the consideration. Kayla did have a knack for romance, and seemingly was always looking for a man or some sort of relationship to fill an empty void she seemed to maintain, but she knew my focus was on the new job and getting used to this city. Charleston wasn't that big, but a welcomed change and light that would hopefully fill the darkness that consumed me. Indiana held a vice around my body; I had to break free from its grasp and this move was the key to, hopefully, opening the lock.

Raising her hands in apology, "Sorry! You're right! Let's just have fun tonight?" Rising from the couch, Kayla was wearing a simple dip neck, red sleeveless shirt, black leather skirt, and heels. She had the ass and knew how to work it; which was obvious, it wasn't hiding behind that skirt. "Ready?" she asked, tussling her long, blond hair over her shoulder, shuffling her phone into her purse.

Swallowing down my nerves, I said, "As I'll ever be."

Leaving the hollows of our apartment, we made our way into the busyness of the narrow sidewalks of the early evening Charleston crowd. The city bustled with throngs of people from every walk of the earth: the eager young couple evidently on their first date, finer dressed married couples heading to the latest restaurant opening, and young college girls laughing about the latest gossip column in *Us Magazine*. Secluded in the lush greenery of the city sat the busy campus of the College of Charleston and among the cobblestone streets, finer restaurants boasted a palate of tastes to be indulged in. Not to be outdone by the vast historical sense it possessed, the robust harbor bordered its streets along the outer edges.

Sweat pearled on my neckline as the muggy July heat tempered my skin. Kayla and I walked along the uneven sidewalks of King Street, finally settling upon a small deli just around the corner from our apartment. Deciding it best to grab a bite to eat, it was a little early to get to the club. Entering the deli, "I'll grab us some food. Will you find us a table?" Kayla called back, pointing to an area near the window. Filled mostly with college students and a few late afternoon business associates, I found a table nearest the door, feeling it the safest option. Kayla greeted the hostess and placed our orders.

The atmosphere of the café boasted modern day accents in its decorum. Settled in a historical building, it had been remodeled with six small red booths, several café tables, and about ten seating areas throughout the bar. It was a quiet atmosphere, with a subtle hint of conversation looming in the air. Based on the number of college students in the small area, it was evident this was a local favorite for small gatherings and study times.

Glancing over at Kayla to find her back on her phone, I realized I hadn't turned my phone on since we had arrived. When leaving Indiana, I decided it best to cut communication until I could get myself settled and my affairs in order. Plus, I didn't want an easy way to be tracked. Finding the saltshaker, I slid it across the table between my hands, trying to pass the time. My observations flowed through the room when my attention fell upon a wire newspaper rack holding the day's local paper. Odd to see news still in print in today's ever-growing advancements of technology; the feature photo caught my eye with a headline reading *Ashton's Final Two Home Games*.

Sports journalism was never my forte when it came to writing, but the fascination of seeing words in print never got old. Squinting to make out the article, it read about someone named Tristan Ashton playing two final home games with the Charleston Sharks before retiring his glove for good. Accompanying the article was an image of the person I presumed to be the man from the article. The image showed someone standing on a pitcher's mound in a Charleston Shark's uniform. He stood in the typical pitching stance of one foot off the ground as he prepared to release the ball. The image made it difficult to make out the details of Ashton's face as the angle was off, but it reflected a man of strength; strong arms, a vine tattoo, and well-toned body that his uniform, I'm sure, did no justice. As Kayla would say, *he had baseball arms*...not that I would know what baseball arms were; jocks were never really my thing.

"Hey?" someone said startling me, not realizing that I hadn't brought my attention away from the wired newsstand. Kayla set down my sandwich, "You look pretty flushed, are you alright?" unaware that my skin had blushed in the few moments of quiet observation, "You've been on edge all day," her voice sincere and concerned.

Forcing my attention to her, reaching and unwrapping my sandwich, "Sorry," taking the first bite, "guess I am still adjusting to the heat and this new life. I still question whether it was right," a slight tone of uncertainty could be heard.

Grabbing my free hand with hers, she gently squeezed, providing me the reassurance I relied on anymore. Taking a bite of her sandwich, she changed subjects, "Are you at least excited about tonight?" pausing momentarily, hesitant to speak, "We can always go home. I just thought it would be fun to get out, see Charleston. We've been moving in for two days, and really need a break. I know with everything that has happened, it's probably overwhelming you," pausing momentarily, "Damn it! I jumped the gun again," letting out a huge sigh, her lips pouting into a duckbill.

"No, you didn't jump the gun," I insisted, trying to pep her back up, "You are right. We need a break away from the apartment, time to refocus and gather our thoughts. It will do me good getting out. I've spent too much of my life cooped up and hidden like some doll stuffed in an attic. I really do need to let my hair down and have a good time. And who better to do that with?" winking over at Kayla, giving her a sly smile. Her persona switching from concerned to excite, she turned back to her phone as I stole a glance back at the paper. Curiosity stormed my thoughts as to the hidden features of the man below the ball cap...*I bet he is gorgeous*, my mind ignoring my need to stay away from men. Shaking my unwanted thoughts of the mysterious man away, Kayla looked up from her phone, her eyes following my glance over to where I was staring. *No response.* She didn't see the photo and went back to whatever she looked at on her phone. I really wasn't in the mood to reflect on my current indulgence. Knowing her, she would put us on an escapade to find him regardless of my wants. I actually doubted we would even run into him.

Taking another bite of sandwich, I concluded that I needed to refocus my attention. I didn't move to Charleston in hunt of a relationship; it was far from what I wanted or even needed right now. My gut churned at the thought of starting something like that. Charleston was a new beginning that didn't need to include a boy or man, however you wanted to look at it.

Kayla finally stuffed her phone away and we chatted about various things we wanted to do with the apartment. Although Kayla and I had been friends for a long time, our tastes in decorating differed. She was more of a bold personality, as I liked simple and elegant. "What about red in the kitchen?" she asked, popping a potato chip in her mouth, "I really like the red tones of this café," her observations settling over the interior decorum.

"I could see that. It would be a nice contrast to a simple living room, with some browns tied in," I agreed, shaking my head positively in response to her ideas. Despite our difference of opinions, we always seemed to come to agreement. She had always had pretty good taste in decorating, I usually just followed suit. Either way, I knew our apartment would look fabulous, no matter how it ended up.

Amber rambled on as I half listened; intruding thoughts of wonder cascaded through my imagination. I tried my best to push them away, but my journalistic mind was curious about this Ashton guy found in the local paper. Only catching snippets of conversation, Kayla rambled on about Facebook and her up-coming course load at school. Giving her an occasional nod, she didn't seem to notice my incessant daydreaming.

Finishing up the last of our dinner, the sun was settling be-hind the west skyline of Charleston, exploding into a fiery red, as shadows cast across the less crowded streets, introducing the impending darkness. Exiting the café, we briskly walked along the sidewalks, window-shopping among the late opened stores that lined the cobblestone drive. "I guess this is the way," Kayla remarked as our feet carried us. "Keith stated to head straight up King and we would make our way there. Ready for a night of fun," rubbing her elbow against mine. My eyes dragged the ground as we walked. Not looking up from my trace of each carved line, I simply nodded my head in agreement.

Even in the growing darkness, Charleston remained busy for a Wednesday night. Evening tourists strolled the streets, tak-ing in the sights and sounds of the city. Charleston was much quieter if compared to South Bend, but it was also a different atmosphere next to the large university town I had just left. A few blocks from the diner, we came across a tiny dessert place. Checking her phone, she noted that we still had some time to kill before the doors opened at *ENVY*. Deciding to indulge the local delicacies, we made our way in for some ice cream. Kayla ordering a strawberry chocolate dip, I followed behind and or-dered my favorite, mint chocolate ice cream. Making our way over to a little café table, spooning the light green mixture and placing the edge on my tongue, a rush of flavor swarmed my mouth; the mixture of mint and chocolate cooling my skin from the heat of the humid Charleston air.

"Mm m..." escaping my lips, I smiled at the delectable flavor. Kayla glancing up, just as she was placing a spoonful in her mouth, "How's your ice cream?"

"Delicious," I smiled, "yours?"

"Good, want to try some," holding her spoon out in offer. Holding up my hand in rejection, I didn't want to ruin the divine taste of this most pleasurable moment. I placed another bite in my mouth. Laughing inwardly, I couldn't remember the last time I had enjoyed something so simple. I had been sheltered way too long.

Finishing the last drop of ice cream, we stood to exit the small dessert shop, asking the waiter the direction of *ENVY.* Darkness had finally settled and the lamps that illuminated the empty streets were lit. Following the waiter's directions, we arrived at *ENVY,* which was only a short distance from our apartment. Reaching a locked side door to the club, we realized the entrance was on the south side of the building. Rounding the corner, the sound of music ricocheted off the historic brick. It was three stories high and obviously an old warehouse; the red brick slowly separating from its mortar and the windows, original, but any light that may have shown was kept dark by drapes; one window lit by a single spot light reflecting the word *ENVY.*

"Check out this crowd," Kayla voiced as we followed the line around the old building. Making it to the back, we waited anxiously to gain access to what looked to be Charleston's favorite new nightspot. "Can you believe this line?" Kayla exclaimed.

"At this rate, we'll be here all night," my lack of motivation to break the past, evident, "You sure you want to go?" I really wasn't in the mood to wait, forgetting that this evening wasn't just about me, or the fact that I needed to cut loose. Pouting, Kayla's look quickly reminded me of why we came, "Yes, please. Only if you're up for it," wrapping her hands around my forearm in a plea of acceptance.

Silently kicking myself for even saying anything, "Of course," I almost whispered, gritting my teeth. The throngs of people around us made me nervous but swallowing my pride I gave into Kayla. She had been at my side a lot lately; giving her this evening was a way for me to pay her back.

Wrapping my arms around my stomach, I shuffled my feet to put my balance on the other foot. The group of girls behind us began giggling. Glancing back, I noticed them whispering to each other and pointing in the direction behind me. Turning to see what they were pointing at, a young man walked towards the edge of the club line, his fiery red hair shining in the alternating street lamps. Standing with one hand in his jeans pocket, he stood with confidence as he laughed with a group of guys ahead of us. Kayla must have heard the giggling as well, and turned her attention in the direction of the young man. Nudging my arm, she began waving the gentleman down, "It's Keith!" almost yelling in excitement.

Keith looked away from the group he was talking to and caught the tiny wave of Kayla. Shaking the guy's hands, he walked down the line, each girl unable to stop herself from gawking over their shoulder as he passed. As his features came into the subtle light, I was surprised that Kayla would even consider him good looking. Don't get me wrong, he was very handsome, however Kayla never had a thing for redheads.

"Well don't you ladies look stunning," a smile spread across his face as he admired the blond-haired beauty on my arm. "Hey Keith," Kayla began, "This is crazy! I can't believe this line to get in!"

"Yea it is pretty crazy. The club just opened not too long ago. Hey I have an idea, but you wanna get in now?" his hands back in his pocket, looking to us for an answer. Our eyes must have gone wide in excitement, a smile of satisfaction spreading across his face! "Um, yea," we said together. "But how?" I asked from the slight shadows, "there's no way we can get through this line without cutting a bunch of people," my negative side, the one not really wanting to even entertain this night out, coming out.

"I have my connections. Follow me," he remarked. Making my way out of the crowd with Kayla, he reached his hand out, pardoning Kayla's lack of introduction, "Keith Mitchell, by the way."

"Amber Slayton," shaking his hand in return; he boasted a firm grip, but quickly turned it to his lips and kissed it in a southern way. Standing next to Keith, he was a tall, slender man with a pale complexion, not helped by his fiery red hair and freckles. Handsome with a southern charm type appeal, he dressed as if he was one of the socialites of Charleston, stalking confidence in his stride.

Smiling as he pulled his hand away, turning back to Kayla, he relayed his message to both of us, "You ladies are with *ME* tonight." Folding his arms in a way that protruded his elbows, we took the gesture to join him on his arm. Each of us curling our arms through his, Keith's confidence was even more exuberant as we got closer to him. Escorting us to the door, Keith flirted with Kayla the whole way, ignoring the thrusts of cheers and flirts in his direction as we passed. Rolling my eyes at his neverending charisma, no wonder Kayla found him dashing. He could put the flirt on in a split second and make a girl melt in the palm of his hand. It was obvious he was familiar with the ladies and what made them tick. For me, it wasn't something I followed suit with, so I wasn't likely to melt at his southerly charm.

Kayla glanced over at me excitedly as we approached the doors to *ENVY*; me responding with a relieved look, thankful we didn't have to stand in the never-ending line anymore. The grunts and jeers began growing as we reached the bodyguard. There stood a tall, clean-shaven, masculine black man, roughly six foot two, and his frame radiating bravado from his stiff stance. Wearing a black, skintight *ENVY* t-shirt that accented every muscle along his posterior chest, he towered over top of my short stature. With glasses pulled to the rim of his nose, he did a quick observation of Keith and us. Recognizing him, he nodded his head at Keith, but furrowed at our appearance.

Quickly answering the bouncer's unspoken concerns, "They're with me, Ray."

Nodding his head back, he unclipped the velvet rope, allowing us entrance into the club. "Enjoy your evening," his voice deep and gruff. Opening the heavy door to the club, the music bombarded my ear canals. Adjusting to the tempo, the heat from the bodies struck next; my mind foggy with music blaring, lights flashing all around and the crowd hot and heavy.

Feeling unsettled among the masses of people, Keith led us to the rear of the building towards a spiral stairwell. I tried my best to make conversation, but the bass of the music made it impossible to hear anything. Reaching the staircase and heading up, the upper level was encased in glass allowing a more private area for VIPS; at least that's what I assumed.

Punching a code into the keypad, we entered the upper level, the door to the encasement closing behind us, eliminating a large portion of the noise from the lower deck. Making our way to the table, I was finally able to ask my question, "So what makes you so special? How do you get prime, instant access into such a hot ticket club scene?" Reaching a plush couch and large table, Keith motioned for us to take a seat. Scooting our way around the table, "I actually know the owner. He's a buddy of mine from high school and he lets me have full VIP rights."

It was peaceful up here compared to the blaring sounds of the rest of the club. Taking in my surroundings, I found the inside had been restored to a more modern appeal, noting the owner had tried to keep most of the original pieces of the building intact, such as the stair case, windows and flooring.

The VIP lounge was housed on a raised platform that adorned six private areas encircling the upper deck of the massive warehouse building. Each area was a different color, to represent a tailored mood I assumed. Three of them faced the dance floor while the remaining lined the back wall, under the third story set of mirrored windows that resembled the old office overlook of the warehouse.

Kayla and I turned and glanced through the glass at the crowd below. Looking to each other, excitement sparkled in our eyes at the prospect of letting loose for the evening. Quickly refocusing my mind, earlier thoughts about locking myself back up in the house like a hermit surfaced. Shaking them away, I observed the swaying of bodies below us allowing excitement to nestle itself within me for the first time in a long time.

Plopping ourselves down on the plush sofa, a sudden nervousness settled over me. Diverting my eyes to the old office overlook, I couldn't help but try and shrug off the feeling of paranoia.

ENVY

F inding only my reflection, along with that of the upper level and moving bodies in the distance of the mirrors, a busty blonde, in a half shirt with a sparkling display of the word *ENVY*, approached our booth. Only about five foot with big hair, tight shorts and a sparkling belly ring, she bounced up with her bubbly personality. Big smiles adorned her features, as she recognized Keith sitting with us. Leaning over, her arms wrapping around his neck, his head quickly turning her direction, "Well hey there pretty lady! Didn't know you'd be here tonight?" Keith remarked in his obvious flirtatious way.

"Got called in last minute," popping her bright pink gum, "Who're your friends?" nodding her head at Kayla and me. Looking back at us, her hand on her hip as she placed all her weight on one leg, "Ahh, this is Kayla and Am..." snapping his fingers, trying to recall my name he only learned for the first time a few moments prior. "Amber," I called out...

"Right, Amber. Ladies, this is Shayla," waving his hands in her direction, "They just moved to the area and I invited them here tonight, to experience the hottest club in town," his attention returning to her.

Catching Kayla out of the corner of my eye, I recalled the scowl I had seen so many times before; jealousy poured from her pores at what was unfolding before us. Looking back to

Keith and Shayla, cunningly, "Leavin' me behind I see..." her face twisting in a teasing manner. She pretended to be annoyed by our presence, gently slapping his shoulder.

Kayla's hands were twisted into a fist though she didn't say anything; just sat there, watching. "Never, darlin'!" Keith grabbing Shayla's hand, kissing it, "You know you'll always be my sweet Southern Belle," winking up at her.

Her lip snarling into a smile, "Well nice to meet y'all, ladies. Welcome to Charleston. Whatcha'll havin'?" drawing in her sweet country twang. Giving our drink orders, Kayla sat quiet. Placing her order for her, Shayla jotted them down, "I'll be right back. Don't get too cozy," winking and blowing a kiss at Keith, sashaying away.

Turning back to us, Keith quickly noticed Kayla's scowl. Rolling her eyes and letting out a puff, "How do you know her? Been together long?" smarting off at him.

A laugh escaping his lips, "Nah, we just flirt," shifting himself to get more comfortable. "I'm not her type," pausing, "wrong gender."

Kayla's scowl quickly melted as Keith's words registered, "Oh..."

Shayla delivered our order, "On the house guys! Enjoy. I'll be back to check on y'all." And she was gone as quick as she had come.

Picking up his drink, "Sweet!" said Keith, downing it in one solid sip. Kayla and I simply smiling at the gesture, but the unease of such a gesture didn't sit so well with me. I wasn't one to trust easy and someone buying us drinks on the house this soon didn't feel right.

Noticing my apprehension, Kayla leaned over to me, whispering low in my ear, "Amber, enjoy yourself. Let loose for once."

She was right. What could possibly happen? No one knew us here and no one knew my past. I swallowed the apprehension down with the next swallow of my drink.

Sipping on her drink, Kayla began asking Keith standard questions, "So are you from Charleston?" breaking the ice. Finding the conversation piece comfortable, Keith began telling us that he was stationed here when he was just a kid and his father was Air Force, maintenance. Growing up in the public-school system, he recently graduated from the local college.

As quickly as we were asking questions, he returned with equal ones, Kayla holding the conversation, informing him of where we from, but not leading into reasons for our big move to Charleston. Silently thanking her, I didn't feel it was any of his business.

Trying to not feel like a third wheel, I returned to overlooking my surroundings. Guess it's the natural inquisitiveness of being a journalist; I took everything in, in full detail. The VIP Lounge tables were filling quickly as young couples and socialite friends took over the area. There was slight conversation that loomed in the air, but nothing as loud as the dance floor thumping behind the glass.

Still taking in the scene, I vaguely heard Keith ask me about my upcoming work venture. "Hey you with us?" my attention finally turning to him, "Ahh, there you are. Thought we lost you. So, I hear you're going to work for *Lowcountry Magazine*? What are you going to be doing?" Keith asked, trying to spark my interest and bring me back to the conversation at the table.

"Just writing small articles on local interests, nothing fancy. More trying to get my feet wet and move up," grabbing my drink and taking a gulp; hoping the cool liquid would ease my stiffness.

"Cool, I know a few people there. You'll like it, I bet," and as quickly as our conversation had started, his attention was back on Kayla. She was always good at carrying a conversation. Me, not so much, my sheltered life never allowing me much socialization with outsiders. Only reason I stayed friends with Kayla for so long was because she lived so close to my house growing up.

The conversation was dying quickly, and awkwardness was settling into the booth. Twisting my fingers in my lap, becoming uncomfortable until a slight nudge took hold of my attention. Looking up to Kayla's concerned eyes, "How about we dance?" Her eyes remaining fixed with mine as she directed the question at Keith.

Shrugging his shoulders up, "Sure. Let's show them what we got." Looking at Kayla, a little excitement swelled within me as we twisted our way out of the plush couch.

Exiting the couch, even though I was excited, hesitation settled in as I straightened my clothes trying to delay going back downstairs. Kayla reached for my hand to drag me towards the dance floor. Arriving at the top of the staircase, the music increased in sound and my ears couldn't help but readjust to the volume of the room. Walking down the steps to the dance floor, Keith was already busting a move as he led us to the center of the room. The heat from the bodies overcoming me as sweat began to bead on my forehead. Taking Kayla by the waist, Keith began dancing close with his newfound friend. Thinking back to what Kayla had said earlier, I began dancing by myself, allowing my body to simply take me away to the beat of the music.

Once I had started, I really began to enjoy the evening. Our group had danced almost the entire night, taking small breaks to the VIP Lounge for drinks. Not hanging around for long, we made it back to the dance floor. Kayla obviously had a thing for Keith; watching them dance, Kayla had her back against his chest, his hands firm on her hip, grinding gently with the rhythm of the current song. His nose nestling in her neck, her head rolling back on his shoulder; her hand reaching along the cusp of his neck, the other hand holding firm over his on her hip.

It wasn't long before a gorgeous man took notice and approached me offering his hand in invitation to dance. Hesitating at first, I gave in; my inner self telling me it was ok to let loose a little. He was a tall, slender man, with a deep olive tone to his skin. Reaching for my hips, his hands were large and firm. Placing my hand on top of his, my other reaching for the back of his neck, we swayed together to the music. Slowly he began pulling me in close along his hard body, the music hot, and our dancing hotter.

Looking up, I found sinful eyes that reflected lustful thoughts. Turning my glances away, closing my eyes, I allowed my body to continue its groove to the momentum of the song. Sweat pouring down my brow, I needed a break. Standing on my tiptoes, I invited him back to the table for a drink. Leading him through the crowd, we made our way up the staircase to the somewhat peaceful VIP Lounge.

Reaching our booth, "This is nice. I've been trying for weeks to get VIP access; how are you so lucky?" he asked with sentiment and curiosity in his voice.

"Oh, my friend Kayla met a guy who has full access. He brought us up here," looking up to the glass windows, I pointed her out on the floor below. "She's right there, dancing with Keith, the red-haired guy," my lips returning to the glass for another swallow.

"Ah," he remarked. "So are you from around here," the question came, noting a slight northern accent in his voice.

Facing him, I caught dark eyes hidden behind the longest eyelashes I had ever seen, "Just moved here. You," returning a similar question in his direction.

Our conversation carried on naturally, he introduced himself as Marco Lucarelli, just moving to the city from New York, and added he was working for a local finance company as their new VP of Marketing. Relaxing a little at this newfound information, I realized it was nice to meet someone else, other than Kayla that was new to the area.

Our small talk didn't last long and we were back to the dance floor, where Kayla noticed Marco. Giving him the once over, she shot me the thumbs up from her position in front of Keith. Rolling my eyes in her direction, she threw her head back laughing at me as I blew her off. Marco grabbed my hip again, allowing us to continue our dancing from moments ago.

The evening faded into morning, and I began easing back on my drinks, knowing I had reached my limit, even though I didn't do much of the party scene. The four of us continued dancing, but haziness began interceding my consciousness. Tapping Marco's shoulder, "I need to freshen up." Marco leaned in closer, not being able to hear me over the loud music, I repeated myself, pointing toward the lady's room to the left of the dance floor.

"You need me to go with?" cocking an eyebrow at me as if it were an invitation to some kind of after party.

Taken back by his glance, "No thanks, I can handle it. I'll be right back," pushing back from him, making my way through the crowds of people lost in their own partners.

Entering the restroom, the door closed behind me as total silence fell. Laying my head against the cold metal door, I savored the few quiet moments I have had this evening. My inner hermit was fighting its way back, but I pushed her away as I didn't want to end the night...not just yet. The air was too quiet and I began feeling the throb of a headache. Staggering over to the sink, the rush of nausea came over me. Reaching the edge of the pedestal sink, twisting on the cold knob, the sound of the water was relaxing as my headache continued to increase.

Knowing I wasn't much of a drinker, I began questioning the amount of alcohol I had consumer, as I laid my head on my crossed arms along the cold porcelain sink. With the feeling of vomit in my throat, I reminded myself I should have stopped a lot sooner. Cupping my hands, filling them with water, I bent forward bringing the coolness to my face. The vomit somewhat subsided as the chill in the water brought down my body temperature.

The music suddenly blasted in the quietness as a young college girl, looking barely old enough to get into a bar, and some guy entered the bathroom, obvious for a quick rendezvous. Shooting an embarrassed look my direction, it quickly diminished as the man nuzzled his nose in her neck; oblivious to my presence he continued his pursuit of the young girl. Pushing her towards the bathroom stall, the door slammed shut as giggles echoed against the bare walls.

Rolling my eyes, I observed my reflection in the mirror. Looking myself over with heavy glazed eyes, I straightened myself up, trying to fix my sweat-beaded hair. Ever since cutting it, it was a hard adjustment getting it just right. Just as I was settled on a look of normalcy, the sound of faint moans began filling my ears and I couldn't bear to listen to late night bathroom foreplay. Pushing from the sink, I prepped myself to return to the blaring room.

The insanely loud music caused my head to swim and my headache quickly worsened. Pain traveled down my neck and the vomit began swelling in my throat; I knew I needed air or I was going to be sick. Dashing my way back through the club, I made way to the front door and exited into the humid mugginess of the Charleston night air. The sudden rush of fresh air filled my lungs, settling my queasiness. Leaning over on my knees, my butt rested against the brick wall behind me. The streets were almost empty, the only activity in the club and the long line of eager entrants to my left.

Rubbing my hands across my face, bracing the brick wall, Marco startled me, "Are you ok?" not realizing he had followed me out.

"Yeah just needed some air," my hands still on my cheeks, taking in deep breaths to continue settling my uneasy stomach. Leaning back over, blowing big breaths from my chest, the slight, salty breeze hit my skin, sending goose bumps up and down my arms.

Walking up closer to me, "Let's go back inside," his hand now on my shoulder, a slur to his voice, "I want to dance some more," he expressed. Sweat beaded under his fingertips as shivers ran down my spine at his sudden intrusion.

Still bent over, he wrapped one arm around my waist, twisting his free hand in the ends of my hair, lifting to his nose to smell.

Panic settled in my stomach and I pushed off the wall, allowing my hair to fall from his hands. Turning towards him, "No, you can go. I need the air," the nausea quickly rising at my sudden movement. The last thing I needed was more heat and loud music. Walking to the curb, bending over, I placed my hands on my knees to try and settle myself.

"Come on baby. Come back inside," hearing his heavy footsteps behind me. Along with the quaking nausea in my stomach, anxiety bloomed more as the intensity of Marco's advances triggered feelings of my recent past.

"Come on Amber!" His hands wrapping around my waist from behind pulling me closer to him; the smell of rum on his breath. His drunken lips on my bare neck as I turned

my head away, doing my best to release his hands from my stomach. Knowing it was a losing battle, his grip held firm, his free hand moving under the waistband of my shorts, doing his best to persuade me into something I didn't want. "Stop," I pleaded, but the liquor took over.

Marco's hands were now on my backside again, as I came back from my daydream, "No, it's fine. I want to be alone," crossing my arms, silently protecting myself; hoping his drunkenness wouldn't allow any further advances. Twisting out from under his hand, walking backwards towards the club, once again greeted by the brick wall.

"Come on, let me stay," coaxing, taking another step forward, his hands resuming their previous position on my waist. A lump formed in my throat as the flashback replayed in my mind; I had nowhere to go.

With trembling hands, my voice faltered, "Back off Marco!" My hands laid flat against the rugged brick; the smell of rum wafting my senses as Marco's breath inched closer to my skin. *Where the hell is the bouncer now?* My eyes searching for any sign of Ray, my clarity fogged by my night of too much drinking. One of Marco's hands began roaming my body freely and I knew from experiences passed, this wouldn't end well for me.

"Don't fight me baby," his grip tightening against my waist as he pressed me further into the brick wall with his hard body. His nose now in my neck, the smell of rum growing stronger as vomit sat at the base of my throat. Whispering along the lines of my neck, "A woman doesn't dance with a man like that unless she wants to," pausing for a moment as his lips pressed the line on my neck, "you know."

Not taking no for an answer, I had to do something but what? I never had the courage to fight back, but my body knew that this was wrong. I tried my best to knee him, do something, but fighting him made little difference. Tears pricked my eyes as I began pleading with Marco, "Please. Leave me alone. Get off," my voice a faint whisper but nothing made a difference against the massive weight of steel that held me against the wall. His hands were now roaming into forbidden territory when a deep, strong voice radioed from the shadows, "The lady said no."

Jerking his head away, Marco searched the shadows to our right, "Excuse me," he replied, annoyance apparent in his deep New York accent. "This isn't your business." The shadow of a well-defined man appeared, his shoulders broad and strong, "Actually it is. Now leave," the voice harsher, not backing down from his demands.

"Or what?" Marco easing up some, my lungs able to gather a little breath. Standing dead still, I silently prayed that Marco would leave and that this would all go away.

"I don't think you want to find out," the unknown man's voice stern in response. By this point, out of the corner of my eye, I saw Ray standing behind the shadowed man; his hands right over left as his muscles protruded from underneath his tight shirt. Reaching up and pulling the dark sunglasses onto the rim of his nose, he silently shook his head left and right as if signaling to Marco that this was the wrong move.

Looking at Ray and at the shadowed man, he quickly looked my direction, eyeing me up down, "Bitch isn't worth it anyways," finally releasing me and heading back into the club. Sneering over his shoulder and pulling the heavy metal door with ease, "See ya tease," he reentered *ENVY.*

Air fully filled my lungs, barely allowing me to catch my breath long enough to whisper thanks to the disembodied voice. Wrapping my arms around my shoulders, my body began shaking violently when the vomit couldn't hold back any longer. Lunging forward to the edge of the street, I expelled all the contents of my stomach. The stranger stepping forward grabbed my hair as my body turned against me.

When I was finished, holding my knees, I used one hand to rub my mouth of any remnants. Reaching back for stabilization, the stranger helped me back to the coolness of the brick wall. Laying my head back, I closed my eyes, the world around me spinning. Quickly realizing that wasn't a good idea, I shifted myself to sit on the ground. Placing my head on my knees, I tried to forget what had just happened, my headache only growing worst.

The stranger kneeling next to me remained quiet as I collected my thoughts. The breeze shifted as an aroma of leather and soap, with a slight hint of whiskey filled the air. I could feel my cheeks flush and skin tingle to the heavenly, soothing aroma. "Are you ok" the voice deep and sharp broke the silent darkness.

"Yea, thanks," my head still on my knees, but turned towards him.

Placing his hand gently on my shoulder, my body didn't clam up in fear at the genuine move, "Not a problem. You looked like you were enjoying yourself...well until just a moment ago." Feeling slightly awkward, and invaded, in addition to my head radiating with pain, I lifted my head slightly as my brow furrowed. Doing my best to adjust my eyes, they were only met with shadows and darkness as they tried to make out the hidden figure.

Wrapping my arms tight around my legs, trying to protect myself, "You were watching me?" You could hear the fear growing in my voice.

Gaining the strength to shuffle to my feet, my head racing, a slight panic entered my bones. An escape plan of any sort eluded me with the fogginess of my mind. Not noticing my unease, he asked, "What's your name," grabbing my elbow to help me steady onto my feet.

Pulling it out of his grasp as tremors raked my body, I questioned whether it was best to answer him or remain silent. My mind making the decision for me, "I'm not in the habit of giving out personal information to men who lurk in shadows," gathering some hidden courage, "if you want to talk to me, step out where I can see you, otherwise I'm going back inside." trying to sound several times more confident than I felt.

Laughing humbly, "I did just hold your hair back while you vomited in front of my business, but if you insist," stepping out from the shadows into the dim street lantern, glancing up to see his face; my eyes locking with the purest emeralds. My pulse racing as the lamps outlined the brazen arms, vine tattoo and well-toned body. My heart skipping a beat as my breath caught in my throat. My wishes to see his face was met as I recognized the man beneath the hat...it was Tristan Ashton.

TRISTAN

"**S**o..." his velvet voice bringing me back to reality. His dark green eyes slowly searched mine for some sort of answer.

Swallowing the knot down my throat, I felt my cheeks betray me as the sudden rush of blood filled them. Pulling away, hoping the darkness covered my newest shade of skin color, "Amber Slayton," I finally answered; a slight crack evident, "Why were you watching me," my body shivering with slight paranoia.

Reentering the shadows, I could no longer see his face, "It's my job. However, when I saw you, I couldn't help myself." I wasn't sure what he meant by his job although he had just mentioned this was his business, but the slow breeze shifted, his scent clogging my mind. My eyes, surrendering my newfound courage, closed as my nostrils inhaled the aroma.

His shoulder rested on the brick wall, facing me, "Are you ok," a slight curiousness in his voice.

"Yes," exclaiming, probably a little too excitedly. Shuffling on my feet, my mind raced as my body quickly concluded that he was intoxicating and damn attractive. My normal anxiety around new people, much less men of any kind, wasn't on high alert with him. What little control I had left, I forced my guard back up, realizing he had been watching me the entire night. My mind raced with questions as to the meaning of his statement.

My quietness must have unsettled him as he shifted on his feet, "Let me restart, I'm Tris..." he began.

"Tristan Ashton, the baseball player. I know who you are," shrugging my shoulders, trying to act unimpressed. My gaze danced across the chiseled features I had been admiring in his photograph earlier, only now the dim light illuminated his white smile that spread across his lips; my attempt of being unimpressed had failed. "Do you really think the hometown hero thing gives you the right to hide in the shadows and watch women like some creepy stalker?" Though I may be drunk, my inner fighter found her way out. I needed to protect myself at all costs and no matter how much I wanted to fight the comfort he gave, I needed to be on alert.

His brow knitted together as his smile faded, realizing his statements had gone too far.

Kicking the ground at my feet, I softened my tone some, "Look, I'm sorry. Thanks for being there and helping me out with that creep, and my most graceful moment on the street," nodding my head in the direction of the club, "but I should find my friend. I kind of left her alone. Will I see you around?" Why did I ask him that? This man had just admitted to stalking me, but yet here my drunk behind was asking him if I would see him again. Catching the whites of his teeth again, I knew his dashing smile had returned but he didn't say anything. I needed to quit drinking...it clouded my judgment too much.

Not wanting to stand around and wait for a reply, I removed myself from the wall as I walked back towards the club doors. Reaching for the handle to pull it open, my hand dropped to my side as my knees began buckling and giving way to my weight. My head piercing with pain, Tristan swooped in and grabbed me before I hit the sidewalk pavement. Huddled in his arms, my head lolled back as I passed out.

THE OVERLOOK

My conscious state faded in and out as the blaring music overwhelmed me, the pain in my head blasting through my entire body. I was vaguely aware that Tristan was carrying me as my body shifted with each step taken on the spiral staircase. Hearing the click of a door, the music completely disappearing behind us, Tristan crossed the darkened room and laid me down on the cool leather sofa. My drunken state taking back over, my eyes closed as I drifted back into darkness. Hearing muffled noises, I couldn't make them out as my body sank in the softness of the couch. Not opening my eyes, my shoulders were lifted as something plush was put under my head for support. "Let's get you some water." A sturdy arm was behind my back, the glass to my lips, I swallowed in sips, pushing away the rest. "Um no, all of it," Tristan remarked pushing the glass to meet my lips again. Swallowing the remaining fluid, my head met the softness of the pillow; my eyes heavy with sleep.

◆ ◆ ◆

The sound of clinking glass startled my restless state. Turning my nose into the now sticky leather, I felt my cheek peel itself off the couch. Raising my hand to shuffle my hair from my face, I felt the couch give way by my waist. Frozen in place, my mental state registered that I wasn't in my room. Lowering my eyes beneath my arm, I found a man's leg. Lifting them above my arm, a hand was extended with two white pills and a glass of water. Finally shifting myself up, I found Tristan's emerald eyes registering concern, but no words spoken. Sitting myself up against the arm of the couch, I tucked my knees into my chest, looking at his open hand in front of me.

"It's aspirin, promise," nudging the pills further my direction. Taking the pills and water, I downed the clear liquid.

"How do you feel," his words slightly husky. Steering my eyes above the rim of the glass, I rested it atop my knee, "Ok, just a headache. Thank you," I lifted the glass in my appreciation. Tristan stood, walking over to a wall of windows that I only assumed were the mirrored wall present in the nightclub. The house lights had been raised; the club was now closed. His back faced me, his one hand held firm in his pocket and the other hand rubbing the back of his neck. Watching over his crew below, he reached over, picking up the crystal glass resting on the bar with his free hand, leaving a ring of condensation. Elegantly lifting the glass to his lips, he sipped and tasted the drink at hand, whiskey I assumed, his motions smooth and effortless.

Rising to take a glance, I glided up next to him. He had the clearest view of the club, including the VIP Lounge area nestled below the windows. He didn't acknowledge my presence, but remained positioned as we both watched his crew clean up the club.

"This is amazing," I remarked, taking in the delicate features of the warehouse building that was now fully illuminated. There wasn't a detail missed, although it was still a nightclub.

"Isn't it," Tristan simply stated, his eyes not leaving their post.

Turning myself back towards the room, I found the office decorated just as nicely. In the far corner stood a masculine mahogany desk with dual monitors, security cameras present on the one screen. Along the wall to the windows, there was an ornately carved bar, stocked with a variety of brands of alcohol, though I couldn't name half of them if I tried. And then there was the couch, a baseball stitched leather sofa, with plush pillows. It had been where I spent my night, passed out and unaware of my surroundings. Anything could have happened to me, but my body reassured me that I was fine and calmness had settled over me.

I made my way to sit back down, grabbing my glass from the table beside the couch. Twisting the empty cup in my hands, my eyes retreated to the man standing in front of me. He was average height, with a body of strength, wearing a crisp, pressed white button-down shirt, with sleeves rolled up to his elbows, and khaki shorts, complimented with flip flops. Not your typical attire for a club like this I mused. I concluded he probably got away with wearing whatever he wanted, after all he was Tristan Ashton, local baseball hero and bachelor – or at least that is how I saw him.

His sandy blonde hair was short, almost military style and he had a hint of a five o'clock shadow peaking around the rim of his chin. His body was chiseled, but with years of playing ball, it made sense. Noticing a slight tension appear in his shoulders, turning to look at me, his gaze caught my observation. My cheeks blushing, a sheepish grin quipped the corner of his lips, unsettling my nerves.

Tearing my glance away, rubbing my neck, "How do you have access to this room?"

"I own the club," short in his response, not giving too much away, though his response did answer the question I held from the prior night as to it being his business. He seemed to be the quiet type, not one to let too much out, not give too much away at one time. Shaking my head in acknowledgement, his dressed down appearance now made more sense.

Feeling like this conversation wasn't going anywhere, I felt it best for me to retreat home. My headache had mostly subsided and I wasn't as shaky on my feet. Standing, "Well I am going to head out," I remarked, pointing my thumb in the direction of the door behind me. In quick reaction, he stepped forward as if to help me. Holding my hand up, he stopped, shoving his hands back into his pockets, "Thanks for rescuing me last night. I hope I wasn't too much of an intrusion," placing the glass on the sofa side table.

"Not at all," he replied, feeling his pockets for something, "Let me take you home. You're not well. I have a car right outside that can take you," finally finding his phone behind the bar beside him.

Refusing the offer, holding my hands up, "Thank you, but I don't mind walking. The fresh air will help me clear my head and walk off my hangover," recalling that it was only a few blocks from the club to my apartment.

"Are you sure? It's never safe for a lady to walk alone, much less alone at night," concern was now evident, his protectiveness slightly catching me off guard. And was it really still night? You couldn't see through any of the interior windows to make heads or tails of what time of day it was. It had to be early morning at best. Uncertainty still loomed with Tristan. He had been there when I needed him last night, but I wasn't keen on letting strangers near my apartment.

"No really it's fine. I will be ok," doing my best to reassure him on my decision. Disappointment and maybe some anger registered, almost acting defeated. I was certain he didn't get turned away often. Noticing his hands clenching, his knuckles flushed white at the tightness of his grasp, he wasn't happy, but I wasn't quite comfortable with him yet.

Walking up to me, reaching behind and grabbing my cell phone from my back pocket; his body extremely close to mine, "Well take my number and let me know when you get home safely." His phone vibrated, signaling an incoming call...I could only assume now my number was in his phone, but not quite sure as I couldn't see the screen. Taking a step back, I sent him a questioning stare.

"I like you, I'm going to worry until I know your safe," he smiled like he could read my thoughts. Placing the phone back in my pocket, I made a mental note to put a key number lock on it. Stepping back to allow me to leave, placing his hand at the small of my back, small tingles lingered along where his palm rest. Catching his glance out of the corner of my eye, I could tell he felt something too. Clearing my throat and catching my composure, I quickly exited the upper level office and out the doors of *ENVY*.

RESTLESSNESS

Leaving the club, the early morning sky had not begun to wake. The streets were empty, still resting from the hurried tourists of the day before. The air was crisp and whatever headache was lingering had all but subsided from the fresh air. My focus had returned to normal and my feet quickened its pace towards my apartment. Thousands of questions swirled through my head as to the prior evening's events, but fatigue caught up and pushed its way to the forefront.

Approaching my apartment, I began feeling a little uneasy and questioned my better judgment on letting Mr. Ashton bring me home. Charleston was still so new to me, but my striving for independence seemed to cloud my better judgment in my decision making. He hadn't tried anything that I knew of, only took care of me when I was quite vulnerable. Shaking off the unwelcomed thoughts I found myself looking over my shoulder until I reached my front door.

Locking the door behind me, I walked straight to my bedroom, peeling out of my clothing, leaving a trail on the floor that started at my door; telling myself I would pick them up tomorrow. My body was exhausted and all I wanted to do was crawl in bed. Forcing my way through the trail of unpacked boxes, I wrestled in the box near my dresser and found my Notre Dame shirt and a clean pair of panties. Turning to my bed, placing my knee on the pearl blue cotton sheets, I crawled to my pillow, driving my face into the puffiness, as heaviness consumed my body and I drifted back into a deep sleep.

It couldn't have been long before I abruptly woke to my cell phone. Glancing at my alarm clock, it registered four in the morning. Swiping for my phone, almost knocking it to the floor, my head pushed into my pillow, I muffled a weak hello.

"You're safe! Thank God!" relief pouring from the man speaking through the phone.

Not lifting my head, "Who is this?" still muffled from the pillow, my eyelids never opening to look at the caller ID. "You know it's like four in the morning?"

"It's Tristan, I'm sorry to have woken you, but I wanted to make sure you were safe. I hadn't heard from you and was worried," his voice slightly hitched from anxiety.

Shifting myself to speak clearer into the phone. "Do you always make it a habit of four in the morning phone calls," the question coming out sleepily. "How'd you get my number anyways? I don't remember giving it to you."

"I called my phone last night from yours," he answered as recollection came to me. My tired body began taking back over, "Well I am safe, Mr. Ashton. I'm going back to sleep. Good night," and I hung the phone up, not waiting for a response. Tossing it onto my bed, I let sleep consume my body as I nestled back into my pillow.

As tired as I was, my body tossed and turned the remainder of the morning and I finally gave up around eight. Getting up from my bed and walking half-dazed through empty boxes, I peeked into Kayla's room to find it empty. I stumbled into an undecorated kitchen, the place still empty, and no sign of Kayla anywhere. Figuring she would have been home by now, I gave up on my search for her and moved into the quest for a coffee cup.

Putting a fresh brew on, the coffee began percolating. Opening the bare fridge, I grabbed the half carton of eggs and bacon. Dragging my feet across the faded linoleum towards the tiny apartment stove, I reached in the cabinet to the right, and pulled out a skillet, placing it on the cold burner. Turning on the stovetop, I waited for the pan to heat up. After a minute, I placed a couple pieces of bacon in the skillet, enjoying the sizzling sounds as it cooked; my stomach rumbling as the slow aroma hit my nose.

The bacon continued sizzling when I heard the lock of the door turn, Kayla shuffling inside. Her clothing disheveled from her acceptable appearance of the night before, the look of lust evident on her face. A smile curling at the corner of my lip as she glided past me, with glazed hung-over eyes.

"UGH!" Kayla let out a heavy moan when she caught my smirk. An early morning Bloody Mary was in order as I retrieved some tomato juice and vodka from the fridge. It wasn't the best but I knew it would be helpful. Plopping herself down in one of the chairs of our tiny four-person kitchen table, I handed her the glass. Taking it in her hands, looking up to me with thankful heavy eyes, she took the first sip. The taste must have been appeasing because before I knew it, it was down in one fluid motion. The next thing I know is the glass hitting the table as I entered with a plate of fresh eggs and bacon. Turning her nose, she stood and made her way to her room. "I need a shower first," calling back as she closed the door behind her. I just let her go; Kayla wasn't one to mess with when she had a hangover. Within seconds, the old rickety pipes began their song of clangs as the shower turned on.

My stomach wasn't up for waiting f or her. Taking the first

scoop of food, my stomach jumped for joy with each morsel. Feeling like I couldn't satisfy my hunger fast enough, I tried to steady myself with each bite, while I looked over the morning's paper. Hearing the shower turn off, I noted that a peppier Kayla reappeared. Walking over, she took a seat across from me, grabbing the spoon and scooping some food on her plate. The dreaded questions I knew that were lurking in her tiny little brain were getting ready to come. I braced myself.

"So, what happened last night? We were dancing and I remember you leaving, but don't remember much past that. It's all a little foggy," she started, her eyes shooting up, a cunning smile perching on her lips.

Myself...hesitant to have this conversation with her. My drunken scene embarrassed me and spending the night in a complete stranger's office; I really didn't feel the need to embrace her interrogation, "Did Mr. Handsome make your night?"

"No Kayla," letting out a heavy puff; she knew very well I wasn't that type of girl, "He wanted a little more than I was willing to share, but did you have fun?" redirecting the conversation to her, trying my best to avoid her line of questioning. The memories of the night before pitted in my stomach and suddenly I wasn't so hungry anymore.

Her curious smile turning girlish, "YES! Keith is amazing," she began rambling; not realizing I had blown off her question. It was for the best, as I didn't even realize what truly happened last night.

Pausing briefly, "I'm sorry I kind of left you...alone."

"It's ok," reaching over and squeezing her hand reassuringly. As quickly as she stopped, she started back on about Keith and how amazing he was. I still didn't quite see what she saw in him, but with Kayla, there was no telling. Her tastes in things changed as fast as she changed her clothes each day. Scooping another spoonful of eggs into my mouth, "I'm glad you were able to have a good time. Keith seems really nice and it looked as if you two hit off." I smiled, glancing up at her.

Returning the smile, her voice picked up in excitement. I listened; trying to show my interest in her conversation, but all I could think about was my early morning conversation with Tristan. It wasn't anything big, but for him to call me all worried raised a little suspicion. I understand people worry, but he had just met me, why the sudden interest? It's not like we were dating or anything.

The sound of my phone interrupting us, I rose from the table and walked to my room to retrieve it, but didn't find it on my nightstand. Following the sound of the ring, I shuffled through my pearl blue bed sheets, finally retrieving it near my pillow. Glancing at the screen, as the caller hung up, I didn't recognize the number. Shrugging my shoulders, I carried it with me back to the kitchen knowing they would call back if it was that important.

"Who was it," Kayla asking over her shoulder.

"I don't know. They hung up before I could find my phone," making my way back to my seat to carry on our earlier conversation. Just as I sat down, my phone rang again, the same number displaying.

"Hello," answering to the unknown caller.

"Hello, Amber. How are you feeling?" recognizing the calmness of the voice, my cheeks betraying me with their rosy color.

"I'm fine. Thanks! May I ask why you are calling me?" biting back slightly; a little unnerved by his forwardness. Kayla shooting me a look, mouthed, *who is it?* Waving her off as I tried to figure out why Tristan was calling.

"Well good morning to you too. Look, I'm sorry about my

early morning phone call. How about I take you out for coffee? My way of..." pausing for a moment, "apologizing for my rudeness."

"I'm already drinking coffee," replying sarcastically, as I turned the handle of the cup on the table. My inner self was silently urging me to take this opportunity. Waiting for his tactful response, Kayla eyed me suspiciously.

Almost pleading, "I really would like to apologize. Please accept my invite." Stopping, almost sounding defeated, "It would be nice to see you again. If you decide to decline, I'll keep bothering you until you agree." I could hear him smiling on the other end, "It may be worth your while to say yes? And I promise to be a complete gentleman." *It was the least he could do.* He wasn't off the hook, not yet anyways.

Instantly a little voice in my head piped up, reminding me of why I came to Charleston in the first place, *a fresh start.* I had sworn off men when I moved here, and I wasn't interested in dating, but making friends would help ease the transition into a new town. *We would be in a public place, surrounded by people. What would it hurt?*

"I guess" still sounding reserved, "Where?"

"I'll pick you up in five," quickly replying, barely giving me time to respond.

Thrown by the amount of time he allowed me to get ready, "Five minutes? Hell, that doesn't give me enough time to do anything," sounding slightly frustrated.

Quickly complying, "Ok, ten. I'll be by your apartment to pick you up."

Flabbergasted, "You don't know where I live!"

Now sounding hurried, "Keith told me. See you in a few." the line disconnecting. Kayla looked at me, surprise on her face.

"Mhm, nothing happened last night, huh," her smirk in a full grin. Staring her down, she threw up her hands in defeat. I didn't have time to talk and I knew her questions would come later. I just needed to go on this coffee visit and try to get Tristan out of my head, focus more on a friendship. Maybe this visit will shed light on some things and I can move on past these crazy emotions I was feeling.

Running to the bedroom, I threw on a pair of jeans, bra, and white t-shirt. Combing through my brunette trusses, that were dirty with sweat from the night before, I had no choice but to throw it up into a make shift ponytail, and slide into a pair of flip-flops; it would have to do without taking a shower. As I was finishing up, there was a knock on the door. My stomach jumping to my throat, nerves filled my belly.

Kayla answered the door as I was re-entering the room, taking a step back and observing the five foot nine, man of steel standing in front of her. Holding the doorknob, not removing her glare, she motioned for Tristan to make his grand entrance into our tiny, disheveled apartment. He hadn't changed from the night before, still in his same clothes. My guess, he had just gotten off from work. Turning her head, she caught the rosiness of my face and her eyes went wide in approval. Motioning with my eyes for her to stop, Tristan caught a glimpse of my embarrassment. Turning back to Tristan, "I'm Kayla. We didn't get to meet last night," holding her hand out.

Grabbing her hand, pulling it to his lips and kissing her knuckles in a southern gentleman way, "I'm Tristan, nice to meet you ma'am."

Kayla's cheeks flushing at the gesture, quickly removing her hand to hide a giggle escaping her lips. "Nice to meet you, also," walking to the kitchen, she called back, "would you like something to drink, Tristan?" Entering the kitchen, hidden by a small wall, turning she mouthed, *damn he's fine.* Simply smiling, Tristan walking towards me. "No thank you, I'm fine. Amber and I are headed for coffee. Care to join us," turning towards her voice. My heart sank; I really didn't want Kayla to join us for some reason.

"No, I'm good. You two have fun," calling back.

Tristan turning his attention to me, "Ready? You look great," his eyes examining my make shift outfit.

Cocking my head to the side, my eyebrows twisting up, "Doubt it, someone didn't allow me enough time to shower."

A smirk wavering his lips, turning, extending his hand towards the door, "Shall we?"

Walking forward, allowing me to lead, he placed his hand at the small of my back, tingles skirting through me, my breath hitching slightly. Pushing the feelings aside, hoping he didn't feel me falter, we left my apartment.

On King Street, the morning sun had risen to its fullest attention, lighting our path down the cobblestone road. The morning was quite humid and local vendors were pulling along storefronts making morning deliveries, while college kids were fast footing to get to their classes. "I know this great little café right up the road. Best coffee in Charleston," he said knowingly, motioning his hand through the air towards an invisible distance. Walking down the old sidewalks, he pointed out different stores and shared certain historical facts about the area. It was obvious he was from here.

"You seem to know your history of Charleston," I noted as I took in each little-known fact of the local area.

"It helps when you grow up here," he smiled, "we should be almost there." It was kind of nice having my own private tour guide. Since arriving in town, this was my first real take of the beautiful city in the daylight. Continuing our course towards the café, there weren't many tourists on the street yet, since it was a little early, but the few we passed, posed interesting characteristics. We passed an early morning dog walker in her yoga pants, tank top, and walking shoes, the diligent runner brushing past us to reach his finish line; and the late college student whose face read that they hit their alarm clock one too many times. Charleston possessed a variety of cultures and characters from all walks of life, each with their own story to tell.

Rounding the corner to the little café, an uneasy feeling settled over me. Looking over my shoulder my eyes searched the passing landscape but found nothing but vendors and oncoming cars.

Noticing my uneasiness Tristan looked back to see what I was looking at. His eyes reaching mine, "Are you ok," breaking my inquisition.

My face twisted in concern, I simply replied, "Yea, I'm fine, let's continue," my hand waving in the air towards the direction we were headed.

Seconds later, "Ah, here we are," pointing at the café', nestled between deteriorating buildings on each side. It was a quiet little café. Most of the morning traffic had dissipated as the rush of college students had thinned out to only a few stragglers running late.

The black and white striped over hang covered the dainty windows and two small café tables were nestled behind a wrought iron fence. "What do you want," queried Tristan, reaching for the café door.

"Just a latte, please." I called back as I made my way to one of the outside tables. The morning continued growing muggy, with an occasional breeze of increasing heat. I was able to get one of the small tables behind the wrought iron fence, allowing me to continue my earlier observations of people passing by. The once empty street slowly growing with foot traffic, people were laughing, couples holding hands, children escaping the grasps of their parents, each passing my tiny table. Arriving with our order, Tristan sat in the chair across the table, setting down my latte, trying not to disturb my observations.

"You like people watching?" curiosity in his voice.

"Yes, how could you tell?" pulling my shoulder into my chin in a flirtatious manner. My attention pointed to him briefly before returning to passersby.

"The smile gave you away," taking a sip of his beverage. A moment or two passed, "What's your story Amber?" he asked me, my eyes quickly catching inquisitiveness knitted around his brow as sudden grief punched me in the gut. Kayla was the only one who knew my past. Taking a deep breath, deciding to act cool...he was only making conversation.

I didn't have to divulge my life to him, "What do you mean my story?" It was a question I was going to need to get used to. People were going to ask why we moved to the area. I just needed to decide how best to respond, and in a way that wouldn't give away too much.

"You know, who you are," a little relief coming over with the clarity.

Considering my answer carefully, I did my best to avoid anything that may divulge too much. Deciding to make small talk, I continued people watching, "I'm from Indiana, moved here a few days ago. Same old story: grew up in a small town with a stay at home mom and stepdad as the local mechanic. Pretty boring I would say," knowing it was far from the truth.

Turning the table of questioning to him, "What about you? Seeing you know quite a bit about the historic city, what's yours?" breaking my observation and turning to face him. He brought the orange and brown colored cup to his lips, silent, contemplating his response.

"Oh, you know, not much to tell," smiling, repeating my lines with his own twist, "Grew up just across the river, went to school here, graduated, never really left. Mom was a stay at home mom most of my life, until she went to work for my father, as I got older," sadness looming in his voice, his eyes diverting into his lap, suddenly growing quiet.

Breaking the silence, "How long have you been playing ball?" Relief pouring over his face as the conversation turned.

"My whole life, really. I joined the Sharks about five years ago. I love the game and hate that my time with it is ending," drinking more of his beverage.

"Why?" as I blew the heat off my cup.

"Why what," avoiding my question, acting as if he didn't hear it.

"Why are you leaving the game if you love it so much?" clarifying my question.

"It's not important," obvious he was hiding something, my journalistic nature peaking, but not wanting to press. It really wasn't my business as I had just met him and I am sure in time, the answer would come if this newfound friendship were going anywhere.

Changing the subject, quickly, "Indiana huh? Where did you go to college?" he asked.

"Notre Dame," I smiled proudly.

"Home of the Fighting Irish. Interesting..." I interrupted him with my own question, "What about you? Did you go to college?"

"Clemson. What did you major in?" returning equally.

"Journalism. You?"

"Ah, that makes sense. Architecture," his answers short and to the point. Shifting my head back, pinching my lips together in a smug, *I'm impressed state*, I continued, "What makes sense?"

"All the direct questions," he replied, taking another sip of his beverage.

Brushing off his nonchalant demeanor, "So why ball?"

"It was a break, a much-needed break." Leaving it at that, he continued sipping his drink. My attention had returned to the increasing number of people looming on the sidewalk. Deciding not to pursue what he meant, *it really wasn't my business*, but Tristan was keeping his end of the bargain with being a true southern gentleman. Out of the corner of my eye, I caught Tristan lifting his cup again to his lips, the motions of his masculine arms mesmerizing me, my eyes glued to each movement. Noticing my lengthy glance, a smile appeared on his lips from behind his cup.

Quickly reaching for my cup to take my mind away from staring, pulling it to my lips, blowing the heat of the latte away, I focused on distracting myself. The mid-morning heat was rising; *coffee may not have been a good choice.*

Slowly drinking the hot fluid, Tristan continued the conversation, "So why Charleston, of all the places you could go?" the dreaded question I hoped wouldn't come.

Trying to devise a plan behind my cup, thinking quickly, "It was Kayla's idea really. She got accepted into College of Charleston for her Masters in Art Education. She found out *Lowcountry Magazine* was hiring, and had me apply. They offered me the job and two weeks later we were moving into our apartment."

Seemingly satisfied with my response, "That's quite a move from Indiana. Do you like it here?"

"So far," looking down in my cup, smiling, "It's growing on me." *What are you thinking Amber? Remember fresh start?* Waving the thought away, I continued enjoying our plain conversation.

Leaning forward onto his knees, turning the cup in his hands, "Amber, I know we only just met, but I like you," the blunt statement throwing my guard off. *What could he possibly mean? Does he like me as a friend, or LIKE me as more?* My eyes, quickly finding his, I could see lust looming, answering my own question of what his statement possibly posed. Forcing myself to drink my coffee, I set my half empty cup on the table. Tristan reached out to grab my hand but in a sudden impulse, I pulled my hand away, hitting my coffee cup and spilling the latte all over Tristan and myself.

"Oh, my goodness, I'm so, so sorry," exclaiming as I pulled my hands to my face. Standing, he gathered napkins as he wiped the coffee off his khaki shorts. Frantically grabbing more napkins, reaching down patting the ground, Tristan reached over grabbing the bottom of my shirt to wipe away the quickly absorbing, running liquid.

Trying to remain focused, bending forward to pick up my empty cup, I continued placing napkins on the mess below my feet, as quietness had settled between us. Kneeling in front me, his eyes watching my every move, he lifted his hand, his fingers tracing the lines of my cheek. Turning into his touch, he whispered, "Look at me." My eyes lifting to his, cheeks red from embarrassment were met with softness as they began searching for answers.

"Say something," he murmured, whispering softly, remembering his confession just moments earlier.

Turning away from him, blushing, "I'm sorry. What am I supposed to say?" unease in my voice, my eyes racing towards the ground, wet coffee stained napkins in my hand, "Tristan, I..."

lost for words.

Cupping my chin, lifting it again so my eyes could meet his, grabbing my shaking hand with his free hand, he rubbed the tops of my knuckles to ease my tension and uneasiness, lifting it to his lips, kissing it gently, "It's ok."

My mind raced a hundred miles an hour searching his eyes and my brain for answers, but I was still lost. His deeps eyes held me in a trance as the knot kept swelling in my throat, finding it hard to breathe and swallow. The heat and intoxication of Tristan's smell had my skin's heat climbing excessively. I was lost in the moment, both of us soaked from my clumsiness. Pulling my chin close to his face, almost as if he was going to kiss me, he brushed my cheek with his, whispering in my ear, "You are beautiful Amber. I don't know what it is," the breath on my ear warm, his scent filling me. Pulling away with a clever smile on his lips, he stood, gesturing his hand to help me up. Accepting, my heart racing as the sparks passed through our palms.

Remaining speechless and red from embarrassment, the heat, and his spoken words I was lost on how to respond; no man had ever spoken such words to me.

"Amber," he said hesitantly, as his fingers found a loose lock of hair to push back.

> *"You know you are the most gorgeous girl in this school," his voice rustic with a northern hint evident. I had just shut my locker when he walked up, his arm resting on the locker next to me. I wasn't used to getting attention from guys at school, much less the guy every girl wanted.*

Coming back to reality, I needed to do something. Panic setting in, I decided it was time to leave. Attempting to take my first step to escape, Tristan grabbed my forearm in an effort to stop me. Dread raked through my body as harsh memories of my past returned.

Let go, I whispered as he held my arm, forcing me in the direction of the front door. "I'm sorry," I cried, please let me go. But my efforts were useless against him. Trying to twist my arm to break free, his grasp tightened and he twisted my arm to lock it against my back. Pulling me into his chest, he whispered in my ear, "I will kill you."

Quickly looking at his arm and then his face, he could sense my fear, releasing my arm, his face softening at fright that must have been evident on my face. I could feel myself growing pale, recalling every detail of my Indiana life. I could feel the blood and color leaving every part of me, "Amber, you don't look so well. Please sit down."

The small command, although not really a command, triggered something inside and I snapped, "NO!" pushing myself past him, finding my way back through the café, I skirted through the line of college students that had entered in between their morning schedules. Exiting out of the café as quickly as possible, my fight or flight instincts began kicking in. Hearing him hustling behind me to catch up, calling my name, I hit King Street, stepping out onto the cobblestone alley, tripping and landing on the hard-rounded stones. Pain shot through my hands, as horns suddenly began blaring, I felt strong, sturdy hands scoop me up by my waist, pulling me to safety against a rock-hard surface, my heart racing from the adrenaline.

Memories choked any voice I had, while Tristan's aroma swirled around me. Still fighting my way out, I pounded against what I realized was Tristan's chest. His breathing was rapid while his heart raced the same pace as mine. He had held one hand tight around my waist, trying to keep me from hurting myself. The other nestled over my ear, trying to get my attention. I had become deaf to the noises that surrounded me as I fought my way through the flashback. Pulling me closer to him, the pressure of his arms slowly settled me as I found my head rested against his chest, our breaths slowing into a matching rhythm.

Once calm, his fingers cupped my chin, easing my face to meet his, the tears pouring from my eyes. Wiping each tear away, his touch soft and gentle, and the fight in me wore off, as his free arm remained wrapped around me, "Are you ok?" His eyes full of sadness as he searched my face for answers, "Amber, why are you crying? Talk to me; tell me what's wrong? If I hurt you, I'm sorry."

Pulling my face away, "You don't want a girl like me Tristan." Expressing my feelings and fears through hard sobs, "I'm not worth the shoes I walk in." a river of tears running through my fingers, my face buried again in his chest.

His hand comforting the back of my head, brushing my hair with softness, saying quietly, "Let me make that decision. I'm not looking to start anything right now. I like you and want to get to know you Amber." He lifted my head to face him, "Will you let me?" his eyes solemnly meeting mine with reassurance, "Let me take you home?"

Nodding yes, I allowed him to embrace me with his arms. When I was finally ready to leave, he wrapped his arm across my shoulder as we made our way back to my apartment.

There wasn't much conversation between Tristan and me as we made our way to my apartment. I wasn't sure what to say or even do to explain what had happened. It wasn't the right place or time. Arriving at the base of the stairwell, Tristan gently kissed my cheek farewell. Grasping the railing to enter, "Hey

Amber, I was wondering, would you come to my game tonight?" Tristan asked. I was taken aback for a second as I watched him shuffle his hands into his pockets, kicking the ground with shoes, acting almost nervous for my response.

I wasn't much of a sports fan but decided what would it hurt, "Sure. I think I could make that work," sending him a small smile.

His smile reached his eyes, "Great. I'll see you tonight then."

Before allowing him to leave, "Hey, I'm really sorry about that back there."

Walking backwards, "It's not a big deal. See you tonight?"

Waving my hand as he turned away, "Yea. See you later," he disappeared among the hustling tourists.

Walking into the apartment entrance and up two flights of stairs, I entered the tiny living room; Kayla ambushed me before I could even fully enter our apartment, "What the hell happened to you?" Glancing down at my coffee-soaked clothes. Grabbing my hand, dragging me to the grey microfiber sofa, she began drilling me with questions along the way.

"TELL ME! When? How? Where?" not stopping to take a breath. I realized it was pointless to keep anything from Kayla at this point. She wasn't one that let up easily, especially after seeing my earlier reaction. I needed to appease her appetite for information. Caving, I recounted our night at *ENVY* and our visit at the café, trying my hardest not to give too much detail or tell her about my freak out episode on King.

Mesmerized by my story, "Wow! Are you going to see him again?"

"Yes, but I don't know if I really want to," embarrassed by what happened earlier however part of me did want to see him again.

Kayla was taken aback, "When and why not?" pausing for a second, "He's hot and you need a good change. God only knows you deserve it," standing to enter the kitchen, she retrieved us a coke from our fridge.

She handed me one and I curled my fingers around the can, "I'm supposed to go to his game tonight. I guess it's one of his last and he wants me there." Taking a deep breath before continuing, "If he knew my past Kayla, he wouldn't want me. No guy wants a girl with a lot of baggage, especially the kind I carry."

Sitting next to me again, touching my shoulder, "Well have you given him the opportunity to find out? If he's truly a nice guy he'll accept you for you, not your past."

Throwing myself back against the pillow cushions, my arm thrown over my eyes, exasperated, "But my past screwed everything up, I'm not even sure I like myself. I'm trying my best to get past it. Charleston was supposed to bring new beginnings, allow me to clear my head. The last thing I wanted, want, is a man to fill it with hopeless dreams. I got screwed badly, and I just don't need any more right now. I need to focus, get my life straight. You know that better than anyone."

Leaning on her knees, her head turned back toward me, "True, but it doesn't mean you can't have a little fun while you're at it." Nudging my arm as she laid back herself, trying to lighten my mood. That was easy for Kayla to say, always rolling with the punches, accepting life one day at a time. You would think I would catch on, but my past haunted me daily. She was right in a way, but Tristan didn't seem like he was in this for the fun. Something said he was more serious. I needed to decide if I really wanted to face that head on?

Glancing down at my watch, it was 12:30, several hours left until Tristan's game. Looking over at Kayla, "I'm exhausted. I think I'm going to crash for a while before the game. Do you want to go?"

"I already am," squeezing her shoulders up in a giddy school-girl way.

"You are? With who," my eyebrows high in curiosity, although I already knew the answer.

"Keith! He asked me earlier while you were out. I guess he doesn't ever miss any of Tristan's games. You know me, I can't pass up a gig to see a man in uniform," winking at me. Smiling, I stood from the couch, "Ok. Well I guess we're all going."

Exiting the living room, I made my way to my bedroom, shutting the squeaking door behind me. Walking to my bed, kicking off my shoes, and peeling out of my coffee drenched t-shirt; I replaced it with my Notre Dame shirt.

Crawling up the foot, finally reaching my pillow, I buried myself in the coolness of the cotton pillowcase. Reaching over, I set the alarm on my *iPhone* for *5:30*. Rolling over on my side, pulling my spare pillow against my chest, breathing in heavily, I tried to clear the thoughts racing through my brain. Closing my eyes and taking one final deep breath, I fell asleep.

GAME NIGHT

Abruptly awakening to the sound of my alarm, raising my hand to press snooze, not trying to lift my head to look for my phone. My hand reaching air, finally I gave up, giving into the late afternoon light that was filling my room. Squinting and finding my phone, I shut it off. There was a new message from Tristan. Sliding the bar to the right, my screen lit up and recanted to my new messages.

> *Hoping you come tonight. I'm sorry for earlier. Let me make it up to you.*

A little excited about the evening, I didn't bother to reply. Easing myself from my bed, twisting my feet from under the sheets to meet the coldness of the hardwood pine floor, my toes wincing at the awkward coolness. Making my way to shower, walking in to the minute space, there was enough room for a sink, toilet, and walk-in shower.

Leaning in to the shower, I turned on the hot water. The pipes whistled their sweet song, as water made its way to the head, beginning their dance as the drops fell onto the blue tiled floor. Stripping my earlier ensemble, I tested the temperature to be sure it was accurate, stepping in, crossing my arms and let the water pound my back, washing away the anxiety of the morning. I will go to Tristan's game, but nothing more, I keep silently telling myself. This had to remain a friendship; I couldn't afford another relationship. I remember him saying he wasn't looking to start anything; maybe there was something to that. Making friends wouldn't hurt, even if my inner goddess screamed every time I was around him.

Spending the next twenty minutes, washing my hair, and lathering my body, I reached around and turned the knob off. Finding my plush blue towel, wrapping my body in it, allowing the fibers to soak up any remaining droplets present on my skin, I exited the shower, skirting over to the mirror. Met with dark eyes, pale skin, and damp hair, I sighed as I wrestled with what to do.

Sighing deeply, I loosened the towel from around my body, and flipped my hair over, running the towel through the wet strands. Allowing my body to air dry, walking to my closet, I pulled out khaki shorts, a white button down, sleeveless blouse, brown belt, and white flip flops; unsure of what to wear to a baseball game. All I knew was, I didn't want to look dumpy.

Back in the bathroom, I grabbed my phone, deciding I needed to lighten my mood. Sliding the bar to the right, I found *iTunes* and began searching my catalog for something upbeat to get ready to. Although crazy, I landed on Brittney Spears *You Drive Me Crazy* and turned the volume up. The chords echoed off the tiled walls. Grabbing my hair dryer, I let the heat dance across my tresses. The tunes trailed on through my small bathroom, the words ironic to my unusual relationship with Tristan. Ignoring them, I continued on my quest for dry hair. Ten minutes later, turning off the dryer, I glanced in the mirror, as Bon Jovi's *Living on a Prayer* echoed through the air.

Smiling, I grabbed my hairbrush, belting the chorus to the song, dancing to the beat, and having my quiet moment of fun. Lifting my phone, I noticed it was after 6 PM and I needed to finish up. Standing on my tippy toes to push my face closer to the mirror, I lifted my hand to pull back the skin on my cheeks slightly pinching to bring some color to them. As hot as it was, I didn't want to wear make-up and pulled my hair back into a shortened ponytail. Ever since cutting my hair, all the strands refuse to fit into the rubber band. Shutting off my phone, I exited the bathroom, and grabbed my Notre Dame ball cap off my bedside table. Placing it on my head, I pulled frayed tail through the back, finally completing my attire.

Reaching behind my back, I shimmied my phone in my back pocket and found my apartment keys. Turning towards the door, the loud squeak announcing my exit, I made my way into the living room. Kayla was sitting on the couch; phone in hand, texting God knows whom. "Ready?" I said, summoning her attention.

Glancing back, "You look cute. Yea, let's go. Keith's going to meet us there."

Arriving at the stadium, I glanced at my phone; it was 6:30 PM, 30 minutes before the first pitch. Making our way to the box office, we bought our tickets and walked over to the tall green iron gates. Walking in with my arm wrapped through the crevice of hers, "Thanks for coming along," I said gratefully, slightly smiling up at her.

"Not a problem," she said, smiling down at me.

"What about me," whined Keith, rushing up behind us as he wrapped his arms around our shoulders.

Rolling my eyes and playfully grinning, "Thank you too Keith. I'm sure Tristan appreciates you being here."

"I wouldn't miss the man's last few games. He needs this and the support before he leaves." Keith remarking

"Why is he leaving?" Kayla asked, being nosy.

Halting, coming almost to a stop, then glancing over at Kayla he emphatically stated, "He should be the one to tell you, not me. It's his business." Returning his attention to our quest of finding seats, Kayla and I shrugged our shoulders as we kept following him. Something was going on, but I couldn't put my finger on it. If things kept going like they were with Tristan, I knew I would find out sooner, rather than later.

Finding our seats just behind the third base line, Keith asked if we wanted some beers and left to get our order. Once out of earshot, "What do you think that was about?" Kayla asked as we sat down.

"No idea, honestly," shrugging my shoulders.

The guys were out on the field warming up as I spotted Tristan looking focused but a little solemn near the dugout. Nervousness shimmied its way into my stomach as I watched him ponder his deepest thoughts. Betrayed by my own eyes, they crept over each line of his masculine features. He was wearing his white, home uniform, pressed and clean, which seemed to be his forte, but his hat was missing, so his golden strands shimmered in the waning evening light.

Lost in my own thoughts, I was interrupted when Kayla piped up, "Do you see him?" Leaning over and pointing my finger in Tristan's direction, her eyes followed towards the dugout; widening in approval as she gently nudged me, "Amber, he's even hotter in uniform!"

I was giggling at her response, smacking at her playfully.

Kayla's attention redirected towards Keith who had arrived with our drinks. Turning my focus back to Tristan, I noticed a smile peak across his lips at seeing me sitting in the stands, only to be interrupted by his coach, "Tristan, you're up!" Grabbing his glove, he met the rest of his team that had line up on the field.

The announcer came over the PA, "We would like to welcome everyone that has come out to watch the Charleston Sharks. Let's give them a big round of applause as they take the field. Will everyone please stand for our National Anthem?"

The fans standing to their feet, men removing their hats and placing them over their hearts, followed by ladies in the same motion. Observing the crowd, the fans were proud of their local team. A young brunette stood on the pitcher's mound as she belted out the vocals to our nation's song. Once finished, the crowd whistled and cheered as the Sharks took their positions on the field for their game against rivals, the Savannah Dunes.

Tristan, taking the pitcher's mound focusing on the batter at home plate, acknowledged the catcher's signal. Rearing back, he released the first pitch of the game. "Strike one," the ump hollered as the batter took a step back to reset his posture and ready himself for the next pitch. Tristan remained focused throughout the game, concentrating on his pitches. As the third batter struck out, the Sharks exited the field. Glancing up to the stands for my approval, I smiled and nodded.

The Sharks went on to play 9 innings, beating the Dunes 10-3. Tristan racing towards the dugout held up both his hands, signifying he would be out in ten minutes. Nodding in acceptance, I turned sitting in my seat.

With his arm wrapped around Kayla, both leaned back against the stadium seating, "Usually after the game we go to ENVY for celebratory drinks. Want to go?" Keith asked us.

"Sure." Kayla and I chimed, replying in unison.

Removing his arm, standing and extending his hand to Kayla, "Great. Kayla you want to head that way. I'm sure Amber wants to wait for Tristan. Can you guys meet us there?" pointing his question at me.

Standing to hug Kayla bye, "Yea, sure. We'll see you shortly." Looking over my shoulder I noted Keith was leading Kayla up the stairs of the stadium into the upper concourse, making their way to the exit. Kayla threw her head back laughing at something Keith had said.

Ten minutes turned into around twenty, as I waited, witnessing a few players from Tristan's team greeting hopeful youngsters, signing autographs. The players were handing the signed balls back to the kids, whose faces were beaming with joy, in awe of the men they had just met. The stadium patrons had all cleared out but a few remaining stragglers. The field operators began prepping the red clay for the next home game. The winds shifted sending the scent of baseball leather and soap in waves my direction. Turning to look, Tristan was hustling down the concourse steps towards where I was sitting. Closing my eyes, breathing in the intoxicating scent of the stadium, I felt Tristan plop down in the seat next to me. His demeanor cool and scent refreshing from his shower, he was wearing blue jeans, a dark green polo, and flip-flops. "Did you have fun," he quipped, tipping the bill of my hat playfully.

Surprisingly calm, I replied, "Yes, thanks for inviting me. I have to tell you a little secret." His brow peaking in curiosity, "I'm not much of a sports fan. This was actually my first baseball game."

Snickering, "Really? Too bad I only have one more, or I would have to coax you into coming for the rest of the season." Gently nudging his elbow against my arm. The playful touch sent pulses radiating around the area of contact. My journalistic instincts kicking in, "And why are they your last?"

His face not giving anything away, acting as if he didn't hear me, "Where are Keith and um..."

"Kayla," I provided, answering him.

"Yea, Kayla?" finishing his question.

Pointing my thumb behind me, "They headed on to *ENVY*. I told them we would meet them there," realizing he ignored my question.

Leaning over, tipping my hat with his finger, "Good, I was hoping to walk with you, alone. Now about this hat?" a smile on his lips.

"What about it? It's all I had!" I exclaimed.

He was snickering at my response.

"Well if you hang here long enough, we may need to convert you," his smile wide, "Ready?" reaching his hand out for mine. Grabbing it, he helped me from my seat. Exiting the row, motioning for me to take the lead up the stairs, he placed his hand at the small of my back. The stairs up were narrow, only wide enough for one person. Making our way to the thorough way between the upper and lower decks, looking over the seating and field, I noticed calmness radiated his features.

"I'm sorry about earlier, Amber. It was never my intent to upset or hurt you," holding my hand, lacing his fingers between mine. Reaching over, grabbing his forearm in acceptance, we headed into the first concourse to exit the stadium.

"It's not you Tristan. Let's just focus on the night ahead, ok?" Passing him a small smile, he dropped the subject as we continued walking. I wasn't sure why I was holding his hand, but it felt so natural. Tristan was sending me mixed signals and at times leading on to wanting more from me, but my mind raced with uncertainty as to whether I really wanted to start another relationship so quickly.

Entering the concourse, Tristan stopped, pulling my hand back towards him. Turning around to him, he placed his hand upon my waist, as he nudged me back against the cool, concrete wall of the darkened concourse. Shuddering from the contact against my warm skin, excitement and fear ran through me, as Tristan leaned his hard body barely against mine. Lifting his hand to reach the front of my cap, he removed it from my head. My eyes shifted to his, as his hand cupped my neck, his finger delicately tracing my cheek. His eyes deep with lust, searching mine, were sparkling with hopefulness. Turning my head to escape his trance, I felt nervous. It had been so long since I had been with anyone, especially someone who treated me the way Tristan has. Nudging my head back to face him, my breath escaped; his rough knuckles tracing as his eyes followed the lines of my face.

His eyes holding my stare, his free hand began at my waist and slid up my arm, barely touching my skin. His hand went back and remained firm on my waist, as he brought his other hand up and pulled my hair loose from my ponytail. Breaking his stare, he leaned further against me, as his nose met my neck, breathing in the scent of my hair draping across my shoulders. "You are beautiful," a sigh escaping, "I know what I said earlier," he said with a small gulp in his voice, "but I can't shake this feeling between us, this connection looming. I know you feel it too. Tell me I'm wrong," the backs of his knuckles brushing the lines of my forearms.

I began relaxing at his gentleness. Shifting his head, he watched his fingers dance across the skin of my arm, making its way back to my waist. His head turning to face me again, leaning in closer, his lips barely touching mine. His dancing fingers landed on the back of my neck, elegantly nudging me forward, asking permission. Unable to resist temptation further, my lips greeted warmth and softness. My hands reached up and wrapping themselves around his neck.

The feel of his hair tickled my wrists. Bringing his other hand to clasp behind my neck, the length of his thumbs resting below my chin, he continued his succulent slow tender kiss. Darkness surrounded us as the stadium lights shut off, allowing us complete privacy in the dimly lit tunnel.

Tristan's hands, gently shifting to my shoulders, broke his course. Whispering smaller kisses on my lips, "Look at me," my eyes opening to meet fire and lust. Brushing his thumb across the pinks of my cheeks barely illuminated by the only light in the tunnel, his eyes took in my delicate features, the slowness and taste of his kiss, mixing with his overwhelming scent. Reaching my hand up, I gently pulled Tristan in for more, his lips firmer against mine, gently coaxing me open as his taste filled my mouth.

Allowing a moment of indulgence, breaking away, "You taste sweet like ripe strawberries on a cool spring day," pushing my hair behind my ear, his hand cupping the side of my face. His nose nestling with mine, "Your beauty is like the sun setting with pink clouds after a fresh afternoon rainstorm. You mesmerize me, Amber," he whispered. Lifting his body from mine, a gush of breath escaping my chest as it rose from the trap of steel that pinned me against a pillar of strength.

Reaching for my hand, "We have friends waiting and as much as I'd like to continue, it wouldn't be very gentlemanly of me to do it here," pulling me towards the stadium exit, my focus hazy with sweet words. Snickering at my entranced state, he led the way to *ENVY*.

The line to the club seemed even longer than the prior evening. Making our way to the front, similar disgruntled sounds resounded as we passed each person. Ray greeting us, removing the rope that blocked out any non-invited entrants, "Mr. Ashton, welcome back. Shayla wanted me to inform you that your friends have found their table and everything is in order," in his gruff, raspy tone.

"Thank you Ray. As you were," nodding in approval. Inside, the music was blaring and the place was stacked wall to wall with people. Yelling over the crowd, "It's college night. We're always slammed." Never letting my hand go, Tristan led to the circle stairway at the back of the building. Entering the VIP lounge, I spotted Kayla and Keith, and pointed Tristan in the direction of their location. Approaching the private seating area, they were locked in a full make-out session.

"Get a room!" Tristan chuckled slapping Keith's back, interrupting their not so private moment.

Looking up, his cheeks redder than normal, "We would if we could get access to yours," nodding his head to the mirrored wall of windows.

"Yea that's not happening," the men exchanged smug smiles, interrupted as Shayla brought over our drinks.

"Here you go guys. Don't y'all have too much fun," placing her hand on Tristan's forearm, "Mr. Ashton, I know it's your night off but a word please," her words running together as she motioned for him to the next private area over. Standing on her tippy toes to reach his ear, Tristan, leaned in to listen as business plagued his features. Stepping down to her flat feet, Tristan returned with directions. Shayla nodding in acceptance turned on her foot, bouncing away.

Calling behind her before she disappeared, he instructed, "Keep them coming. Put them on the house tab!" Throwing her hand back in acknowledgement, she continued on her mission.

Making his way back to our booth, "Everything ok?" I questioned.

"Yea, just club stuff. I'll be right back," kissing my cheek and turning towards the stairway that took him to his office.

Breaking my stare, Kayla garnered my attention, "Sit! Relax, let's have a good time." Sliding into the booth, I returned the smile.

There was subtle conversation in the air as I waited for Tristan to return and Shayla to come back with our drinks. Keith and Kayla were busy making small talk, while I sat with my hands in my lap. We were seated at the black sofa station. The micro-suede was adorned by damask style pillows and there was a simple, small black coffee table and a lounger, adorned with the same damask fabric, but held plain black pillows.

Having some time to think, my mind wandered back to the concourse. Shayla returned with our drinks. Not waiting for the others to drink up, I downed my gin and tonic in one swallow, my body was still warm from earlier. Shaking my head to bring my attention to Keith and Kayla, they were staring at me.

"Good walk?" Keith jokingly asked.

Redness upon my cheeks, I hadn't realized that I had stared off, daydreaming. "You could say that," I said shyly, bringing my drink to my lips to hide my smile, searching for any trace of liquid left. Within minutes, Tristan made his way back down the stairwell, meeting Shayla at the base of the second level stairwell. Handing her an envelope, she turned and headed towards the opposite side of the building, down the winding staircase.

Hands in his pockets, Tristan shuffled towards our table. Sitting next to me on the sofa, placing his arm around my shoulders, he sent me an innocent smile. Turning to Keith, they began exchanging details about Tristan's game from earlier, as Kayla and I chatted about her upcoming semester. I could tell she was antsy for details but knew it would have to wait.

Mid conversation with Kayla, we were interrupted, "Do you want to dance? I missed out the last time you were here," winking at me, Tristan grabbed my hand pulling me from the comfort of the sofa.

Shocked by his forwardness, "Hey now, you were some stranger in the shadows, but seeing I don't have a choice, sure," giggling, as he led me to my feet and then the dance floor.

Laughing at my response, he led me down the winding stairway to the crowded dance floor. Heat had enveloped the room from the swaying bodies. Tristan began dancing to the song, me following with the beat. Turning and dancing up behind me, grinding softly into me, his hand was firm upon my waist. Our bodies moved together, his nose nuzzled in my neck; my mind lost in the sensations of the rhythm.

With songs changing, I looked over to find Kayla and Keith dancing; Kayla looking over at me, a coy smile displayed. Turning around in Tristan's hands, pulling him in close to me, my hips moved in rhythm as his hands wandered freely.

Dancing the next three songs, we returned to the VIP Lounge where fresh drinks sat. Taking a sip, my tongue caught an unfamiliar taste, however my judgment was clouded and I ignored my taste buds, finishing my drink.

Noticing the bitter look on my face, Tristan took my drink away, "Slow down darling," he suggested, setting it back on the table, "Or you won't last the night. Plus," his arms pulling my body into his, his nose level with mine, our foreheads pressed together, "I'd like to continue where we left off." Kissing me gently, the few drinks unveiling a more ambitious side of Tristan. Smiling into his kiss, my hand finding his chest, there was a slight tension under my fingers. On my tiptoes, I leaned into him, so only he could hear, "or we could finish right now," a slightly courageous side of me showing, motioning my eyes at his private room as I bit my lower lip.

Surprise evident, "Now I wouldn't be a true gentleman to take his fair lady in my office," raising his brow at me.

"Well I'm not a fair lady, kind sir," lacing his fingers in mine, pulling him towards his private office. Coming up behind me, his arms folded around me when everything suddenly went dark.

THE HOSPITAL

The smell of latex filled the air, my eyes doing their best to adjust to the bright fluorescent lights above me. Shifting myself to get comfortable, I felt a heavy hand on my forehead, rubbing my hair to the back of my head. Finding it a little bizarre, the sound of the plastic mattress ruffling from underneath me, I concluded this wasn't my room or my bed. With each movement, my head throbbed with pain and my voice was hoarse, barely choking out, "Where am I?"

"Shh," Kayla was insisting, "You're in the hospital," continuing her soft rubs of my hair across my forehead. Kayla had seen me one too many times in a hospital bed. My heart began racing as panic struck at the sound of hospital. Opening my eyes to the bright room, I lifted my hands to relieve the tension in my head, the IV line halting my arms, "Hospital? What?" my head lolling back and forth, looking around, "Where's Tristan?"

Kayla placing her hand in mine, to calm me, "Slow down. Tristan is right outside. He hasn't left all night. You passed out at the club. The doctors are running some tests, but believe someone spiked your drink last night. Did you see anything suspicious?"

"Drugged?" thoughts to Indiana invaded my memory. This was something that would happen there, not here. Why here?

"What? No? Who," struggling to recall anything.

"The cops are on their way to ask you some questions. Tristan is pissed that this happened in the club, but he says his first priority is you right now." Kayla still calm while the doctor entered the room with a police officer.

"Ms. Slayton, I'm glad to see you're awake. How are you feeling," the doctor questioned while reviewing my charts. He was young, mid-twenties, stood about six foot, with shaggy brown hair, his name tag read, "Alexander Timble, MD" Grabbing an instrument from the wall behind me, lifting my eyelid, shining a bright light in each one, checking the dilation of my eyes. "I'm ok. Just a massive headache," I answered as he switched off the little light and replaced it on the wall behind me.

Shuffling his hands into his coat pocket, "We'll get you something for that. In the meantime, this is Officer Caudell. He has a few questions for you, are you up to answering them?" I nodded my head yes. "Good, I will be back in a few minutes. We're going to keep you for observation overnight and then release you in the morning."

Officer Caudell took the empty seat next to my hospital bed. Reaching in his pocket, he removed a tiny spiral notebook and pen to jot some notes. Looking up, he asked everyone to leave before starting his questioning. Kayla kissed my forehead as she stood to leave the room.

Officer Caudell was a tall, skinny, black man, with a marine haircut. His voice firm, as he began his questioning, "So Ms. Slayton..."

"Please, Amber," I said, politely correcting him.

"Ok, Amber, what do you recall from last night's events?"

"Nothing really. We were dancing, having a good time. Tristan and I were leaving and the room went dark." Jotting some notes down as I recounted my foggy memory.

Not looking up from his notes, "Do you remember seeing any-thing suspicious? Did any of your drinks taste funny?"

The question triggering recollection, "Now that you men-tion it, yes. We returned to the lounge and found fresh drinks. As I drank mine, I vaguely recall something funny, but nothing out of the ordinary. I drank it anyway."

His eyes shooting up, his head still cast down, "Why?"

Shrugging my shoulders, "Why not? I had already had several, my better judgment was clouded."

After a few more questions, he finished, giving me his card with a case number, "Call me if you recall any more details. I'll send your friends back in."

"Thank you, officer," with the officer exiting the room, Kayla returned to my side.

"What did he say?" she asked placing her hand back in mine; I laid my head back on the flat hospital pillow wondering where Tristan was?

I was looking her direction, telling her, "Nothing really. He just asked me some questions about last night, took some notes, and that was it.

"*Ssst*," my head radiating pain in response to the noise in the room. Reaching behind me, Kayla pressed the call button to summon someone.

"Yes..." came a voice calling over the speaker.

"Amber has a headache. The doctor stated he would bring her some meds," Kayla fussed impatience evident in her tone.

"Yes ma'am. We're working on it," the speaker going quiet. Within a few minutes a grumpy, grey haired woman entered the room, carrying a cup with medication in it. Shoving the concoction in my hands, "Take this!" Hesitantly, lifting my hands, I took the water and meds and downed them quickly. Lying back on the flat hospital pillow, I covered my eyes with my arm and welcomed the slight darkness.

Knock, Knock! Not lifting my arm, I heard the doctor shuffle in. "All your charts look good. We did find *Rohypnol* in your system. Luckily you weren't left alone with anyone or you could have been in serious danger. Your friends rushed you straight here when you passed out. Are you feeling ok?" His words like knives, piercing through my temples.

Shaking my head to jolt the million thoughts away, removing my arm, "Just my head."

Shifting on his feet, replacing the chart at the end of my bed, "Nurse Mary brought you some meds. They should start working in no time. We'll write you a prescription to take with you tomorrow after we discharge you. In the meantime get some sleep. Before I leave, do you have any other questions?"

Groaning slightly at the constant noise, "No, thank you."

Dr. Timble left the room. Hearing heavy footsteps enter, taking Kayla's place, Tristan sat next to my bedside, his grasp firm but yet soft on my arm. His fingers dancing on the inside with his smell mixing with the latex calmed me but also announced his presence.

"Are you ok?" his voice light, "How do you feel?" lifting his hand to brush my hair softly, as not to place any more pressure. Not removing my arm, my eyes heavy, "I'm fine, just a headache. I'll be better when I get home."

"Kayla said she will take you home. I will try to come by in the morning to see you. I have an out of town game, so I will be gone for the next couple days," his voice still light and soft.

Removing my arm, squinting in the harsh light, "Ok," smiling at him he leaned forward kissing my cheek good bye.

"I'm going to head out too," Kayla remarked, "Get some sleep."

Kissing my forehead, everyone left, leaving my room in darkness as I fell back to sleep.

I was greeted with the early morning sun cascading in the hospital window. The stale smell of the hospital loomed in the room as the new nurses began making their rounds.

Dr. Timble entered the room, "Well Ms. Slayton, everything looks great. Any questions?" Kayla entered the room right at the end of the conversation and took the seat next to my bed.

"Ya, when can I go home?" I remarked.

"We are working on your discharge paperwork. Nothing but rest for the next 24 hours, minimum visitation Ms. Slayton." Sending a stern warning to Kayla.

Responding, "I'll make sure of that." The doctor nodding at her response turned and he left the room. Walking back in, a different nurse entered with my discharge papers, followed by a candy striper with a wheel chair.

Kayla standing, "Here, let me help you," making her way to help grab my elbow for support.

Lifting myself, turning, my feet dangling over the hospital bed, "Where are my shoes?" Kayla, finding my garment bag, took my flip flops out to place them on my feet. The nurse removed my IV lines and shut off the monitors. Standing and taking two steps, I turned and sat down in the wheel chair, placing my forehead on the tips of my fingers, closing my eyes. Backing us out of the room, we made our way to the elevators and out of the hospital.

RECOVERING

Upon returning to our apartment, the shades had been drawn and peace filled the air of the somewhat empty space. Glancing over at Kayla, "Keith came over and helped me prepare the apartment before you got home. Now let's get you in bed to rest." Keeping her arm wrapped through mine, she led us through the dark apartment into my room. The curtains had been drawn and only a small amount of light was trying to peak through the loose crack.

Crawling into my bed, Kayla pulled the loose sheets over me, as I lay my head on my pillow. Closing my eyes, I heard Kayla tip toe towards the door, she quietly closed it behind her as I drifted off to sleep.

Waking into darkness several hours later, I stretched my aching arms above my head. Reaching for my phone, my hand pulled back empty, I came to the realization that Kayla must have taken it. Easing myself up, I shifted the blankets off of me, turning my body and placing my bare feet on the cold hard floor. Walking to the bathroom, I flicked on the light as the dull fluorescent illuminated the small space. Looking at myself in the mirror, my face was pale and my hair matted from my restful sleep. The creak of my door interrupted my thoughts as Kayla entered carrying a glass of water. "I'm glad to see you're up. How do you feel?"

"Good." Reaching for the refreshing cool glass. Sitting on the toilet, I took small sips.

Leaning against the trim of the doorway, folding her arms together, "Well bad news."

Looking up from beneath my eye lashes, "What?"

"Tristan's game is rescheduled to tomorrow due to rain, so no game tonight. He will be out of town for an extra day," a slight pout on her lips.

"What?" scoffing at her, "Well that sucks. What are we going to do?"

"Well you are going to rest...doctor's orders," she reminded me looking down at her phone. Sending her a sarcastic grin, blowing me off, "At least you will be able to rest, but we can just sit around, relax, and watch movies for the night."

Sitting around did sound pleasant, "Sounds good," I said, reaching my hand out to her, "Now my phone?" she smiled as she slapped the rectangular device in my hand. I sent Tristan a quick text, letting him know I was good and I stood to change into something clean and comfortable.

Finding the right attire, I retired to the living room where I found Kayla already in her comfy clothes and starting one of the dozen girlie movies we had on hand.

The next couple days were productive as Kayla and I worked on unpacking the apartment and getting most of the boxes put away. Keith came over for a short stint and helped out some. It was nice having the help and we made a huge dent in the mass chaos of our apartment. While there, we made plans to attend Tristan's game that night together.

Stripping out of my dust ridden, dirty clothes, I entered the shower to wash away the hard work of the day. The busyness kept my focus on something productive, rather than dwelling on things of the past and the uncertainty of the future.

After about 30 minutes, I was fresh and ready, the hot water washing away any sign of days past. Deciding on a linen khaki skirt and teal green spaghetti strap shirt, with my Sperry's, it would be something comfortable to bear the heat of the summer. Leaving my brunette tresses down, I shifted them in the mirror, spraying them into place with my hair spray.

Exiting my room, I noted Kayla had opened the curtains in the living room, allowing the warm orange tones of the evening to wash through our apartment. She was wearing linen capris and a blue spaghetti strap shirt, with flip-flops. Her hair pulled back in a loose ponytail, topped with her new College of Charleston ball cap. Smiling in approval at my ensemble, she grabbed her keys, handing me my phone and we exited our apartment towards Tristan's last game.

Meeting Keith at the stadium, we arrived just in time to hear the announcer welcome everyone to the game. A slight headache peaked from earlier in the day, I brushed it off reflecting on how well rested I felt. Making our way to our seats, Tristan came over from the dugout. Easing himself over the fence, he gave me a small peck, "Are you ok," landing back on his feet. "I'm fine," responding, as he rubbed the base of his neckline. "Good, I gotta run," back on solid ground, he hustled back to the dugout; the game wasn't far from starting.

The loud speaker crackled with the announcer welcoming everyone to the game, the players taking the field. Fans in the bleachers stood for the National Anthem holding hats or gloves to their hearts, same as the prior game. A young girl, about seventeen stood on the pitcher's mound, belting out the words to our Nation's song. When finished, the crowded stadium roared into applause and the teams took their places. Tristan took the pitcher's mound and threw out the first pitch of his last game.

Tristan had no issues striking out his first round of opponents against the Savannah Dunes again. As the players crowded into the dugout, watching, I noticed Tristan grabbing his helmet. He seemed to be slightly resisting solemnness taking over his demeanor. He placed the helmet on his head, grabbing his bat, and walked onto the field, the crowd erupting in applause as he reached home plate. Tristan readied himself as the opposing pitcher got the signal from his catcher on the mound. The pitcher reared back, releasing the pitch, only for it to barely miss Tristan. I stood, angrily as the crowd grew furious at the wild pitch. Tristan shook it off, lifting his hand to quiet the crowd as he returned to his stance. I could see the anger flash as he was ready for the next pitch.

The pitcher threw the ball and, CRACK, the sound of the bat making contact with the fierce pitch echoed through the stadium. Fans grew quiet as they watched which way the ball was going. It was headed towards the left field foul post where it barely scraped by into fair territory, landing over the fence line. The crowd exploded in cheers as Tristan rounded the bases enjoying his homerun. He was met at the dugout, by hands held high, and pats on the back of a job well done. Glancing over at me, grinning at his success, I returned with an equally wide-eyed smile.

Lasting nine innings, we won by two runs. The teams exited the dugouts, and took to the field to offer their good game handshakes to one another. The announcer coming over the loud speaker, "As many of you know, tonight is Tristan Ashton's last game here with the Charleston Sharks. We ask that our hometown crowd and welcomed visitors keep Tristan in your thoughts and prayers as he leaves for Afghanistan in the coming days. We have enjoyed watching Tristan through the years and wish him well on his future endeavors. God speed and thank you for all you do for our country."

My ears must have been deceiving me, it couldn't be true. The hurt stabbed me like a rusty knife and my heart sank as applause erupted through the stadium, followed by whistles and cheers. Sinking into my chair, Tristan exited the dugout and lifted his hat off his head in recognition, thanking the crowds, when his eyes met mine. Tears about to erupt, my head throbbing worse, my mind couldn't comprehend the fact that he was leaving. He had kept the worst part of it from me. I knew he didn't owe me an explanation, but why start anything or pursue anything with me?

Kayla's hand found my shoulder, as we sat there quietly. Tristan's eyes held mine as if he could see the insides of me shredding with the unsettling news. His face registered the wrongness of the situation unfolding between us. My mind racing with a million questions, I strongly questioned why I had even gotten involved in this. My fingers folding into the palms of my hands with the anger growing within me, my past haunted me daily and now the man who had begun winning me over was leaving.

Seeing my face, Kayla asked, "You're pale and you look as if you are going to pass out," her hand on the back of my shoulders, "Amber, did you know?"

Tears strung with anger, "No. Why would I? I just met him. I knew it was his last game and even asked him why but every time he avoided my questions." Unfolding my fingers to try and calm myself, my eyes cast down as I began grabbing the end of my linen skirt. Squeezing my hands tight, my hands moved onto rubbing down my skirt, doing my best to keep my anger and hurt at bay.

Trying her best to console me, I heard the clicking of cleats coming down the stadium concrete stairs. The wind shifting, the aromas of baseball leather, sweat, and soap announcing Tristan's arrival, "Could you excuse us?" asking softly of Kayla and Keith. Kayla rising quickly to her feet, pointed her dainty finger at him, "How could…"

The words escaping me faster than I realized, yelling at her, "Stop, Kayla!" My tone shifting slightly to a low mutter, "I will take care of this," still facing the field. It was time I stood up for myself and quit letting Kayla do my dirty work. One thing I learned from my past was to defend myself and this was my chance.

Halting on her hanging words, stomping her foot, clenching her fist in defeat, "We'll wait for you outside the stadium," she hissed through clenched teeth.

"No need," Tristan refuting her, "I plan to take her home. We need to talk."

Kayla reared to speak, stopping her before the words could leave, "It's fine, Kayla. I'll call if I need something." Staring him down and then at me, Keith tried grabbing her arm to leave, however she pulled away stomping up the concrete steps, Keith trailing behind her.

"Let go of me," I heard her screeching at Keith as she angrily left the seats. Waiting for them to disappear from sight, my body was ready to erupt like a volcano as tears pierced the corners of my eyes. Tristan sat next to me not speaking, reaching for my hand. Pulling away, I reached for the hemline of my skirt again, and then shifted to curling my fingers together.

"Why?" stuttering, breaking the silence that was swallowing us. "Why didn't you tell me when I asked you? Why are you…" before finishing, grabbing my chin he turned my face towards him, fear, hurt, anguish all looming in his eyes. Releasing my chin from his grip, I looked down knowing I couldn't face him without letting every emotion burn through me.

He remained quiet, unsure of what to say I am assuming. I couldn't handle the silence and the secrets any longer. Standing to walk away, he grabbed my wrist to stop me. Fire burned under his grasp, my face growing pale with fear, he let go, "I'm sorry. Please let me explain." Hesitating for a moment, I sat back down, not removing my eyes from my lap. Crossing my arms, it was now or never, my time to find out. I needed an answer to his evasiveness.

Tapping my feet to try and calm myself, Tristan begged, "Look at me, please," but I couldn't do it. Repeating his plea again, I forced myself to finally meet his gaze. I found the same fear and sadness in his eyes from moments ago. I could see that he felt wrong for what had happened, that this wasn't something he wanted.

Reaching for my clenched fists, forcing them to release and grasping my hand into his, "I'm sorry, Amber. I didn't plan for this to happen. No one knew about my career except for the league and a few people. I got called up last week for a classified mission and decided it was time to leave the league. I didn't plan to meet you or anyone for that matter. When I made the decision to leave, my plan was to play this game and leave Charleston behind, with my focus on the war."

"So why even pursue someone? Why not tell me yesterday when I asked?" I bit, the words spoken through the tightness of my jaw.

Releasing his hands from mine, he ran his hands through his short hair, down to his face, rubbing firmly. The military cut made sense now. Searching for answers to a question he knew he didn't have the answer to, my heart was aching, anger pounding through me. My guard went up and I knew I didn't need to get any closer.

"When you walked into the club that night, I don't know

something hit me. Your beauty truly captivated me and my mind wouldn't give up. My mind raced with every possible scenario of why this would be a bad idea, but something inside me pushed me. I couldn't give it up, no matter how hard I tried," his words soft as his hand cupped my cheek.

Resistant, he could feel the tension beneath his fingers, "You have hurt me Tristan. This isn't something I needed with just moving here, but you have been so persistent. You have me so confused. How am I supposed to handle this? What am I supposed to do? Tell me!" He tightened up and remained silent. Squeezing my fingers into a tight fist, my mind couldn't handle any more rejection, "You don't want a girl like me, anyway. I'm so screwed up. I guess I just don't..." before finishing, he cupped the back of my neck and brought his lips to mine, pressing a kiss to my lonely lips. His kiss was warm, full of compassion and heartache. Lifting my hands around his neck, finding his short hair, I pulled his mouth closer to mine, my anger melting. Lost in the moment, he pulled away, kissing my chin to my ear.

His forehead nestled to mine, "Let me make that decision, Amber. I know what I want, and screwed up or not. I'm sorry I didn't tell you sooner. I should have, but please don't give up on me yet. This isn't easy for me. The last thing I wanted was to start a relationship before leaving, but I couldn't give up trying when I know the effort is worth it."

The heat and smell of the man was like a drug to me. Tristan began nibbling my ear lobe, brushing soft kisses down my neck. Resisting temptation, my body betrayed me as my head turned towards him. He was reaching his firm hands along my back for support, shivers racing along my spine as his hand tightened against it. Heat radiating from every pore in my body, I lifted my head back losing myself in the pure ecstasy of his touch. My hurt lost in his overpowering trance of seductiveness.

With unfinished moments from the night before, lust surrounded our every move. Whispers of kisses plagued my skin, and clouds of touches echoed along my arms. I could feel him smiling in my neck, even losing myself in our passionate embrace. Pulling away, "Tristan, what are we doing?" resting my forehead against his, my eyes closed, a small amount of fear still evident in my voice. Thoughts plagued me; could I really do this? Could I start something and continue this new journey with someone I just met?

"I don't know Amber. Whatever this is, I want it. I want to know you, all of you. I don't care about your past. What I see in front of me is what I want," his words plundering my thoughts, knowing if he knew the truth, he wouldn't be saying that.

Tears crept back as Indiana made its appearance again, "Tristan, no. I can't do this." Shoving him away from me, my heart raced with fear and anxiety. I couldn't do this; I couldn't let someone hurt me again. I couldn't let Tristan in on Indiana. He would never understand and he would never accept me for what happened. I stood again to leave only to be stopped by Tristan placing his hand at my waist.

Looking to his eyes, I was met with sorrow and remorse, "I'm sorry Amber. I know you've been hurt, but I want you to know you can trust me. I would never, could never hurt you. When you are ready, I am here to listen with an open mind. I need to grab my stuff but we can go."

I remained quiet as he stood to leave behind me. Motioning for me to lead up the stairs, tears tried to leave my eyes, but I was done crying. I had cried so much in the past months it was useless to continue. Anger, insecurity, you name it had all settled in the pit of my stomach. I wanted so much to believe what Tristan was saying, but Indiana had me like a vice. I didn't know when it would be right to tell Tristan, really didn't know if now would be good with him leaving. Indiana reminded me constantly of what I left and I knew there wasn't a chance that anyone else would treat me any different. I wanted Tristan, so much, but I just couldn't bring myself to move forward with this, not with him leaving in a matter of days or weeks. Reaching the top of the stairway, he ran off to grab his items from the locker room. Now was my chance to walk away, now was my chance to escape, but my feet remained glued to the pavement. I couldn't move, couldn't do it.

Within minutes he had returned to walk me out of the stadium. Memories replayed from our last time along this same trail. His hands, his smell, his lips, but as we reached the gates to exit, the memories remained in the darkened concourse.

INDIANA

Exiting the stadium and walking towards my apartment, quietness surrounded us; the only sounds filling the air were passing motorists and the occasional chatter of passersby. Questions hung over us, but neither of us wanting to face them. Tonight could have been the most sinful, best night of my life and the man I couldn't get away from was leaving. I gave in to Indiana; it was time to tell the truth; to let Tristan in on a secret that had been plaguing me since the beginning. Breaking the silence between us, "When are you leaving," nervous, I dreaded the answer, my face falling to my feet.

"Friday, 0600 sharp," kicking the rocks on the sidewalk; not revealing too much,

Folding my arms across my chest, doing my best to protect the shattering of my heart, "When will you be back?"

"I don't know," he admitted.

My feet stopped. He didn't know; how could he not? What exactly did he do for a job that he didn't know when he would return? This whole relationship really didn't make sense at this point. Who would want to live like this? So many questions hung in my mind.

Growing weak from my emotional high, "I need to sit down." Shuffling to the closest park bench, sitting, I rubbed my face, trying to remain calm. Tristan stood next to the bench with his hands in his pockets, shuffling back and forth; it was obvious he didn't know how to approach the situation.

Swallowing the knot in my throat, "I came to Charleston to start over, clear my head and get away from some things in Indiana." My gut was screaming at me not to do this, not to even mention Indiana. Tristan's eyes focused on me, still holding his stance, "Within a few short days, I meet you and now you're leaving. My head is so messed up now, I don't know what to do," agony in my voice.

Sitting down, pulling me close to him, I tried to push away, but his strength got the best of me. I couldn't budge. Anguish set over me at the tightness of his grasp, my body growing tense, "There you go again. Why are you so tense? What is it?"

It was time; it was time to get this over with. Telling him the truth would end this and allow me to move on and heal like I need to. I didn't need any more hurt or a relationship at that. I know the time we had spent together had been amazing and he had helped me gain a confidence I never knew I had, but I still didn't know if reliving Indiana would truly make things any better, or if I was hoping they would make things worse?

"I told you I'm screwed up," answering brashly, "You don't want a girl like me. I have issues you wouldn't understand."

Grabbing my hand, kissing it in a reassuring way, his voice calmer, "Try me Amber. We all have a past...I have a past. We're all screwed up in some way. Just tell me."

With a heavy sigh, it was now or never, the words began rolling off my tongue, "I left Indiana and took a job at *Lowcountry Magazine*, after Kayla helped me apply for the position. It was a way to restart my life, the first thing I had control over since Casey."

The tension grew immediately throughout his body. The

only thing I could hear was the racing of his heart, or was that mine? I could see the questions fall across his face as he tried to process who I was talking about.

"Casey?" he swallowed, "Who's Casey?"

"My husband..."

THE EFFECT
INDIANA HAS

T he giant rock that had been sitting on top of me had finally lifted at the revelation of his name. Tristan, on the other hand, looked like he was about to pass out. He didn't say anything, still trying to process what I had just revealed.

"Husband?" his voice broke, "husband...you're married!" he stood hurriedly, "Amber, what the hell? Why didn't you tell me?" He began pacing as he tried to make heads or tails of the information I just gave him. I could see the dreaded words all over his face.

"Well soon to be ex-husband. I left Indiana to escape him, to escape my life and his control over it," rubbing my palms on the back of my neck, as I leaned forward on my knees.

Pulling his cheeks down as he rubbed his hands over his face, "What do you mean escape? Why did you leave him?"

Taking a deep breath, I was ready to finally tell my story, "Towards the end of college, Casey and I married. I was in love with him and couldn't picture my life without him, even though we fought constantly. When I moved in with him, the fighting grew worst and the abuse soon followed. It wasn't physical at first, mostly mental. He degraded me and broke my will down even further. My parents didn't see it; no one did, other than Kayla. She was constantly telling me I could do better and that I needed to leave the SOB. I just couldn't make myself go. He had me on a tight leash and with his angry temper I knew he wouldn't let me go willingly."

"So, what was the deciding factor," still remaining guarded, his arms now folded across his chest.

"Casey had a porn addiction. After we moved in together, I walked in on him several times watching it and you know... I didn't understand it, I was his wife and he could have me any-time, why did he need porn? So, I tried my hardest to make myself approachable, but always got shot down. He only wanted me when he couldn't have me. He slept all hours of the day and night and we barely had a marriage, but I tried to make it work. After several months of continuously coming onto Casey, I finally gave up. I couldn't take rejection anymore and started to distance myself from him.

He got deeper in the porn. If I turned him down when he wanted it, he locked himself in our bedroom and told me not to bother him until he was finished. It crushed me. One night I told him that if he didn't stop, I would leave. He told me I would never leave him and punched me in the face. At that moment, I knew I needed to get out, but didn't know how or where to start. All I knew is that if I stayed any longer, it would get worse."

Tristan grew angry as tears began streaming down my face recounting my past. At that moment, I wanted Tristan or some-one to hold me, but all I could do was wrap my arms around my-self to try and fill the empty void.

"How did you leave?" his fists now tightened into a ball, his knuckles white as the bones tried to break through the tight skin.

"When he punched me, I stumbled back against the wall hitting my head which knocked me unconscious. It freaked him out, so he called for an ambulance, since I wasn't responding. Even though he knew Kayla hated his guts, he called her in a panic and told her they were taking me to the hospital. He told her that I tripped over the dog, while walking in the dark hallway and he heard me fall.

She rushed to the ER and got there with a police escort before he arrived. They wouldn't let him near me. Even though I tried to tell Kayla he didn't mean it, she could see right through me. I tried to convince her that I fell and that Casey hadn't hit me. One of the cops was her boyfriend, so he knew she meant business, even though he was crossing the line, denying my wishes. Casey left the hospital, pissed off, no less.

Kayla stayed with me through the night and coaxed me into leaving. I knew she was right; I had to get out. But with losing so much control over my life, I wasn't sure where to start. So, in the coming days she helped me pack my things. Her boyfriend kept Casey at bay, so he wouldn't interfere. She helped me apply for the job and I left town within three weeks. Kayla's the only one who knows the full truth."

Tristan's knees gave way and he found himself back on the bench, remaining silent. I knew he was angry and I feared he was angry with me, I didn't know what to do. My inner conscience began questioning whether it was right for me to even tell him.

Although I felt relieved, Indiana took back over, "I told you I was screwed up Tristan."

Standing up from the bench, still clenching his fists, he punched the brick wall behind us. The sound of his hand crumbling with the wall scared me and I knew it was time to leave. I quickly got up and began walking towards my apartment. *Shit!* I heard him gasp from behind.

Running up behind me, Tristan grabbed my arm to pull me in towards him. Looking down, I saw the blood trickling from his knuckles. Grabbing my chin with force, the tightness of his arms filled me with fear as I could feel his anger pulsing through his body. Trying my darnedest to remove my chin and escape, he held it firm and kissed me hard and deep, his kiss raw and angry. Biting my lower lip, I pulled back, finding my strength; I broke my arm free and slapped him across the face. He let go rubbing the red handprint embellishing his cheek. Our eyes caught and I could see the hurt that filled them. Rubbing his hands through his short hair, he threw them down in defeat and turned the other way, leaving me there on the darkened street alone. Crossing my arms at the sight of his back, I turned around and walked home, realizing I had received the rejection I feared most.

Finding my way back to my apartment, disappointment and resentment perched her ugly head up as thoughts plagued me with each step. I tried to clear my head, reminding myself that he would be leaving Friday, he left me on the street alone, he couldn't handle the information I just gave him. I told myself this was good, this was best. Crossing my arms across my body, Indiana lost her battle as solemnness surrounded me; part of me did want to see where this could go with Tristan. I knew he was mad about the situation and not with me, or at least that's what I wanted to believe.

Making it to my apartment, before inserting the key in the lock, the door swung open, Kayla grabbed and hugged my neck as if she hadn't seen me in days. Keith stood behind her, obviously concerned. Stepping back in surprise, I could see Kayla's tear-soaked face from crying with worry and anger. This wasn't like Kayla; she was always the strong one.

Noticing that Tristan wasn't with me, Keith asked, "Where's

Tristan?"

Glaring over at him, my snarky side showing up, "He couldn't handle what I told him and he left me on a park bench. I walked home alone."

"Ah, damn. I'm going to go. I'll call you tomorrow," Keith said, kissing her cheek good night and hurrying out the door, pulling his cell from his pocket on the way.

"O...k...," she replied, closing the door behind him. Her face covered with invisible question marks.

Grabbing my arm, she led me over to the couch. Pushing me down, she remained standing, her arms crossed as her foot stammered, "What the hell Amber? Are you ok? I've been worried sick about you since we left the stadium. What did he say?" she spit angrily, spewing so many questions at me I couldn't respond.

Pushing my hands across my face, "Oh Kayla, what the hell have I done?" resisting the urge to tell her the next part, biting my lower lip, "I told him about Casey!" You could hear the dead silence in the room, Kayla's eyes widening with shock.

"YOU DID WHAT? Amber, why? You came for a fresh start, why the hell would you tell him that? It was going so well, well until tonight," she began pacing the floor in front of me, her finger tapping her lips as she processed the information.

Slouching against the back of the couch, "Because he needed to know, Kayla. He needed to know how messed up I am before he got too attached; before I got too attached. Plus, I needed him out of my life anyway. He's leaving and doesn't know when he will be back. I don't need that type of relationship right now. I need to stay focused until my divorce is over and then see where my life takes me. Tristan is a distraction I don't need."

Crossing her arms and throwing me an *I can't believe you are saying this* look, "Before he got attached...or before you? What a cop out," anger pounding in her voice. Not looking at her, she had a point. Pressing on, "Amber, Casey's a douche bag! He's out of your life. Your divorce will be over in two months. Then you won't have to worry with that SOB anymore. You need to embrace what is here and not let your past haunt you. Tristan is a good man and I don't see him being Casey." She was right that he wasn't like Casey; he was open, sweet, and gentleman like. I just don't know how to process what I was feeling and deal with him leaving at the same time.

"What did he say when you told him?" she continued.

Draping my arm over my eyes, pressing my head into the plush cushion, "He punched the wall. I stood to leave, when he grabbed me and kissed me too rough. I slapped him. He walked away, leaving me alone. I left and he didn't follow. It's for the best; he can leave and have no distractions. God knows he doesn't need any with going to war."

Taking a seat next to me, "Amber, that's a lot of information to take in. He probably never expected to hear you had a husband that you left in Indiana, no matter the circumstances. Maybe he needs time to register what you told him. Maybe he's angry at what happened to you. He doesn't seem like a bad guy. You're not giving him a chance," her soothing words, her way of trying to reduce my anger.

Snapping at her, "I DON'T NEED TO! He's leaving. Why the hell even worry with it?" Kayla threw her hands up in defeat as someone began knocking on our apartment door. Rising to answer, I escaped to my room; not waiting to see whom it was. Walking to a box nestled in the corner, I began rummaging through it, looking for a fresh t-shirt. Pulling the cotton shirt over my head, a wave of baseball leather, sweat and soap filled my room as I was pulling the fresh shirt on, causing me to freeze. I knew Tristan was at my door and the last thing I wanted was to face the man I had just divulged every bit of my past to.

Walking up behind me, placing his hands on my shoulders his nose breathing in my hair, laying his forehead against the base of my neck, he whispered, "I'm so sorry Amber. I asked you to trust me, and then this happens. Please look at me."

Tension filled beneath his fingertips through my shoulders. Refusing to leave my post, my grip remained firm on the lid of the box; I needed to stand my ground. I said my piece and I couldn't let myself get involved, not with him leaving in days, not with Casey still in the picture, not with my life in such chaos. Though in the midst of this anguish, part of me wanted this relationship, wanted this to work with Tristan.

Letting out a heavy sigh, "I know you're mad, but please I need to do this. I never wanted this to happen, Amber. I had no intention to start something with my leaving so soon, but once I saw you Amber, my life changed. Every part of me felt drawn to you in a way that wouldn't let go. I was wrong in how I reacted, please." running his fingers through the length of my hair, twisting and sliding it across the palms of his hands. Grabbing the ends of my hair and bringing to his nose, breathing in my scent, "Strawberries, so delicious, so sweet." He whispered as my inner self began melting; releasing my grip I turned to face him.

Crossing my arms to protect myself, I turned and I found warm eyes, reluctance deep in my throat. Wrapping his arm around my waist, pulling me close against him, my arms still crossed across his chest. My face fell to the floor as guilt began nestling in my gut. Easing my chin up, "Look at me. Always look at me. You're beautiful and this beautiful face should always be held high," his hands cupping my face, his thumb rubbing my jawline, "You survived and escaped an ordeal that no ordinary person could imagine. I know Casey beat your will and self-esteem down and I'm going to make sure it's the last time that ever happens. You're gorgeous and you should be proud of the woman you are," the words stirring heavily in my brain.

Swallowing my pride, "Casey always degraded me, told me I was fat and needed to lose weight. He controlled what I ate, wore, everything, I'm not sure I can live up to your standards. Plus, why even get involved with me? I don't know if I can do this Tristan."

The words pained him, responding coolly, "He's not here, Amber. And I'm not him," pausing briefly, "Plus this is a decision I don't take lightly. This is one I have fought against for days, but it's one I can't let go. You're worth the fight, the wait, every-thing...I just know it." Breathing deeply, "He's out of your life for now," rubbing my shoulder, "I have an idea...let's start by work-ing on getting past it for good. I just need you to trust me. I know that me leaving is a shock to... I don't even know what to call it," pulling back as his hands returned to my waist, looking for the air to make sense of everything, "but something inside me told me that you are worth every bit of this challenge we face. Again, I never intended to start a relationship within days of leaving, but I just can't let this go." Seeing the remorse in his eyes, all of this was a lot to take in; even I know that.

I am not sure how I expected him to react, or anyone for that matter, once I divulged the truth. I should have been more understanding of his reaction, "Again, I'm sorry for how I reacted. I wasn't mad at you about your past; I want you to know that. I was angry because I didn't understand how a man could treat a woman that way. Part of my job is to protect every part of the people I care about, and the moment I saw you, I knew you would fall into that realm. But I let my anger take over my better judgment," his body registered defeat.

It was time to take Indiana down completely. Standing on my toes, at this moment, I felt this was right. It was time to take a chance, to overcome the fear of the unknown and possibly embrace this newfound relationship that was developing. From the first moment I met Tristan life had changed for me. He had always treated me with respect and it wasn't something I could ignore. He was starting to grow on me and I knew for sure, if I was truly honest with myself, I couldn't just let him go either. There was something different about him. Not that I had much experience in the dating scene, Tristan was unlike any guy I had ever been with. I had always heard stories of the good guys and at this moment, this felt like he was one. Standing on my tip-toes, I wrapped my arms around Tristan's neck and kissed his lips. His arms wrapping tighter around my waist, pulling me even closer to his rock-hard body, "So does this mean you forgive me? Can we restart?"

A smile peaked at the edges of my lips as my hands reached to touch his chest; he grabbed them to stop me. Throwing me slightly off guard, Tristan raised my hands to his succulent lips, kissing my knuckles.

With accepting eyes, Tristan led me to my bed. Turning my body towards him, his hands reached into the strands of my hair as he pulled me into his kiss. Our motions dancing together, the attraction growing with intensity between us, Tristan's fingers whispering touches along my arm, finally resting on my waist. Our movements dancing together, he slowly walked me with my back facing the bed. Gently nudging me forward, finding the cool cotton sheets, my body relaxing, Tristan took over.

My body sinking into the mattress, Tristan eased himself on top of me, his kisses crossing the lines of my face. His nose brushing as his lips sighed across my neck. Reaching for the bottom of my shirt, Tristan lifted the cotton off my body allowing the material to escape and cascade to the floor. The coolness of the room waving over my skin, Tristan's heat mixing.

Not being able to take anymore, reaching up, I began unbuttoning Tristan's jersey. Reaching for my hands to stop me, wrapping his fingers around my wrist, kissing my fingers, he placed my hands at the top of my head. Kneeling up, Tristan began unbuttoning his jersey. Wiggling out from underneath him, I kneeled before him, reaching over I tried again to assist.

His shoulders grew tense, as my hands gently pushed his fingers away, "Let me," I whispered.

Hunching his shoulders, defeated, he stated, "Amber, you're not the only one with a past," the confession consuming his demeanor. Reaching for my fingers again, kissing the tips he placed my hands on his shoulders. Rocking back onto my heels, I watched as he continued unbuttoning his shirt, while I reached for his collar, pushing it off his shoulders. In the dimness of the room, my eyes journeyed over his exposed chest, catching glimpses of a pale mark on his shoulder. My head turning curiously, as my fingers reached to trace the five-inch mark on his shoulder. Stopping me, "Don't," he said firmly. Pulling back, the dimness illuminated the rest of his body and I saw five other scars across his chest.

Hanging his head, his fingers rubbing the lines of his forehead, my eyes read agony, "What happened?" trying my hardest not to reach out and trace them.

"I'm not ready to tell you Amber. It's not something I can talk about, not yet," he said shamefully.

Lifting his chin for his eyes to reach mine, "Its ok. In time, you will be able to tell me," wrapping my arms around his neck, leaning in, kissing him softly; doing my best to reassure him. His shoulders relaxing, he continued hugging my waist, pulling me in tighter as he made love to me.

Laying his body next to mine, his nose found the crevice of my empty neck. Whispering softly, "Now this was the right time," leaning a kiss onto my temple, his breathing becoming lax. Closing my eyes, dragging my fingers down his back, I felt myself drift into slumber in the comfort of his arms.

TRIGGERED

I woke to the sound of the key lock turning. Pulling the
comforter tighter into my chin, I closed my eyes,
hoping he would see I was asleep and not try anything. Realistically, I knew that was far from reality. He
had been drinking and I could smell the waft of alcohol as
he entered the bathroom of our master bedroom. Grum-
bling under his breath, he hunched over as he forced his
shoes off, untied.

Peeking out of the corner of my eye, trying not to show
that I was awake, I watched him peel his shirt off, and
strip down to his boxers. Walking to my side, I quickly
closed my eyes, as I felt his cold finger push a strand of hair
back to see if I was awake. Silently, I was praying that he
would just go to bed and let the drunkenness take over.

The bed dipped down from the weight of his body as
his hand slid across my hip. My heart quickened its pace
knowing what was coming next. As a natural reaction, my
body tensed under the tips of his fingers. A small smirk
escaped him, as he pulled the blankets off me. Still trying
my best to fake sleeping, I could feel his eyes burning as

he examined me. I hated when he drank, because I never knew which way an evening would go once he got home.

Tonight, I quickly found out the answer. The bed lifted back as his weight shifted off. Peeking again, I quickly regretted my decision as a hand forcefully met my cheek. "You bitch," I heard him growl as my hand replaced where he left his mark. Looking up at him, he calmed his composure as a devilish sneer crossed his face, "You think you can fake around me, you're wrong," slurring his words through gritted teeth.

Pushing my hip towards the bed, me flat on my back, I did my best to resist, "No Casey! I wouldn't...I just felt you get off the bed and didn't know you were home," trying my best to stall what was next; kicking my legs as he began stripping me of my panties.

Forcing my arms down, tears pierced my eyes, "You will never win," he growled in my ear, as he licked the side of my face, the smell of alcohol invading my nostrils. Vomit rose in my throat, but I swallowed it down as tears continued to well in my eyes.

"Are you crying? Bitch, I will give you something to cry about," flipping my legs and forcing me to my stomach. Pulling my hips up to meet him, his elbow pressed into my back as he released himself and forced into me from behind, "This will teach you to lie to me, to fake being asleep." Pulling my hair as he jerked hard into me, "Don't

ever think you can get away with anything. I will always know."

When he was done, he pushed me back into the bed as I curled into a ball still feeling the weight of him on top of me. He rolled over to his pillow, possessively holding his arm across me so I wouldn't move.

My body jerked as Tristan tried his best to wake me, "Amber...Amber...wake up..." swatting at something heavy on my stomach, my hand quickly clasped between rough hands. The light turning on quickly, it was only a dream. Quickly pushing myself up against the wall, I was disoriented from being half asleep. Pulling me close to him, I quickly realized that I was ok and sobs began pouring into his chest, his arms tight around me. I didn't want to be touched, but the comfort of his arms softened the urge to pull away. Shifting to see me, rubbing his hand across my face, "Amber, are you ok? What happened?"

"No, I can't," I couldn't control the tears. The realization of what my life was before, now that I had left it, began tumbling back. I didn't want to relive it, didn't want to see those things again. "Shh, it's ok. I have you," lying me back, I met my pillow and the weakness of my body consumed me. Tristan rested his body slightly behind me, careful not to put his arms on me for fear of how I might react. The heaviness of sleep consumed me before I could bring myself to talk about my nightmare.

I didn't dream again the rest of the night, but instead tossed and turned. Giving up at what felt like midmorning, I found Tristan sleeping next to me. Questions logged my memory as to what this was, where this was even going, or if I could even do this with everything I had been through. Shifting slightly, I glanced at the alarm clock on my nightstand, it wasn't as late as

I thought, only three in the morning. Pushing the anguish and memories of the prior evening's nightmare away, I rubbed the tiredness from my eyes.

Tristan stirred, murmuring something unrecognizable. A hint of courage perked up as my nose met his, slowly kissing his lips to wake him from his slumber. Heavy eyes wakening, "Thank you," I whispered.

"Shower with me," not the response I was expecting.

Giggling softly, "It's three in the morning."

His hazy eyes finding mine, his hand reaching my cheek, "I know, but shower with me. I'm dirty from last night's game and all I want to do is be near you," his words soft and coaxing.

Lifting myself to sit on the edge of the bed, the dimness of the light cast shadows along the curves of my body, "You're so beautiful, your body is like the breathtaking view of the Alps," his analogies always spoken at the right moments causing me to melt a little further.

"Please, I'm not beautiful," my hands curling along the edge of the bed, my chin resting against my shoulder, glancing back to find Tristan leaning up on one elbow, observing me as I shifted out of bed. Continuing on with my insecurities, "I have big hips and my breasts sag."

Pressing his body against my back side, kissing my shoulders, his hand dancing down my arm, reassuringly, "No Amber, your body is beautiful, and I plan to show you every chance I get," remarking under his lips, as they brushed along my skin, "I know you won't talk to me about what happened earlier, but just know that I will work every day to show you the beauty you bestow and treat you the way you should have always been treated. I can't imagine the heartache and pain you suffered at the hands of Casey, but just know, that will never happen here."

Releasing myself from his tender touches, I stood to walk to the bathroom, Tristan shuffled, following behind me. I didn't know how to respond to his commitment, but knew that he wasn't like Casey. I wasn't sure where this would go or how long it would last, but quite possibly what I needed.

The glass shower wasn't very big in the small bathroom, but would make due for two people. Turning on the hot water, I stepped inside, my body clinched at the heat pelting my skin. Glancing over my shoulder, I observed the body that hid in the dimness of our lovemaking. Lined with muscles, shaped by years of playing ball and fighting war, my cheeks blushed, "That hint of red is beautiful on your skin," he stated as he gently kissed my pink cheeks, climbing in the shower behind me.

Reaching for the shampoo, "Turn around," he demanded. Complying with his demand, he poured the golden liquid into his hands, reaching up and began massaging the lather into my hair, his fingers relaxing as they wrestled any dirt and sweat away. Working the lather down to the edges of my hair, he slightly nudged me forward under the spray continuing the care as he grabbed the body wash pouring it onto my blue loofah. Pulling me back from the spray, scrunching up the loofah, producing a foamy ball, he washed my body. The soft bristles tickling my skin as every bit of anxiety washed down the drain, "Done this before?"

"Once or twice, why" he questioned.

Tensing, almost regretting my next question, "Just wondering. Do you do this with every girl?"

"Never with a girl that I am not fond of," he remarked. Regarding him coyly, beginning to relax again under his tender care, his touch soft and delicate, my head hazy by the aroma of lavender mixed with Tristan's scent. Turning his back to rinse the loofah, I reached for his shoulders to steady myself.

"Are you ok?" he asked tenderly, taking my hands from the front, concern in his voice as he tilted his head back in my direction.

"I need this Tristan. I need you. I need to know that everything will be ok," it was so surreal to be feeling such emotions in such a short time frame. I needed answers though, reassurance that this was real, that the feelings felt were mutual. Pulling my hand from his shoulder, kissing my knuckles, "Yes, we can make this work Amber. If you are willing so am I." Still holding onto his shoulders, my nose nuzzling at his back, I noticed he didn't try to withdrawal. Courageously releasing his shoulders, I guided my fingers smoothly down the fine lines of his back, kissing each contoured muscle.

Turning to face me, my hands naturally moved to caress the lines of the front of his body. Pulling my hands into his, his long fingers closed around my wrists guiding them behind me. Trusting myself to his next move, he gently pressed me against the cold tiles of the shower stall, the instant coolness sending shivers through me, as I felt the warmness of Tristan's breath along my ear. Responding to his touch, my head remaining turned against my shoulder so his kisses could continue their path along my neck. Releasing my wrists from behind my back, he gently brought my hands up to wrap around his neck, as his fingers slid down the backs of my arms.

His eyes met mine. With no words exchanging between us, he brushed my lips with soft kisses. Closing my eyes and breathing in his scent, my stomach wrestled with excitement.

After moments of intensity, he grabbed my hand bringing me under the now cold spray, as I cleaned myself up. Chills covering my body, I opened the glass to exit. Grabbing a towel, I stepped out and wrapped myself in it, closing the shower door behind me, allowing him to collect his thoughts. A moment later, opening the glass door I handed him a towel, and shot him an inquisitive look, "I'm sorry," I whispered.

He was kneeling in front me to meet me eye to eye, "Touching my chest is off limits. Just like you aren't ready to discuss Casey, I'm not ready to discuss some of my past either."

"I'm sorry. I know it bothers you. Will you ever..."

"Maybe...." Not allowing me to finish my question.

"What happened to you," the question escaping me before I could stop, even though he just told me he didn't know when he could share.

"Amber..." rubbing his freshly shampooed hair in frustration, standing back up in front of me, "I have a frightful past that I am not ready to share." Rubbing his face, he held his hand out for mine, "Here, let me show you where you can touch me." Wrapping a fresh towel around his waist, he curled my fingers closed only keeping my index finger open. Beginning at the sides of his face and his neck he began tracing a path across his body making sure to exclude anywhere near his chest. When he was finished he pulled my hands around his neck, his hands finding my waist, "You can touch my back and anything below my waist, also," sending me a wink, trying his best to lighten the atmosphere.

Still wrapped in my towel, I sat on the toilet. Wonder struck me as I tried to comprehend what he meant by a frightful past. My lack of military knowledge allowed my head to run rampant with ideas, but I truly had no clue how bad it could really be. Grabbing a dry towel, walking over to me, he began drying out any loose moisture that was falling into my lap. Even though I was exhausted, I was ready to change the subject and return his favor.

Grabbing the top of his towel to pull it off, I placed my hands on his waist, tugging him closer to me. Kissing his stomach along the crevice of folds, his hands reached the back of my head, breath escaping his lips. Glancing up, Tristan's eyes dark and green, met mine waiting in anticipation for what I was planning to do. Tristan's grasp tightened on my neck to stop me, "Amber, what are you doing to me?"

Ignoring him, I continued my slow torture across his body. Responding to my moves, Tristan collapsed to his knees in front of me, laying his head on my lap, breathing heavily as if he lost his mind. "Amber, why do you torture me?" Smiling down at him, my hand wrestling with his damp hair, he kissed my legs.

Reaching for my hand, he walked me into my bedroom. Pulling my shirt over my head, him following suit, we climbed into bed. Snuggling in behind me, his arm under my neck, his other around my waist, he pulled me in close to him. Brushing the hair from my neck, breathing in my fresh clean smell, I could feel his body lax behind me. The smell of him was like a drug that settled any restlessness in my body and soon we both drifted off.

My body must have sensed emptiness as I woke not long before the sun rose. Exhausted, I stretched my sore aching muscles. Turning over, finding the bed empty, I examined the empty pillow next to me. Searching the room, I could feel eyes upon me. Edging up on my elbows, I reached over to the bedside table to turn on the light. Barely filling the room, I found Tristan sitting in the corner observing me as the quiet surrounded us. Breaking the silence, "What are you doing? Come back to bed," rubbing my eyes, yawning.

Breaking his concentration, he stood from his chair, walking to the bedside, and slid under the covers behind me. Cradling my body like earlier, he nuzzled his nose in my neck. Rolling over to face him, looking up, my eyes caught darkness, "Go back to sleep. You need your rest." He was right, again, but questions burned at the edge of my tongue.

"Before I do, can I ask you something?" my mind was telling me to leave it alone, but my journalistic side wasn't giving up.

"Anything," as he traced kisses along my neckline.

"Why won't you share with me what happened?" Tensing at my question, a deep sigh came from his throat as he rolled on his back, putting his arm over his eyes, trying to ignore what I asked. His face reflected shame, horror as if he was reminiscing through old memories.

Lifting my head up on my hand, supporting my weight with my elbow, I reached over to touch him, hoping that since he had a shirt on, he would let me, but no, the tension grew even more. Grabbing my hand, kissing my knuckles, "Tristan, I'm sorry if I upset you. It's just that I feel like I have shared a terrible part of my past with you and just want to know just as much about you. I can't help it; call it the journalist in me." Doing my best to ease the tension growing thicker in the room, I said, "I know you told me you might tell me, but I can't stand not touching your body the way you can touch mine. I need that just as much as you need it. I wish you would tell me why I can't," almost pleading with him.

Uncovering his eyes, easing himself up into the same position, facing me, his eyes looked to mine, still not answering my question. This time his eyes were filled with hurt. He leaned forward, grabbing the nape of my neck, kissing me, his kiss passionate and slow, I knew he was avoiding my question and answers would just have to come later. Kissing my forehead, his hand still on my neck, "Go back to sleep. There will be plenty of time to talk soon."

Anger reared her ugly head as emotions cascaded, "When Tristan," my voice probably louder than it should be. My tongue betraying me, "You're leaving in, God I don't know how many days," adrenaline poured through me, as any bit of exhaustion had now left, "I've poured part of my past to you and you can't seem to do the same for me! I don't want to press you, but don't try to tie me over with there is plenty of time." Now I was out of bed and on my feet, pacing the floor.

"I know darling," lying back again, rubbing his hands over his face. Growing quiet, coldness fell as I realized I pushed the issue too far.

Not sure why I couldn't let it go, this whole relationship thing was so new to me and for once I started feeling like I had a say in my life, in this relationship. Maybe it was my way of gaining a little bit of control on something that I didn't have control of before. If leaving Casey allowed me one thing, it was finding a voice that was hidden behind bruises and sheltered living.

I couldn't understand why I could share part of myself with him, but he just couldn't bring himself to me. Feeling the cold and bitterness that Casey showed me on a regular basis, my defenses went up and I knew I was about to regret what I was about to do. Folding my arms across my body, halting my pace, "I think you need to go home."

His arms flew to the bed as his head twisted in my direction, "You don't mean that. Please don't do this Amber." Rushing out of bed, meeting me on my side, "I don't know what you want from me. I didn't ask you to tell me what happened to you, you chose to share that with me. I would think you would have the same respect for me?"

"I'm sorry Tristan. How would you feel if you could never touch a part of me," I shouted, my brows pinching together.

His face twisted with dismay, "I would be hurt and it would kill me," his hands now rubbing the back of his neck. "I know this isn't easy Amber, but please understand. This isn't something that is easy for me to talk about. I don't open to many people, not when it comes to that. In time Amber, I know I can tell you, but I can't right now. So please reconsider, don't ask me to leave," moving forward to pull me into him, I stepped back out of his grasp.

"I can't Tristan," swallowing the huge knot now in my throat, "The last few days have been overwhelming and I can't lie next to a man who is giving me the cold shoulder. I've spent a lifetime with someone else who did that and I'm not about to start again." The hurt on his face caused the worst feeling in the world for me. I didn't want to hurt him, but how can I deal with another cold shoulder?

Throwing his hands up in defeat, "Fine," he growled, grabbing his clothes off the floor and putting them on. "Whatever you want, but we're not over," his finger pointing at me, "Not by a long shot." He stomped across the room, slamming the door behind him, causing me to jump.

Sitting on the edge of the bed, my hands in my palms, Kayla entered the room finding a seat next to me. Knowing not to say anything but just be present, she had done this a million times through our friendship and knew to tread lightly and just wait for me to break the silence. After several minutes of not speaking, she couldn't take it anymore, "Amber, what happened? Do I need to drag you away from Charleston now?"

"No, Kayla," I mumbled through my hands. I didn't really want to talk about how stupid I was being or to hear her tell me how dumb I was.

"Tell me what you need? I'm sure whatever this is, it's all a misunderstanding," leaning forward to try and get my attention.

"I just don't get it Kayla," my hands sliding down my face, the dam breaking, "He won't let me touch him."

Pulling back in surprise, "What do you mean touch him?"

"Ugh! Never mind," exasperated, pushing myself off the bed to enter the bathroom.

"Oh skip the crap Amber," she always called me out when I was being irrational.

"Kayla, I've poured my soul out to him and he won't do it in return. I just don't get it. I'm trying not to press him, but I'm so confused by all this...whatever this is" reentering the room, finding my seat next to her. Grabbing the lotion by my bed, I poured some in my hands to try and keep myself busy while Kayla interrogated me, "I asked him to leave."

I could see the confusion on her face, as she wasn't following the conversation, "Ok, slow down Let's start over. First, what do you mean you can't touch him?"

"I can't touch his chest. He has all these scars, so I was curious and asked him about them. Anytime I would try to touch them or ask him, he clammed up and wouldn't tell me anything," I told her, my temper slowing down.

"Ok, so what's his reason," she asked, slowly putting the pieces together.

"He says he's not ready to tell me. He says it has to do something with his past," I still couldn't understand why it was ok that I could tell him my sordid past, but he couldn't do it with me. What was so terrible that he couldn't share?

"Amber, men are complicated. Have you ever considered it could be war related? Maybe something pretty bad happened to him and it will take him time to open up. I know you shared a big part of you, but it's a whole lot different if he was hurt by something in the war, especially if there are external scars," she pointed out reassuring me, placing her hand on my shoulder. She did have a point that I had never considered. My lack of understanding was hurting my better judgment in this newfound relationship, as I am sure that my being married was new to Tristan. "I am sure he will tell you in time, but give him a chance. He's really into you, don't let him slip through your fingers," her hand tightening against my shoulder.

"How can I trust him?" Kayla was quiet for a moment.

"Are you afraid he's going to turn into or become a "Casey"?" she asked.

I wasn't sure what to think. So much about Tristan was different, but "Casey" kept me from wanting to accept anything different. When he grabbed me, he wasn't being forceful, but it was a form of control, a trigger from when Casey would grab me in the same manner, but this felt different. Everything about the last few days was overwhelming. Tristan wasn't something I wanted to give up, no matter how hard I tried to tell myself that I didn't need this. I was so lost and confused.

"Maybe," I was finally admitting the unspoken truth, although that wasn't everything that I was feeling.

"Amber, he's not Casey. In the few minutes I've been around him, and from what Keith has told me, Tristan is nothing like Casey. Yes, he has a past, but so does everyone. Keith told me that Tristan struggles with some serious stuff, but wouldn't divulge. Tristan will tell you in time and when he is ready," she always had a way of clearing things up, but I just didn't know if this would work.

Flustered, "I don't have time Kayla. He's leaving Friday! I just don't need to get attached, not now," trying to convince myself over and over that was the best decision, "How can I meet someone and then they leave, not knowing when they will be back? I just need to focus on starting my job and getting Casey out of my life," my fingertips holding the weight of my forehead, as my mind tried to decipher between the blossoming feelings for this relationship and the anxiety of what was to come.

"I know Amber," sighing, rolling on her back, "Just, I don't know, talk to him. Things will sort themselves out," pausing for a second. "How about we go shopping later today, after we get up, and be tourists for the day? It may help clear your head," she was always good at trying to distract me.

"I guess," trying to sound reluctant. She was shutting me down. She was right; maybe I needed to just ask him, but he just didn't seem to want to open up. Maybe I needed to redirect my approach to him. Sometimes I hated being a journalist. Although I lacked in the social scene and girlfriends, I always struggled with pressing people until I received the answers I needed.

My eyes beginning to drift, I laid against the pillow, Kayla pulling in beside me, "Now get some sleep. I'll be right here." Reaching over I shut the lamp off, cascading darkness into the apartment room. Staring off into the empty blackness, my arm rested under my head as my mind wondered of things to come.

CHARLESTON

Waking at almost midmorning, leaning over to my bedside table to check my phone, I hoped that I might have a text or missed call from Tristan. The phone registered blank. Easing myself to a sitting position, I stretched my arms back, pressing my shoulder blades together. Walking into the bathroom, I found Tristan's jersey lying on the floor, number nine and Ashton written across the back. Picking it up, I held it to my nose, smelling him. Always relaxing me, it was a nice reminder of the few good times we had the last couple of days.

Setting it aside, I sat on the toilet, placing my head on my knees as I recalled the mix of emotions from the last couple of days. Finishing up, I began my morning prep to prepare for the day ahead. As I flushed the toilet, I flushed the rest of my emotions with it.

Standing in front of the mirror, I brushed my hair. Grasping the edge of the sink, taking a deep breath, I concluded that I couldn't just let him go, no matter how hard I was trying. It seemed so silly to me to be so attracted and somewhat attached, so quickly, but there was something about him that I couldn't waiver. Like right now, I wanted him here, to hear him, feel his breath, smell his scent, and feel his touch.

My knees betraying me as my body dropped to the cold tile

floor, pulling my legs into my chest. I began sobbing, my conclusion clouded with fear and uncertainty. Sitting and crying on the bathroom floor, I tried to rid myself of every thought of Tristan from my mind, but it was pointless. A trace of him lived in every part of my tiny space in my apartment. No matter where I went, there was a version of Tristan there. It was driving me crazy and the kaleidoscope of emotions wasn't making things better.

Giving up trying to figure out what my brain thought was best, I exited the bathroom to get dressed. Putting on a pair of khaki shorts and pink top, I chose comfy clothes for our day of shopping and being tourists. Walking into the kitchen, Kayla was sitting at the table, reading the morning paper. There on the front page, in big words displayed, "Ashton Heading to War." Stabbing my gut just a little, I tried to shift the thought from my head, continuing on my quest for coffee and a small snack. It was already so late in the morning, I figured we would eat while we were out.

"There's cereal in the cabinet. I picked up some this morning." Kayla said, not lifting her head from the paper. "The paper has an interesting article on Tristan, if you want to read it."

"No, I need to clear my thoughts," knowing it was pointless to read anything. Nothing would change how I felt about him leaving.

"Ok, its here if you want. It may answer some of your questions," I will admit I was curious, but I needed to focus on the days ahead. Finding some crackers, I scarfed down a few and drank my coffee.

About an hour later, Kayla and I made our way down to the busy street, somewhat expected this time of year with the influx of tourism in the area. The day was gorgeous as the sun was shining high above the buildings; the heat was another story. Blistering hot as a cloud swarmed overhead, immediately causing our skin to feel the sun's rays. Not paying it any attention, we made our way down King Street, entering and exiting several of the local shops, stopping along the way to buy a couple of things. "I hear there are some really cool vendors on Market," Kayla remarking as I held a chevron print shirt up, judging if it would suit my wardrobe.

"Sounds good, do you know how to get there," I said, deciding against the shirt, placing it back on the table.

"I believe it's right up the road," said Kayla, pointing in some far-off direction outside the shop.

"It is," said a middle-aged woman interrupting our conversation, "Just around the corner ladies," our attention now focused in her direction, "Where are you from?"

A little caught off guard by her forwardness, simply replying together, we said, "Just moved here from Indiana. Thank you for the directions."

"Sure thing. Enjoy the city, but be careful of the heat. It will get to you. Have a wonderful day," our backs turning towards her as we exited back into the midday heat of the city. Before moving here, I visited some local blogs, finding Charleston had been marked as one of the friendliest cities in the nation. Never really experiencing such friendliness in the northern part of my world, it was remarkable to see the courteousness present in this city. It seemed everywhere we visited in this town, people were always willing to answer our questions or help us when needed.

Several minutes later, after combing several blocks, Kayla and I found Market Street. Known for unique Charleston gifts, we entered the end greeted with a magnificent building, displaying the words, *Daughters of the Confederacy* across the top. Canvasing each vendor table as we walked through, we dodged oncoming tourists, children loose from their owners, and bulky backpacks on backs. My eyes wandered toward a vendor selling jewelry near the end of one of the buildings. Out of the corner of my eye, a sliver of light sparkled off a silver ring. Picking it up, observing the delicate work, the ring had a hint of green that layered the carved in lines like diamond plates, *home plate*, instantly it reminded me of Tristan. Running my fingers over the carved surface, pondering, *should I buy it?* Deciding against it, I began to place it back, as, "Nice ring," echoed in my ears.

Kayla looking over my shoulder, hinted, "Are you going to get it?"

Sighing heavily as I shrugged my shoulders, "No, but it is nice." Placing it back in its original place, I didn't even know if I was going to see him again, "Come on, let's keep going," I motioned towards the rest of the market.

Finishing up the Market, Kayla had bought herself a small sweet grass basket to send home to her parents, along with a maxi dress she found. Continuing down the street, passing parked cars on our left, realizing the harbor was just beyond our view, we were eager to find a place to eat. Approaching the water's edge, we were greeted with a quiet little restaurant settled on the harbor, *Fleet Landing*. Not knowing much about it, we decided on it since we were famished and ready for some lunch.

Pulling one of the double doors open and entering, the ombre haired hostess greeted us, "Hello ladies! Welcome to Fleet Landing, table for two?"

"Yes, please. May we sit outside?" Kayla asked, "It's such a gorgeous day and the view I am sure is spectacular."

"Yes ma'am. Right this way," grabbing two menus. Following the hostess through the single door, out onto the wooden dock, we were seated right at the guardrail, on a bench styled table. Handing us our menus, she stated, "Your server will be right with you."

"Thank you" we replied, opening the menus, scanning the local offerings.

"Hello ladies," our observations interrupted as a stockier gentleman, holding a notepad, greeted us. "Would you like to hear our specials for the day?" nodding; he proceeded to read off the list written on the notepad in his hand. We both decided on the Mahi platter and ordered two sweet teas. "I'll be right back," he said grabbing our menus from us, turning to head to the kitchen to retrieve our drinks.

Clasping my hands together, Kayla and I took in the beauty of the Charleston Harbor. The view of Patriot's Point right across the way nestled below the Arthur Ravenel Bridge, such exquisite beauty. The water sparkled across the harbor as the midday sun shone overhead. The water's edge lined with buildings and historic homes, Charleston exhibited beauty unlike any other town I had seen.

Following along the harbor, my eyes settled upon Waterfront Park, finding Tristan sitting with another woman on the wooden swings that lined the docks. My heart was racing and skin blushed as subtle anger began stirring in the pit of my stomach. She was blonde, petite, and beautiful! *Who the hell was she? What was she doing with Tristan?* Kayla catching the fumes escaping my ears couldn't help but to see why my demeanor had done a 180. Her face growing pale as her eyes set upon what was unfolding before me.

"It's probably a friend, Amber, "grabbing my hand in reassurance, trying to calm me down, "Don't judge. Casey always did that to you. Plus, you don't want to see him anymore, remember?" her snarky remark befuddled me. She could be a complete smart ass; however, she had a valid point. I couldn't understand why the jealousy surrounded me when it came to him. My emotions once again playing Jekyll and Hyde with my head, not really making up its mind on which way I wanted to go.

As hard as it was, I tore my glare away from the unfathomable relationship blooming in front of me. The way she laughed at his gestures, the slight touch of her hand on his, her slight nestling along his shoulder; the epitome of jealousy broiled within my inner being. The sight of them also made me sad, made me reminisce what could have been. Shaking the thought away, my Mr. Hyde reminding me he's leaving any day.

Kayla snapped her fingers to regain my focus, "Hey!! Did I lose my best friend to some far-off land? Hello! I am talking to you!"

"Yea, sorry! I'm listening. I guess I was right about his role with the ladies! He doesn't waste any time, does he?" I smarted off.

"Amber, drop it! You don't want anything to do with him. Again, you are jumping to conclusions. For all you know, it could be a sister! Stop judging," steam slowly coming out of her ears as she was practically lecturing me. Why did she have to be right, especially now? The waiter placing our food in front of us, bringing the focus back to lunch, "Here you go ladies." Seeing the food made my stomach churn but I needed to eat. Between the heat of the day and the long walks, I was famished.

"You're right! I will stop. Let's eat lunch and worry about the rest of the day," I was remarking as I reached for my fork.

"I know I am right…" Kayla's lips thinning as her smile spread. She carried the conversation through lunch as we chatted and laughed about our day. Finishing up our plates, we paid our bill and headed out the door. Walking to the end of the parking lot, I didn't want to head towards the Waterfront knowing Tristan was there. Motioning to Kayla in the direction of the apartment, the uneasy feeling that had lingered with me for the last few days appeared again. Looking over my shoulder, I only saw the restaurant and the new port terminal. Turning back forward, my eyes focused to the ground as I collided into a wall of muscle.

My hands reaching bare, strong arms, "Excuse me," my eyes finding the man's face, registering, "TRISTAN!"

"Amber!" His hands firm upon my forearms to keep me from falling back. Steadying myself, his eyes fell to mine in sadness.

"I'm so..." trying my best to apologize.

Cutting me off before I could finish, "Its fine." Suddenly I became aware the woman he had been seated with at the park was still standing next to him. She was wearing a pale pink summer dress with white strappy sandals. Her perfect blonde hair sat below her shoulders, while her nails were perfectly manicured.

Realizing the tension growing in the moment, Tristan quickly cleared the air, "Amber, this is Rebecca, my sister," his words turning my Mr. Hyde back to Jekyll, my embarrassment evident as I recoiled. Catching the smirk on Kayla's face, she was silently laughing at my discomfort. Turning back to them, I observed the resemblance they shared. It was so obvious, they looked almost identical; same sandy blonde hair, hers just longer. Her eyes, piercing green just like his.

Shrugging off my jealousy, extending my hand to hers, "Hello Rebecca, it's nice to meet you. I didn't know Tristan had a sister," I swallowed my pride.

"Hello Amber," taking my hand in greeting, a smile creeping across her lips, "I've heard a lot about you. Tristan is quite smitten over you." Tristan shooting his sister a stare of *don't*, but she ignored it. "We were just headed back to his condo to grab some lunch. Care to join us?" Shuffling on his feet, Tristan threw his hands into his pockets like he does when he is nervous. Gazing up from his brow, he awaited our reply.

"No, I'm sorry," sincerity in my voice, "We just ate, and are on our way to do some more sightseeing," I said, pointing back at the restaurant.

Not giving up us joining her she queried, "How about dinner then?" A look of hope appeared on Tristan's face. "Sure, it sounds lovely," my inner Jekyll skipping with joy as Mr. Hyde fought to creep forth.

Forgetting my manners, Kayla reminding me she was still present with a tap, "I'm sorry, Rebecca, this is Kayla," she smiled, extending her hand to shake Rebecca's.

"Oh yea, the girl Keith is smitten over. Now it makes sense. How about Keith and you join us Kayla? It would be nice to get to know the women capturing the dearest men in my life's hearts," smiled Rebecca as she continued to put the pieces together.

Kayla glancing my way, responding, "I'll have to check with Keith."

Waving her hand in my direction, "Oh, don't bother dear, he's already coming. He normally joins us on Saturday nights for dinner."

Her eyebrows lifting in upward motion, "Hmm," escaping her lips as she pondered what Rebecca had just shared. "Well alright. Do we need to bring anything?" Kayla continued in conversation, finalizing the details for dinner with Rebecca.

Stepping forward with one hand behind his back, the other extending towards an empty space away from Kayla and Rebecca, I nodded in acceptance as we walked just out of earshot. Leaning in close, his breath warm against my cheek, the salty breeze shifting Tristan's aroma my direction, "I'm sorry," he began, "about this morning. You're right. I shouldn't have reacted that way. Last night was a lot and I'm not ready," pausing, trying to find the right words, "to share my past with you, yet. You thought you had a past; I'm way beyond that. Please understand. One thing I promise is to tell you when I know it's the right time and there's a lot at stake if I tell you now. One thing I can tell you is I am a man of my word and I, again, promise I will tell you. You have to give me time," *time…the one thing we didn't have.* Pulling my shoulders back, Tristan placing his finger on my lips before the words could escape, "Yes I know we don't have a lot before I leave and that is something we will work through. However, I will keep my promise to you! Just give me a chance," He pleaded.

Crossing my arms in a protective way, I did my best to be understanding at that moment. Sincerity was evident, "Let's take things slow," he suggested, reaching and pushing a loose strand behind my ear, "You don't know how much I respect you for sharing such a hurtful part of your past with me. Opening yourself up like that, I know wasn't easy. But I am going to be honest; it also isn't easy for me to know you are still married." I could feel the blood flood from my face, like a dam had broken, a knot swelling at the base of my throat. He needed reassurance and if I truly wanted this, which to be honest…I did…it was time for me to put everything aside and learn to trust again. Casey was no longer part of my life. I had only been away from him for a brief time, but I knew that my marriage was over. I knew I couldn't go back to the control and the abuse that came with him; not after the way I felt with Tristan and the respect and dignity he bestowed upon me.

My arms still crossed as I slid my foot across the loose gravel, "Ok," I agreed, responding in acceptance. Relief poured over his features. Hearing the release of breath, he was holding, I continued, "Let's take it slow. You don't have to worry about Casey," trying to reassure him and nip this doubt quickly, "Although, yes, I am technically still married, our relationship is over. He abused me, controlled me, I couldn't take another day with him, not after what he did to me. It's unforgiveable. Please understand that, but also understand that it hurts me to not know just as much about you as you do me. Also know this isn't going to be easy for me to understand and deal with you leaving," my hands now out in front of me as they did the talking for me.

Placing his hand upon my arm, "I do," he rubbed it up and down, "Thank you for accepting the invitation to dinner," glancing over to catch Kayla and Rebecca deep in conversation, "I hope you enjoy your day with Kayla. We'll have plenty of time to talk more tonight," lifting my hand to his lips and placing a simple kiss upon my knuckles. Locking his fingers with mine, we walked back towards Kayla and Rebecca who were laughing at something unbeknownst to us.

Catching us out of the corner of her eye, Rebecca turned to us, "You guys good," she queried inquisitively.

"Yes, we are," looking over at me, a smile spread across his lips.

"Well we must go get ready then. Tristan..." Stepping away from me, her arm locking in his, "We shall see you both tonight?"

"Yes," Kayla and I responding in unison.

"Until then, enjoy your day ladies," waving with a nod they turned the opposite direction of where we were heading.

After saying our goodbyes, we spent the rest of the day wandering the cobblestone paths of Charleston. Returning to our apartment, the rush of cool air attacked my sticky, sweaty skin upon entering. Needing a shower to ready for the night ahead, I quickly felt refreshed from the rushing water. Rummaging my closet for something elegant but sexy I finally settled on a sexy red scoop neck shirt and knee length black skirt. Also finding my killer pumps, I accented with my short black pearl necklace and matching earrings. Walking back to the bathroom, I threw some curl in my hair and put a little make up on. I normally didn't wear make-up but tonight seemed like a special enough occasion. My goal was for Tristan to know that I was serious about moving on and to continue to reassure him that Casey was out of my life.

Taking one last look in the mirror, I nodded my head in approval. Before walking out of my bathroom, my eyes fell upon Tristan's jersey on the small shelf where I had laid it earlier. Pulling it to my nose, I breathed in the aroma I felt I couldn't get enough of. A smile creeping across my lips as the prior days replayed in my head, I folded it up and shoved it under my arm. With the intention of returning it to him, I exited the bathroom, grabbing my purse and phone on the way.

Entering the living room, Keith was seated on the sofa waiting for us, "Hey, when did you get here?"

Startling from his thoughts, standing, he strode over to me, placing a kiss upon my cheek, "Well hello gorgeous," giving me a once over, "Uh, not too long ago. I'd figured you guys could use your own personal guide to Tristan's place." Suppressing a smile, I motioned my hand in the air, waiving his words away.

Right behind me, Kayla walked out in an equally sexy outfit. Keith picking his jaw up off the floor, left my side rushing to her; lavishing at her beauty. Playfully pushing him away, he nestled her arm into his, giving her a kiss on her cheek, "Keith," she giggled, trying to get him to stop.

"Ready ladies," holding out his other arm to me. Nodding and accepting the invitation, we were out the door into a night of tell all.

We were walking through the early evening streets of Charleston, the sun was waning on the western skyline, golden hues of yellows and oranges hinting at the buildings. Keith was beaming as Kayla and he carried on a melodic conversation, me taking in the onlookers staring at us as we walked by. Men passing couldn't help but turn their heads in our direction, taking one final look before returning their attention back to their wives or girlfriends. "I told you," a sly smile lying across his lips, "You ladies are rocking it," the two of us giggling as we continued basking in the unwanted attention.

Tristan's condo was located in a newer section of town facing the harbor. Living on the top floor, we entered the elevator, Keith inserting a key card that allowed us access. "How come you have a card," Kayla asked.

"I watch Tristan's place while he's gone." answering her. The elevators opening to the penthouse, we walked into the open, lavishly decorated room, boasting masculinity but elegance at the same time. The living area adorned a large, gas-burning fireplace on the only closed off wall; the remaining walls full windows displaying magnificent views of the Charleston Harbor. A brown leather sofa and matching loveseat sat in the middle of the room with a coffee table, and an elegant arrangement of fresh flowers; summer colored roses, calla lilies and camellias.

Above the fireplace, a family photo hung with a younger boy, resembling Tristan, a young girl resembling Rebecca, another girl, a nice-looking gentleman and gorgeous lady standing behind them. Walking closer to the photo, the same quality trait displayed among all of them, deep green eyes.

Removing myself from observing what I assumed was a family photo, I grew inquisitive at the absence of Tristan. "Make yourselves at home ladies. Would you like anything from the bar?" Keith asked, making his way over to the kitchen area. Kayla requesting a glass of Chardonnay and I a Shiraz, he obliged us.

Walking to the window, sipping the smoothness of the red wine, looking over the harbor, I heard laughter coming from the opposite side of the room as Tristan and Rebecca entered. Turning to the sound of their laughter, Tristan's appearance stole my breath away. Wearing a crisp, pressed button-down shirt, with grey slacks, he was just showered and had shaved off what was left of his five o'clock shadow.

Making his way to the bottom of the stairs, I could feel the temperature rise in my face as he walked towards me. Sipping my wine to hide any change in color, Tristan leaned in kissing my cheek, whispering, "You look positively gorgeous my darling," placing his hand upon my hip, my head curling into his softened words.

Peeking out of the corner of my eye, up to him, "As do you," turning back to the immaculate view of the harbor, "This view is gorgeous, Tristan," I was remarking as Tristan's hands curved around my waist, my hand naturally lying on top of his. My eyes danced across the endless views of the Cooper River emptying into the Atlantic Ocean on the horizon. Leaning against him, his jersey shifting in my arms, "Oh, I wanted to return this. You left it at my place," handing him the jersey.

Pushing it back in my direction, "Keep it. I don't need it anymore," smiling at me. Pressing the jersey to my chest, kissing my cheek, he walked in the direction of Kayla and Keith who were standing at the opposite display of windows, leaving me to my thoughts, "Kayla you look ravishing," finally reaching them, kissing her gently on her cheek.

"Amber I love your outfit," Rebecca, wearing a formal but simple summer dress; her beautiful sandy blond hair pulled back in an exquisite bun, broke through my thoughts, "Very fitting for the evening. So, I hear you just moved to Charleston," catching me a little off guard with her forwardness.

Taking another sip, responding coolly, "Yes, just a few days ago. It's a very nice city. Getting to the end of unpacking, thanks to Keith's help yesterday. From what I have seen it's a nice fit for Kayla and me," hoping that would satisfy her appetite. I really didn't want to get into why we were here, but I'm sure, as close as Tristan and she seemed, she already knew why. Eyeing me suspiciously; she turned towards the rest of the guests, "Well let me go see how dinner is coming along," clasping her hands together, "I'll be right back," walking out of the room towards the kitchen area.

Returning back towards the open windows, the view was beautiful as the sun was setting in the west, providing a nice orange tone that sparkled and danced across the tops of the crests of water and boats.

Sneaking up behind me, "You like the view?" wrapping his arms around my waist, nuzzling his nose in my neck. "Mm mm... strawberries and cream, so delicious and irresistible." whispering so only I could hear.

Nibbling my neck, goose bumps tracing my skin, giggling, "Yes the view is beautiful; almost breathtaking," answering him.

"Like you," mumbling under sweet kisses, "Come with me, I want to show you something." Offering his hand, our fingers lacing as he led me up the stairs to the upper floor. "We'll be right back," he called back.

Reaching an entertainment room, it adorned a typical bachelor pad with pool table and wet bar. Along the opposite wall, a collection of books bordered by more windows faced the Arthur Ravenel Bridge, the view just as breathtaking. Basking in the glorious sunset unfolding before me, Tristan turned on a low melody, something classical, but I didn't recognize it. Walking up to me, requesting my hand, "Shall we dance," placing his other hand on my hip, gently leading me into a slow sway. Stifling a grin, I placed my hand in his, sauntering to the tune.

Grabbing the glass of wine from my hand, setting it on the bar, returning to his lead, "I thought we should talk a minute. We really didn't finish our conversation well this morning," swaying us to the slow melody that quietly filled the room. Looking at me intently, "I want to know everything about you and you know everything about me. However, it will take me some time to open up, but believe me when I say, I will," repeating the similar conversation from earlier.

Sighing as the melody ended, Tristan kissed my hand and led me over to a white leather sofa that faced the TV, hanging in the middle of the library. Sitting down, I placed my hands in my lap, curling my fingers into loosely closed fists, smiling but nervous. Not knowing what to expect from this conversation, I knew he has reservations about Casey and I wasn't sure where this might go.

Bringing my glass of wine back and sitting next to me, "Look at me. Always look at me," he stated lifting my chin so that my eyes met his, reflecting invitation and questioning at the same time. I was slowly coming to learn that as degraded as I was, keeping my head down reflected the shame that I felt. Tristan was helping me to realize just how much I casted my eyes down.

"Where should we begin?" My voice was barely a whisper as I took a sip of my wine.

Sounding just as nervous as I, he asked, "What do you want to know?"

Mr. Hyde deciding to try his luck, "Since you want to start slow, how about what you do for the military?" his shoulders tensing slightly, a small gulp passing through the knot in his throat.

Releasing his breath, rubbing the back of his neck, "I'm sorry, it's a highly classified project I can't discuss," I could tell he wasn't happy with his response; his hands reaching and rubbing his face.

"Classified? So, you can't tell me anything at all," really trying my best to remain open minded and calm; but Mr. Hyde was peaking his ugly head, "It'll remain a secret, just like the rest of your sordid life?"

"Look," pulling his face down with his cheeks, approaching my response carefully, "I want to be open with you, but there are some things I am not allowed to discuss. As a journalist, you should know this," punch in the gut, but I knew he was right.

Time to change my questioning, "Ok what branch of service are you in?"

"Army," he simply answered still not giving too much away. It was obvious that I was probably going to get nowhere with these job questions.

Sighing heavily at the lack of information, "You really don't know how long you will be gone?" somewhat frustrated at this point.

Rubbing the back of his neck still, holding my hand and facing the palm up, he began tracing the lines, "No. Last I heard it was going to be a quick mission. Those are normally a month or two, but rumor has it, it could be longer. I will know more when I get there and can assess the situation." His voice slightly buckling as the not knowingly seemed to eat away at him.

There was just one thing eating away at me and with a heavy sigh, I braced myself for an answer I knew wasn't coming, "Why can't I touch you? I've seen the scars, is that why?"

Darkness clouded his features as if recalling the terrible ordeal, "Yes."

Deciding to press, "What happened," now turning his hand in mine, my fingers lacing with his.

His stare was blank as the memories still replayed, swallowing hard, moisture soaking his eyes, "Not yet, I'm not ready to visit that part of my past. I've spent years wiping it from my thoughts, pushing it to the back of my head. It's a dark place and it puts me in an even darker place. Please don't," almost pleading with me.

Taking my hands and cupping his face, to bring him back to me, "Hey, ok...I'll drop it."

His features softened some, but seeing the effects my questions had, I knew this was unchartered territory for him.

Standing to give him a minute to recoup, I walked over to the books. His non-answers were torture to my mind; someone had hurt him in a way that he struggled with recovering from it. His pride could shatter just by him recalling what happened.

Running my finger across the line of books, I found collections of classics, from *Moby Dick* to *Jane Eyre*. Tracing the canvased binding of each book, "You like to read?" I asked trying to lighten the mood, looking back over my shoulder to find him observing me as I read each title.

My eyes traced each book, examining the ages. There were first editions to later editions, an array of different genres and authors, an impressive assortment. Hearing him shuffle to stand, his hands finding my waist from behind, "When I have time. It allows me to escape; to go to another world and leave the one I'm in. That was until I met you." My heart fluttering, I turned into his words, finding pain that lingered.

Rubbing his hands ever so slightly up my arms to my shoulders, he kissed my lips softly. Brushing my cheek, his eyes searching through me, "In time, I promise," a promise that had been repeated all day, his way of making sure I knew he would tell me when he was ready. It was now my turn to make sure that I held up my end of the bargain and give him that time. Raking his finger down my bare spine, his gentleness made me quiver, goose bumps forming under the trail of his finger.

His nose pressing against my cheek, quietly whispering, "You truly are radiant," his breath soft and warm, "but it's time for dinner." Turning back to him, kissing my lips, he broke away, leaving me in a cloud to gather my thoughts.

Walking towards the windows, settled near the bar, Tristan poured himself a glass of whiskey. Realizing he left me in a daze, he came over, smiling ear to ear. Quickly coming out of my trance, Tristan grabbed my hand, leading me out of the library, down to dinner.

DINNER

B ack downstairs, entering the dining area, the rest of the guests seated, waiting to be served, "Just in time," Rebecca exclaiming, as the first waiter appeared with our appetizers. It was simple calamari, the finest no less. The mood was light, each of us carrying on in conversation; learning that Rebecca and Tristan were twins, their parents were one of the wealthiest business investors in Charleston, owning half of downtown, and the condo was their latest venture with Tristan heading the designs.

Placing his hand upon my knee in a simple gesture, his smile light. Kayla spoke about her art education class at the college, Rebecca relaying that she knew the head of the department well. Of course, that excited Kayla even more, and Rebecca provided some of the inside scoop of what to expect from her upcoming lectures at the college.

The main course consisted of fresh shrimp linguine with roasted asparagus and creamed potatoes. The first bite against my tongue caused a hushed, *mmm*. His eyes peering to me from the corners, I reached the napkin to my lips, "The food is exquisite, Rebecca. This is divine."

"Yes, Rebecca," Tristan stated, giving my knee a slight squeeze in agreement, "You did a fine job preparing tonight's' menu."

Rebecca beaming at the compliments held her glass up, "A toast to new friendships and great beginnings," the rest of us following, glasses chiming one another.

Finishing up dinner, the waiters cleared the tables as they presented us with a dark forest truffle, topped with fresh strawberries. Impeccable like the main course, I couldn't help but moan again with the taste floating on my tongue. I had never had food like this and felt awfully spoiled to be enjoying such a course. With the next bite on the tip of my tongue, Tristan watched, a small laugh escaping. Touching my fingers to my lips I laughed off my embarrassment.

Going in for another bite, I noticed Kayla and Keith sharing in each other's desserts, playfully laughing. In that moment, I couldn't recall the last time I saw Kayla this happy. Sure, she had her fair share of romances, but what was blossoming between the two in front of me was new. Looking over, I found Rebecca sitting with lonely features observing her brother and brother's best friend's shared moments. Breaking the tension, "So Rebecca, are you dating?"

Turning to me, shaking her head matter-of-factly, "Not at the moment. I just got out of a bad relationship. And let's just say, well...good riddance. I plan to keep cool for a while and focus on some projects I have planned."

Peeking my curiosity, "What are you working on?"

Perking up at my question, Rebecca began rambling on about a non-profit she had started known as Charleston Against Drunk Driving, an initiative to raise awareness and stop people from drinking and driving. Before I could dig into more detail about the non-profit and her reasons for starting it, the staff began clearing our place settings; our cue that dinner was over. Standing, we made our way to the living area, Rebecca staying behind to help finish clearing the dining area. Grabbing their belongings, Keith reached his hand towards Tristan, "Hey man, I think we are going to go. Thanks for the delightful meal. It was awesome as usual."

Kayla following with her own compliments, "Yes Tristan, your sister's and your hospitality has been wonderful. Thank you so much for the invite, it was truly wonderful," impatience evident in her voice, making her way to the elevator.

Patting Keith on the shoulder with one hand and shaking with the other, "Well it was our pleasure. You both enjoy your evening," then reaching and hugging Kayla.

Proceeding with my own farewell, "Are you sure you're ok?" Kayla whispering so only I could hear.

"Yea, I'll be fine," easing her concerns, "You'll be the first one I call if I'm not," giving her a wink as she pulled away. Turning towards Keith, he placed his hand at the small of her back, escorting her to the waiting elevator, whispering something in her ear. Kayla playfully hit his chest as the waiting doors opened and they entered in.

Coming up behind us, "Well that's my cue. Good night brother," Rachel hinted, gathering her purse in her hands. Walking to Tristan first, hugging him tightly, and following up with me, "Amber it was a pleasure. I look forward to seeing you again." Stepping back and looking us both over, "You two are divine as a couple. Amber, Tristan will take good care of you. If he doesn't, he'll answer to me," winking in my direction as Tristan shuffled her out the door. I couldn't help but laugh as Rebecca waved farewell while the elevator doors closed in front of her.

Striding back over to me, scooping me off my feet, giggling at his romance, Tristan escorted me up the stairs. Placing his nose to the edge of my loose hair, "You know I have never invited another girl into my home."

My hand catching my mouth, shocked by his confession, "Really, why?"

His brow furrowing, "I like my privacy. You're the first girl, other than Kayla and my sister who has ever been in my home."

Curious, I asked him, "So where do you take the girls you date?"

"I don't take them anywhere. I haven't dated much in the past few years," pausing, contemplating my question. Sending me an accusing stare, "Do you think I am some guy who brings a girl home every night?"

Passing him a look back, "You do have that sweet southern Gucci type about you."

Shaking his head, denying my accusation, "I'm not that kind of guy. I'm a one-woman kind of guy and right now, I am pretty sure I am holding her," his nose nestling back into the crevice of my neck.

Opening the door to his bedroom, the spacious room romantic and crisp, a four-post mahogany bed with a white comforter adorned the far end; the walls a pale grey. The atmosphere definitely suited Tristan's personality of simple and clean. Carrying me over to the bed, laying me down, the coolness of the comforter playing across my bare skin. Propping himself beside me, with one hand holding up his head, he looked down at me as I could see a hint of fear tracing his eyes.

"What?" shifting myself to match his position.

His eyes searching mine, "You drive me crazy, darling. You're everything and more. My life was empty, pointless until I met you."

Waving off his negativity, "That's not true. You are an amazing ball player and man who fights for what he wants. You designed this gorgeous condo," my hands and eyes wandering around the room, "Any girl would be lucky to have you, but... why me," biting the inside of my cheek.

"You're worth keeping, almost," that word *almost*, I knew he was referencing Casey. I needed to act quickly and show him Casey was a distant memory, at least getting there. The divorce was, of course, my only hang up, but that didn't mean that my emotions or feelings were still tied to him. Reaching to push his shoulder, hesitating while looking for permission, he nodded in acceptance. Climbing on top, his back reaching the bed, I grabbed his wrists, pinning them above his head.

Smiling up at me, "Hmm...I like this side of you," his neck extending, his lips barely touching of my neck.

Smiling at my coyness, my eyes meeting curiosity, "Let me ease your worries." Leaning down, my lips brushed soft kisses on his neck, speaking softly, "Casey is my past and you're my present. Let's forget the past, shall we?" Finding his lips, pressing soft kisses, I continued to tease as I brushed against his. Straining to reach deeper against my lips, pulling back, whispering, "No sir, it's my turn," smiling along his neckline. Wrestling his wrists under my grasp, my hold wouldn't budge. Giving up, he eased into my slow teasing.

Sliding one of my hands down his arm, my hand reached for his chest. Stopping myself, knowing I shouldn't continue. Swiftly grabbing my hand before it had the chance to do anything, "Wait!" breathless, Tristan shifted himself to a sitting position, me straddling his lap, "I want to show you that I trust you, that you are everything to me." Unbuttoning his shirt, my eyes grew hazy as the bare skin revealed itself from under the fabric. Allowing it to flow off his shoulders, cascading in a rumple on the bed behind him, his scars were prominent on his chest, "Let me see your hand." Obliging his request, he turned the palm towards his chest. My heart began racing at what he was gesturing. Tension was tight in his arms, my hand moving in slow motion towards the one thing I had wanted since the day I first laid eyes on them. Suddenly everything stopped when his cell phone chirped from the nightstand table. His head plowed back into the bed, his palms rubbing the frustration from his face. Lifting me off of him, rolling onto his side, he reached the phone, "Hello," his face growing pale with news from the other line.

"Are you sure? When," his free hand rubbing through his short sandy blonde hair, his paleness turning to anger. "I'll be there in 30," he quipped, hanging up.

Turning to me, "Amber, I'm sorry, I need to go. Let me walk you home."

"What's wrong? Everything ok," I asked, lifting myself off the bed, heading towards the bedroom door.

"It's *ENVY*, someone robbed the place."

ELEVATORS

"**I** have to go. The police are asking for me," he stated frustrated.

My hands directly covering my mouth, "Oh my! Ok, I'll grab my purse."

Reaching his shirt from the bed, he began covering the beauty that hid beneath. Buttoning each button back and grabbing his keys and phone, I gathered my purse. Interlacing his fingers with mine, we descended the stairs, entering the elevator to head out. Inserting his card, he punched the down button in frustration. Jumping at the forwardness, a deep breath escaped him, his demeanor relaxing. Facing forward, quietness loomed like a heavy cloud of rain on a summer afternoon. My self-control getting the better of me, as my eyes could see the reflection of frustration still evident in Tristan's expression in the steel doors. Taking advantage of the mirrored image, my eyes took inventory of the whole package. Moving up the bottom half of his body, Tristan cleared his throat, catching me in my quiet observations. His features quickly changing to enjoyment, a hint of pink flushed my cheeks as embarrassment crept through my stomach.

Watching from the reflection, Tristan's attention turned to the back of me as his hand found the bareness of my back, tracing the lines exposed. Rubbing his knuckles softly down my spine, "I really like this shirt," goose bumps forming a trail from where his touch vanished. Slowly sliding his fingers up my back, reaching the small loose strands of hair at the base of my neck, twirling them in his fingers, I continued watching, trying to keep my breathing even.

Moving closer to me, I could feel the strength of him against my arm. Glancing at me in the reflection, a smile perched as his eyes turned sultry before moving behind me, his lips finding the base of my neck where his hands had just left the loose locks of hair. Softness trailed watching his hands finding my hips, pulling me closer into him.

My hip felt empty where his hand left to pull the keycard from the elevator slot. Coming to a halt, the emptiness filled quickly with his hands, his lips never stopping along my neck. No longer able to control my breathing, my breaths grew heavy as the air thickened in the elevator. Turning me and pushing me into the elevator wall, lifting my arms to reach around his neck, his face never met mine, but watched as his hands began tracing my bare arms. Closing my eyes and resting my head on the aluminum wall of the elevator, all I could do was take in the heat of the moment.

Finding the back of my leg and lifting it to wrap around his body, his mouth close to my ear, pulling my hair from its holder, "Envy will have to wait."

MOM

Adjusting himself to a more manageable appearance, I assisted by smoothing out the wrinkles present among his shoulders. Following suit, he reached over, inserting the card back into the slot; the elevator beginning it's decent. Lifting my hand, kissing it, the elevator doors opened to the first floor and we made our way outside, "It's really ok. I can walk myself home," I remarked.

"Nah," Tristan answered nonchalantly, "Last time you didn't let me know you were safe. Plus, the club is only a few blocks from your place."

"Fine," I sighed, as we were walking down King Street towards my apartment. The night was cool for July; the stars present but not quite in focus with the lights of the city. Clouds slowly moved in, hovering over the moon present in the early evening sky, something heavy looming in the air. Looking over my shoulder, there was nothing but a few tourists. Sensing my tension, he asked, "What?"

"Something's not right. I keep getting this feeling like I'm being watched. I've had it for several days," I commented, turning back to face the direction of our path.

Slightly squeezing my hand tighter, he promised, "I'll keep you safe darling." Lifting his arm around my shoulder, "Come on, let's get you home."

Arriving at my apartment, he kissed my cheek, "I'll call you when I finish up." Before I could respond he hurried off in the direction of *ENVY*.

Making my way upstairs, I entered the apartment hearing the faintest of moans coming from Kayla's room. Quietly making my way to my room, stripping out of my clothing, I had Tristan's jersey in my hand. Deciding I would wear that, I rummaged through some boxes to locate my laptop and battery cord; I needed to catch up on some emails.

It had been almost a week since our move and I hadn't even turned on my computer. Pulling it out, plugging it in, plopping myself on the edge of my bed, I waited a few minutes to allow enough battery juice to give me enough charge to turn it on. Coming on, the dialogue to set up the new Internet wireless appeared and once connected a ping came over my Mac. Pulling up my e-mail, not to my surprise, an e-mail from my mom was the first and only one:

> *Amber I am worried sick! You have not called or gotten in contact with us since your move. Luckily Kayla informed me you were ok! Call us sweetie. We are worried.*

Sensing the anguish in the e-mail, I knew I should have called sooner, but I dreaded it. Kayla helped keep my mother at bay, knowing she was the last person I needed anything from. I also made sure to not have my phone on much this week. I was avoiding any conversations with Casey as best as possible. Plus, anytime I seemed to have it on, she didn't call.

When things went south with Casey, I didn't leave much detail. I simply told my mom things were over, and being like most moms, she pushed for answers. I figured she would have gotten the hint while I was laid up in the hospital. Like most old-fashioned women, she didn't believe in leaving a man, God knows she stayed with my stepdad this whole time.

She was a fair woman, small in frame. She married my dad during college and had a whirlwind love affair. Within a year, I was born. Shortly after I turned two, my father was killed in a car accident. It devastated my mom and drove her into a deep depression. About a year later, she met my stepfather; Casey reminded me a lot of him. He was demanding of my mom, very controlling; I would hear them fighting late at night.

I saw my stepdad hit my mom and always threaten her if she left. He always pounded into me to obey your husband, do what he says, blah, blah, blah. I didn't know why she stayed with him, and I feared I had become just like her through the years. I never brought it up, it was pointless but after being controlled for as long as she had, I knew it would be even harder for her to accept it. I knew she could do better.

They weren't the wealthiest of people. My mom was a homemaker and left college to stay home with me. I was the only child. My stepdad owned a machine shop in town. It was the one all the locals went to, so he stayed plenty busy.

When I was six, my mom and stepfather got into a terrible fight after he had come home from a three-day bender at the local bar. She had sent me out of the room so I wouldn't be around him, but I remember peeking around the corner as I watched him punch her in the stomach. He hit her so hard she collapsed on the floor unconscious and they had to rush her to the hospital. There was so much damage they had to do a hysterectomy or she would have died. I wouldn't call it a blessing, since no man should beat his own wife, but there would be no more kids that would have to endure the heartache and pain I was raised with.

Picking up my phone, I dialed her number, dreading what was

ahead.

"Hello?" my mom answering. *Thank goodness*. I didn't want to talk to my stepdad.

"Hello, mom..." resistance evident in my voice.

"Amber, finally! Are you ok? Why haven't you called? I've been worried sick," panic and anguish mixing as she drilled me with questions.

"I know, I'm sorry. Everything is fine. Still trying to get settled in Charleston," I said after a long pause, calming her and myself at the same time.

"When do you start your new job?" settling the excitement down some, I was hoping this would be the start of a normal conversation.

"Monday morning. I'm looking forward to it; ready to get in a routine," I stated nonchalantly.

A small glimmer peeked in that the mention of the elephant in the room had not appeared, however, "Casey stopped by, asking about you. Honey, he's devastated you left. You know...you should give him another chance. He misses you and really does care. Won't you reconsider moving back and fixing things?" I never understood why my mom never supported my decisions or me. Why she was so hung up on Casey. Yes, I did marry him, but I couldn't endure any more of how he was. I couldn't end up like her, sad and abused.

The glimmer was gone and rage filled me, "Mom! Do you not remember me laid up in the hospital with a broken nose and concussion? That should be plenty of reason to leave him. I'm sorry mom, you might be able to live that life, but I can't," I shouted, my tongue lashing at her.

"AMBER MARIE SLAYTON..." she screamed back, disbelief present in her voice.

Getting off topic, "Never mind. Look, Casey and I are done. My divorce will be final in two months and I need to move on with my life. Start fresh. Charleston is that answer. Will you for once support what I want and not what everyone else wants," I snapped, ending the conversation.

"I guess," I could see her pacing the floor, her hands swallowing the air. Exchanging a few more words, I hung up the phone with her. The dread of knowing Casey was asking about me irked me. He needed to get over it and realize we were done, but deep down I knew Casey wasn't going to go without a fight. I was actually surprised that I hadn't heard from him since I moved.

My adrenaline was so high, now was the perfect time to finish unpacking what was left. Shuffling through the boxes, finding photo frames, books, my extra phone charger, clothing, etc., I finished the last box at a quarter after midnight. Picking up my phone, I hadn't received a call or text from Tristan and as late as it was, I wasn't expecting one.

Kayla and Keith were still busy in the next room. Climbing up in my bed, finding my iPod on the bedside table, I placed the headphones in my ears, as I normally did anytime Kayla had a midnight romp; lying against the pillow, I drifted off to sleep.

THE FINAL STRAW

What is this? Hovering the mouse over the latest site in the computer's recorded history. Easy girls? Clicking the link, horror covered my screen as busty blonde-haired women, shaking their breasts, showing off their asses flashed across my screen. My heart sank as I realized what Casey had been viewing.

"WHAT THE HELL?" Casey yelled upon entering the room. "What are you doing? Don't I have any damn privacy?" Evident he had been drinking. He was an angry drunk and catching his latest viewing venture just fueled it. His tan forehead furrowing as he watched me watching the screen.

Turning to him, tears filled my eyes, "Casey, you told me you would stop. What is this? Why do you need this? I just don't understand how you can look at this? It's filth! This isn't a marriage. You're tearing us apart," screaming at him, my heart ached knowing he hadn't stopped watching the porn. I couldn't even look at the screen, as I felt the vomit swell in my throat at the disgust.

Grabbing the back of the seat, Casey threw the seat and me away from the computer, "Shut up Amber. You don't know what the hell you're talking about. You need to keep your damn nose to yourself."

As the chair came to a stop, turning to face him, "It's disgusting Casey and if you aren't going to stop, I'm done! I'm leaving," standing to storm out of the room.

Grabbing me up by my waist before I could leave, "The hell you are! You'll do what I say! You find it disgusting; well I find it absolutely satisfying, especially since you don't give me any. Come on babe watch it with me," his hand now tight on my jaw, forcing my face in the direction of the videos that were playing on the screen, the sound of moans filling the speakers. Shutting my eyes tight, Casey drew his tongue along my neck as the smell of alcohol filled me. The vomit was growing higher and all I could do was fight to get away. "Oh, hell no; you aren't going anywhere," holding his grasp around me, pointing his index finger so hard in my chest, I felt the bruises forming, "You won't leave Amber. You say you will but you won't." Calming his voice to a low tone, pulling my hair and wrapping it around his wrist, and jerking my head back, "I've got you babe, on my tight little leash and you aren't going anywhere!" Pushing me against the wall, he pressed his hardness against me, releasing my hair as he began ripping my clothes.

Waiting for my opportunity, I kneed Casey in his groin.

Collapsing in pain, he held onto his manhood. Free from his grasp, turning to the door, I scrambled, "Watch me!" I hollered back.

Snarling and lunging forward, a sudden pain gripped the back of my head as I felt my hair tearing away from my scalp. Casey had my hair again, pulling me back towards him, like a dog on a leash, "I said you weren't leaving Amber." Twisting the tresses in his hands, tighter this time against my scalp, "Do you understand?" Tears pouring from my eyes as the strands began tearing even more from my pores, fear tightening in my stomach.

Reaching back to try and ease his hand, failing, "Yes Casey, I'm sorry, you're right. Please let me go. You're... you're hurting me. Let me go," I pleaded. His hand tightening harder, as angered poured from him, he drug me through the room. I knew he was taking me to our room to rape me, as he did often on one of his drunken rages. Entering our bedroom and lugging me forward, I tripped over my feet, screaming...

"Amber, wake up," Kayla shouting, shaking my shoulders, "AMBER..." the shaking jolted me from my nightmare. Wrapping her arms around me as tears poured down my face, she held me tightly. Keith looked in from the doorway, his face paler than normal. Turning away, he was back within a minute to join Kayla beside me on the bed. My whole body shaking uncontrollably as I tried to force myself out of my dreamlike state.

My face now in her hands, bringing my attention directly to her, "Amber, are you ok?" smoothing my hair, looking me over.

My breathing heavy as my hands replaced hers on my face, the gasping sobs pouring from me as the adrenaline high began tapering, "It was the same dream Kayla. I felt like I was right there." Trying to regulate my breathing, "I talked to my mom tonight. Kayla, he wants me back," my crying uncontrollable again. "I can't go! My mom wants me to come home to be with him! I CAN'T KAYLA! I JUST CAN'T!"

Keith got up and moved to my other side, now holding my hand, trying to comfort me the same. He sat quietly as Kayla continued to comfort me the way she always had, "Shh...I know, I know," pulling me into her chest, rubbing the tangles of my hair, soothing my fears. There was a knock on the apartment door. Disappearing out of the room, Keith returned with Tristan right behind him, looking as if someone had torn his heart out. Seeing him, I began whispering to Kayla, "He can't see me like this." He had enough doubts about our relationship; I didn't need him seeing me upset over Casey!

Kayla didn't say anything as she shifted from my side, Tristan sitting next to her. Wrapping his arms around me, pulling my head against him, I couldn't stop the rush of emotions that overcame me. The bravery and pride I had been swallowing for weeks had broken away, the dam was gone and everything that I had gone through came rushing back. Hiding my face into Tristan's chest, "I'll leave you two alone," Kayla stood, as Keith came over, squeezing my shoulder.

Shaking Keith's hand, "Hey man, thanks for calling," he whispered, looking up to him.

"No problem. Take care of our girl," he said in a hushed tone, leaning over and kissing the top of my head.

Looking back from the doorway, "We'll see you guys tomorrow. Amber, talk to Tristan. You need him now," said Kayla closing the door behind the both of them.

My face now hid in the palms of my hands, "Tristan, I don't want you seeing me like this," I said, trying my best to catch my breath.

Tristan was clueless to what was going on, "Shh… are you ok? Did someone hurt you?"

In all my years with Casey, there was never a time he cared for how I felt…it was always what he wanted, when he wanted it. I never had an outlet for my emotions and now my reluctance to divulge too much was overpowering, "No, it was just a dream; a really bad one."

"How often do you have them?" I assumed he was going to ask me about the details of my dream, but he didn't.

"Every so often," wiping my eyes, "It's not a big deal. I have dealt with it this long; it's something I will have to learn to live with."

Baffled by my nonchalance, "No Amber, you need to talk to someone," he said, expressing his concern, "I know someone who can help."

Lifting my face from my hands, "Help? Help you with what? Your pa…"

"I battled with nightmares for a long time. Let's do this; we'll talk about it in the morning. Right now, we need to try and get some sleep." He cut me off.

Moving towards the top of the bed, Tristan pulled the blankets down, signaling for me to get under. Finding my way to my pillow, "You won't leave?" I queried.

"No darling, I'll be here until you wake," crawling in with me, we settled into the evening.

DAY OF REST

The early morning sun peaked through the crack of the curtain, my heavy eyes blinking at the invasion. Emptiness filled my body, panic setting in, I turned over to find Tristan still lying next to me, a sudden rush of relief pouring over me.

"Did you sleep," I asked, stretching my body under the layer of blankets?

"No," reaching over to push back a strand that had dropped across my brow.

"Tristan, you need to sleep," I yawned the last few minutes of sleep away, my hand finding his cheek, rubbing across the freshly grown stubble.

Turning and kissing my hand, "Comes with the territory." He said. "It's all good; I'll sleep when I die. Are you ok?" always turning the questions back to me.

"Better since I'm waking next to you," I said quietly, leaning over and kissing him gently, "What happened at *ENVY*? Is everything ok?"

"Everything is fine. The police are handling it. Are you ok?" concern now evident, as I didn't really answer the last time.

Not answering right away. "I'm fine. I'm sorry you saw me like that."

Trying to convince me, "I think you should talk to my therapist. She may be able to help you sort out some stuff."

"I might take you up on that, but right now I'm ok," I nipped the conversation quickly, not wanting to discuss the option of a shrink any further.

Changing the subject all together, "What do you want to do today?" It was the day before starting my new job.

Lying back on my pillow, staring at the ceiling, "I start my new job tomorrow. Really, I just want to relax and lounge all day. I've got a full day ahead of me," realizing I hadn't had any time to prepare myself.

"That's right. I got an idea. I'll be right back," with a quick peck on my lips, jumping out of bed, reaching for his cell in his pants pocket, he exited the room.

Calling back to me, "Nice shirt, by the way." Looking down, I had forgotten I had worn his jersey to bed; me smiling like a schoolgirl.

While Tristan was busy making his phone call, I got up, raising my arms to stretch my limbs, standing on my toes stretching my legs; I started towards the bathroom. Walking in turning on the shower, removing his jersey and the rest of my attire, I stepped into the heat of the water, laying my head on my arms on the opposite side, the water pelting across my back, the emotions of the night overcoming me. Tears filling my eyes, *why am I crying?* Maybe it was the emotional rollercoaster I had been on for what felt like forever; I really don't even know how long my emotions had been out of check.

I had just left Casey around a month ago and already my life was turned upside down again. Tristan was so different from Casey, but Mr. Hyde was peaking back up; my past a constant reminder that my life was resistant to accept it would be any different. I needed the time to think, if Tristan could just give me that.

Stepping back from the wall, I let the water cascade onto my body and wash away as much of the worry and anguish that I could allow it. Finishing up my shower, turning the water off, I opened the door and was greeted by Tristan wrapping a towel around me.

Kissing my cheek, "Get dressed. You have about 20 minutes."

Confusion furrowing across my brow, "Why?"

Wrapping his fingers around the edge of the door, his face peaking around the corner, "I know the owner of Mystique Day Spa. They are closed today, but she is bringing in her crew to give Kayla and you a day of pampering," he winked at me, vanishing into my room.

Surprised by the gesture, entering the room behind him, "What? Really? You shouldn't..." Pressing his index finger to my mouth to hush me.

"Yes, I needed to. It's my pleasure. Now get dressed. You have twenty minutes to get there." Kissing him quickly, I ran to the closet to find something to wear. This was the answer to what I needed; the man definitely had one up.

FIRST DAY ON THE NEW JOB

Waking the next morning, feeling fresh and relaxed, Tristan out did himself with our spa day. We were pampered to the core: full body massages, pedicures, facials, the works. When Kayla and I returned home, we found a bottle of wine, pizza, and two chick flicks with a note that read:

> *Enjoy your girl's night! Talk to you soon. ~Tristan and Keith*

It was short, sweet and to the point. Kayla and I indulged and spent the night on the couch in our pajamas, watching the two movies Tristan and Keith had picked out. Retiring around 10 PM, I hadn't slept so peacefully in weeks. Waking up refreshed and ready for the new day ahead, I needed to start this job with a clear focus and Tristan had provided that.

Walking into my closet, I pulled out a pencil skirt and white button-down blouse. Sliding on my grey pumps, walking back to the bathroom, I applied light makeup and left my hair down. The look was professional but not overdone. With my appearance finally to my approval, I grabbed a cup of coffee from the kitchen and headed out the door. Hitting King Street, the morning was humid, but cool, an obvious cold front settling in. The sky was filled with ominous dark clouds, looking as if it was going to rain. Before moving here, I had read that flooding could be vicious downtown, if the tide was high. Hopefully it would wait until I made it home.

Strolling down Broad Street, I entered the two-story brick building, just half a block down from the *Four Corners of Law*, as they called it. Advancing the creaking flight of stairs, I was greeted with the words, *Lowcountry Magazine* on the hunter green, wooden door. A bell chimed when I opened it, the receptionist greeted me.

"You must be Amber," standing and extending her hand, "Mr. Klein is expecting you. Go on in," pointing me in the direction down the hall; the hallway walls lined with various awards and key pieces from prior journalists. The building was old but remodeled to a modern venue, although the smell of old paint hung in the air. Finding my way to the frosted door and knocking lightly, I entered Mr. Klein's office.

"Got to go, I'll call you soon," he said, hanging up the phone upon my entrance, standing to greet me. Shaking my hand, he gestured for me to sit. Taking a seat in a plush burgundy wingback, I glanced around his office, a picture of a young boy with fiery red hair and braces snagging my attention. He was holding a fish and a man, a younger version of Mr. Klein, stood behind him with a proud smile on his face.

"Ms. Slayton..." Mr. Klein started.

"Please Amber," correcting him before he got too far into the conversation. He was my boss so formal pleasantries weren't necessary.

"Ok, Amber. Welcome to *Lowcountry Magazine.* We hope you will find the environment here..." waving his hand in the air to grasp the right word, "…pleasant. We have a desk set up for you at the opposite end of the hall with a laptop, monitor, docking station, and some office supplies. Feel free to decorate and re-arrange as you see fit. Human Resources will be in touch with you shortly to sort out any remaining paperwork and minor orientation. I mostly deal with e-mail, so expect to get several from me throughout the day," pausing briefly, I shook my head to acknowledge I was still following along.

Continuing on, "We don't allow any personal e-mail here in the office, so please keep those at home. All of your assignments will be sent via e-mail. If you have any questions, please feel free to ask. I do have an open-door policy, but prefer e-mail, so there is a paper trail of conversations. If the conversation needs to be held outside of e-mail, please notify me in advance and we will try to accommodate."

Nodding my head in understanding, the details sounded fair. I had never worked for someone who was a stickler for a paper trail, but being a publisher of a magazine, it made sense. "Do you have any questions?" Shaking my head side to side, "Well since that is all settled, welcome to the team," extending his hand across the desk as he stood, "Your first assignment is due by Friday. The details are in your e-mail," ushering me out of his office.

I made my way down the hall to my desk, excited to get to work. Having my first assignment already would help refocus my mind on something else. Finding my desk in a cozy corner of the building, there was a window overlooking a quaint lit-tle flower garden in the alley behind the building. My laptop docked, I turned it on, the ping of e-mail startling my thoughts, my eyes immediately reading *First Assignment* on the brightly lit screen. Sitting in my chair, I quickly scanned the details con-tained within:

Again, welcome aboard Ms. Slayton. Below you will find

the details of your first article.

We need a quarter page review of a local spa here in Charleston. Please be detailed and thorough. No worries on the required length. Write what you feel and we will cut out what we need.

Mr. Klein

Memories flooded me as I recalled my most recent spa treatment at *Mystique Day Spa*. Writing a quick reply, I asked if they had ever done a review on the place and to my amusement Mr. Klein informed me that no one had done one yet.

Turning to my desk, I found normal first day paperwork lying and waiting. Spending the next hour, I familiarized myself with the typical first day stuff: some Human Resource forms, insurance, W-2's, and personal information sheets; also, a non-disclosure agreement. Once finished, my phone buzzed in my purse. Reaching below my desk, I retrieved my purse, digging to the bottom to find my phone. Pulling it out, I didn't recognize the number displayed. I answered, "Hello?"

"Hello babe, how are you?" recognizing the husky voice on the other end, I could feel the blood rushing from my face, growing pale.

"Casey?" The words barely escaping my throat as fear clenched it tight, "What do you want?" The question coming quicker than anticipated, "How did you get my number?" Already knowing the answer to my own question. I had gotten rid of the phone I had when I was with Casey, due to all the monitoring features he had placed on it.

"You sound angry. Don't you miss your husband? Remember our vows, until death do us part?" I could hear the smile creeping upon his lips as he reminded me of the one thing that held me from living a normal life. "You left in such a hurry; I am surprised I could track you so easily. Guess it helps when your mom loves me. You do remember you have a husband, right? Or did you forget since you have been squandering with some local joke of a man?"

"I can't talk right now..." My throat grew tighter as realization grew that he knew about Tristan, but now wasn't the time to discuss this.

"Why? Because you are at work, you know I don't like you working. It's not good for you, or any woman for that matter to do a man's job. Women belong at home, cleaning the house, cooking dinner. Not gallivanting across town, schmoozing with the locals, especially the ones you are associating with. They don't come from the life like we came from, they're not like us," he continued to ramble on.

I was trying my best to remain calm, no words coming. Questions flooded as I tried to think of how he knew so much about my life in Charleston. I knew Kayla hadn't talked to anyone. Suddenly it crossed my mind, he had to be in town, but why hadn't he shown himself.

Interrupting the silence, "You didn't think I would find out, Amber? What's his name? Oh yea, Tristan Ashton."

"You don't know what you're talking about? I left you Casey, end of discussion. I don't need this or you in my life. The divorce will be over in two months and you can move on," biting through my clenched teeth, still trying to remain as calm as possible. Peaking around the corner of my office, I quickly made sure no one was listening or coming down the hall.

"You can't hide from me. You may have moved, but you'll

never be rid of me. I own you; never forget that," his voice stern and forceful, "Get rid of him Amber. I'm the only man in your life," the phone disconnecting before I could say anything else.

My knuckles were white as they held my phone tightly; I couldn't move. I was finally getting used to this new place, growing friendships, and yet Casey still had a hold on me. He would never let me go. I needed to get some fresh air, but the clock reflected I still had an hour before I could go to lunch. The buzz of my phone startled me back to reality. Looking down, it was Tristan calling.

"Hello?" my voice shaky, the tightening in my throat still hadn't quite wore off.

"Darling, are you ok? You don't sound good," he remarked, noting the fear must have still been evident.

"I'm fine," clearing my throat, gathering myself back together, "How is your day? Thank you for yesterday, it was magnificent," quickly changing the subject to something other than me.

"I'm glad you enjoyed yourself. I called to see if you wanted to grab some lunch," he didn't skip a beat.

With Casey's voice fresh in my head and Mr. Hyde in full force, I knew he meant business. Casey knew about Tristan, and I let Mr. Hyde take over, "I really can't," Jekyll dying at my response.

"Well darn," he said, pausing briefly, "Hmm, how about I bring lunch to you? I'm right around the corner." Silently I told myself that it wouldn't hurt for him to come to me. Somehow Casey knew about Tristan, but maybe him coming here wouldn't set off any flags.

"Sure, that would be nice. Let me check and make sure visitors are ok," reaching over to email Mr. Klein.

"Oh, don't worry darling, I know Mr. Klein. Be there shortly," he finalized as the line clicked off, leaving my fingers dangling in the air, unsure of what to do.

Looking back to my desk, I began shuffling my papers together to organize the chaos a little better. It was a welcomed distraction from my phone call. About five minutes later, Susan, our secretary buzzed my desk phone.

"Ms. Slayton, I didn't know you knew Tristan, he's here to see you. I'll send him back," she said, sounding a little bit too excited.

"Thank you, Susan," I replied, my finger releasing the button on the phone as Tristan rounded the corner, a white paper bag clenched in his hand. Nerves nestled in my stomach, him noticing my disposition was still off as the blood hadn't quite brought the color back fully.

"Amber, is something wrong? You're pale. Sit down," he said, concern evident as his eyes continued to study my features.

"Yea, I'm fine. Just famished," I suggested, trying to waiver his concern, "What did you bring?" hoping my answer would ease his concerns further. Although the look he gave me told me he didn't believe me.

Taking the seat in front of my desk, he set the bag down, "I brought you a chicken salad sandwich on whole wheat toast, chips, and water," he said, pulling the contents out of the bag.

Reaching for the sandwich and unwrapping it, I said, "Sounds wonderful. Thank you."

"Anytime, darling," he said, beaming with pride as he began eating.

"Tristan," Mr. Klein's voice trailing in from behind him.

Standing and extending his hand out, "Mr. Klein, it's great to see you, sir."

Returning the gesture, "Same. How are you? How's your sister?"

"Fine, sir. She is doing well. She asked about you the other day. She said to say hello," Tristan said, his hands shuffling into the pockets of his shorts, Mr. Klein following his example.

"Well, please return the favor," Mr. Klein said, patting his shoulder and then extending his hand my direction, "I see you have met Ms. Slayton, our newest employee."

"Yes, sir. I met Ms. Slayton a few days ago at *ENVY*. I'm sure she will be a good fit for your company," both men's eyes turning to find me with a mouthful of sandwich. Pulling the napkin to my lips, smiling as I swallowed the food down.

Extending his hand to shake Tristan's in a farewell gesture, "As do I, carry on," turning to walk away, stopping abruptly, "If you see that boy of mine, tell him he owes his dear old dad a phone call," his hands returning to his pockets of his *Armani* black suit.

"I'll be sure to tell Keith to call you," Tristan remarked as he turned to sit back in his chair. Mr. Klein leaving us to our lunch. I suddenly realized that the little boy in the picture was Keith, Mr. Klein's son.

"That's Keith's dad? I thought his dad was Air Force," I whispered to Tristan, his attention returning to me.

"His dad is, or was. Mr. Klein is Keith's step dad. Keith's dad and mom split up when Keith was 3. His dad was gone all the time, so Mr. Klein stepped in as the father figure. He retired about four years ago, when he took over the magazine," he said, popping a chip in his mouth.

Holding my sandwich up, ready to take a bite, I said, "I saw his picture in Mr. Klein's office, he was a cute kid! The fiery red hair should have triggered the connection," finally taking my bite.

Coughing with laughter, "Keith hates that picture, the braces and everything. I rag him about it every once in a while. He just raises his hand and pushes the conversation in another direction. I've threatened to show it to his girlfriends," Tristan said, sipping his drink to help ease the food down.

Continuing with small talk, we finished up. My mood settling from my earlier phone call with Casey, I was ready to talk to Kayla. I needed to finish up some items and I would be out the door.

Gathering the trash and standing to leave, "Got plans for dinner?"

"Nothing. Why?" I sounded a little startled as Casey's words replayed in my head. I came here to leave the control and, in that moment, Mr. Jekyll took back over as I decided his call was not going to change that.

His eyes kind of diverted to the floor, almost acting nervous, "The Sharks are holding a going away party slash gala tonight. Kayla and you are invited," putting his hands up to prevent me from saying anything so he could finish, "Don't worry about what to wear; I've got you covered. Please say you will go."

Responding a bit over excited, "How can I say no? Wait, how do you know my size and what I like?"

His eyes returning to mine as a sly smile crept on his lip, "Well if you don't like what I picked out, you can wear something else. I'm sure you won't be disappointed," leaning forward, kissing my cheek, "See you tonight then?" he said, turning to leave.

Smiling as he exited down the hall, "It's a date."

PROOF

The clock signaled quitting time. I finished up all my first day paperwork and had already called Mystique Spa and spoke to Charlotte, Tristan's friend about a possible interview. She confirmed an appointment for Thursday, before lunch. Shutting down my computer, I grabbed my belongings from under my desk and exited my office. Heading down the steps of Broad Street, I had a quick errand I wanted to run before heading back home.

Trying to hurry as fast as I could in my pumps, I rushed through the crowd of tourists on Market Street to the vendor I had visited on Saturday. I wanted to give Tristan something to thank him for everything he had done for me in the past few days. He really was different from Casey, but Mr. Hyde continued to tie my emotions to him. I was trying my best to get Casey out of my mind and out my life, but today's phone call didn't help. I was determined to not let that stop me.

Reaching the vendor, I found he still had the ring I eyed on Saturday. Buying it, tucking it in my pocket, and rushing back towards King Street, to my apartment, I made it up the stairs and dashed towards my room.

Reaching the bedroom door, "There's a package for you," Kayla yelled from the other room. Thinking it was my dress; I rushed back to the living room, but found nothing there.

"Where is it?" I hollered back, my eyes scanning the area for a box of some kind.

"On the table, the yellow envelope. It's kind of weird, there's no return address. I didn't want to pry," she answered, the sound of makeup clanking on the counter from her room.

My heart sank, as the reality of Casey's phone call replayed. Not knowing what it could be had me worried. Picking up the package, my hands shaking, it was heavy and thick. Walking to the stove, grabbing a steak knife to cut the seal open, reaching inside, I pulled out the contents. There was a piece of paper on top of thick sheets behind it.

If you want your lover boy to keep his career, you better listen and do as your told. I still own you. ~C

Terror gripping my stomach, I removed the piece of paper to see the contents behind it. My hands grew weak causing the contents to drop to the floor. Horror surrounded me as the evidence reflected that Casey was in Charleston.

Not realizing I had screamed, Kayla rushed out of her room, in just her bra and underwear. "What is it? Are you ok?"

My hands shook as one reached to cover my mouth. My legs becoming jello, my body sank against the cabinet. Making her way to my side, her face grew pale as she saw the pictures of Tristan and me scattered on the floor. There were pictures from *ENVY*, the stadium, our apartment, and his condo, even from lunch today. Confused, she sat down beside me, wrapping me in her arms. Tears beading at the corners of my eyes, I sobbed into Kayla's shoulder.

Rubbing my arm, "Amber, what is this?" I handed her the note, confused. "C? Casey? How? Why? I'm confused." I began sobbing harder. "Calm down Amber, what's going on," she pried.

Lifting my face from my hands, I began recounting our phone call from earlier, leading to this, reaching forward to pick up the pictures, her look was one of fury. She was pissed, "How did Casey get your number? How did he know?" Before I could answer, her face reflected that she knew my mother had given it to him.

Her lips pinching tight, "Amber you need to set your mom straight. She's not being supportive. Her husband is a total ass hole, who controlled her life and yours. I hate to say it but unless she starts supporting you, you need to cut your losses."

My mom always did what others thought was best, not what was best for me.

"And tomorrow we change your phone number. Don't give it to your mom!" You could sense the steam escaping from Kayla's ears as she bolstered with anger.

"I don't know what to do Kayla. We have this banquet tonight and I don't know if I should even go," remarking as I rolled my head back against the cabinet door.

"You need to talk to Tristan. If this man is threatening his career, he has a right to know," she stated firmly.

Kayla was right. The last thing I wanted was for Tristan to lose the one thing he loved. I didn't know what Tristan did, but I knew it was serious, serious enough he kept it secret and even left the game he loved so much to go back to war.

"Come on, let's get dressed," shuffling to her feet, forcing my arm up with her, "Screw Casey! You're still going and the last thing he wants to do is come into a party full of ball players. The men will be here shortly to pick us up. You can talk to him then."

COMING CLEAN

Kayla was right, Tristan had a right to know. Gathering myself together and the contents that were spread across the floor, I went to my room to get ready. Laying the envelope on the bed, I found a long white box that contained my dress. Opening the lid, the latest design from Vera Wang's Summer Formal Collection was inside. It was an off the shoulder, champagne colored, low cut V-neck that dipped down the front and back. It was long and there were shoes to match. I knew I didn't have anything nicer. Lifting the dress in admiration, a black box sat at the bottom, catching my attention. Reaching for it, I opened it to find a 2-carat diamond infinity necklace and note:

> *For a woman with exquisite beauty, may this be the first of many more. ~Tristan*

My breath hitching at the sparkling beauty,

"Do you like it," he queried.

Surprised, I turned to find Tristan standing in my doorway, watching me as I opened the box. Dressed in a black tux with a grey vest, clean-shaven, his hair was groomed, gasping, "Tristan it's too much. Everything is too much," the emotions of the day catching up with me as I wrestled to fight back tears.

"Nothing is too much for a beautiful woman such as you," he said. His words sweet as he walked over, removing the necklace from the box, "turn around."

Complying with his request, I turned so that my back was facing him. Brushing my hair to the side, Tristan brought the necklace around my neck, clasping it closed, as his fingers floated down my back. Turning around to face him, my eyes found grace and passion in the darkness of his green eyes. My hands reaching and tugging at his vest, the events of earlier clouding over my face, I did my best to conceal the emotions. Tristan must have sensed a shift in my demeanor as my eyes met the ground. Touching the necklace lying against my collar bone, taking a deep breath, Tristan grabbed my hands in silent reassurance, "Tristan we need to talk," I said, my eyes catching his smile fading as the sparkle slightly dulled in his eyes.

His hands growing tense in mine, "What's wrong? If you don't like..." putting my fingers to his lips to stop him from continuing.

"No Tristan... the dress, the shoes, the necklace, it's all beautiful. I feel like the luckiest girl," I said, sighing deeply.

"Well you are," he said, always trying to reassure me. Moving closer to me, wrapping his arms around me, warmth nestled at the pit of my stomach.

Forcing myself to move out of his hold, I sat, regaining my focus on the bed, while he remained standing; his hands immediately entering the pockets of his suit pants.

Finding the envelope on my bed, laying it on my lap, I placed my hand gently on the top of it. Tristan's eyes shooting to the envelope that laid beneath my palms, shifting from one foot to the other. Fighting the bile of vomit sitting in my throat, I swallowed hard, taking a deep breath, forcing myself into a conversation I didn't want to have, "Remember at lunch when you saw me today?"

"Yea you didn't look well, but you said you were hungry, so I didn't think much of it," shrugging as nothing seemed amiss, his eyes still on my lap, occasionally flipping to meet mine, but not really leaving my lap.

"Well I wasn't completely honest with you," I could see his shoulders stiffen as my gaze remained steady on the floor. Rubbing the furrow between his brow and finally sitting next to me on the bed, grabbing my chin, he turned my head towards him so my gaze would meet his.

The sparkle in his eyes had somewhat returned; his shoulders seemed to relax, "Whatever it is, tell me. You can tell me anything," his hand now lying on top of hand that sat atop the envelope.

Looking back at our hands, "Right before you called, I received an unexpected phone call from C..." before I could choke the words out, he finished, "Casey. Why is he calling you? I thought you guys were done," confusion evident as his brow knitted further together.

"So, did I, but after our conversation today, it sounds as if he isn't ready to let me go." I proceeded to tell him about my earlier conversation with Casey. After divulging most of the details, I told him about the events of when I got home, "Kayla told me about the envelope on the table and that's when I found these." Finally lifting my hands off the envelope and handing it over to him. The envelope seemed to weigh heavy in his hands, pulling the contents out, he found the note and read it.

As his eyes scanned it, grabbing his arm for some form of confirmation, "Can he do that, Tristan? Can he ruin your career?" Tristan didn't respond. I could tell by looking at him, he had seen the photos before, except the ones from today, those seemed new to him. His eyes studied each photo closely,

"Amber, when you told me you were married, I never explained why I got so angry. While I am a Christian man and believe that God brings people in our lives for a reason, I wasn't upset with you that you were married. I guessed you had good reason to leave a man you vowed to devote your life to. I was angry more with myself because I knew I was running a risk with my career, one I wasn't sure I wanted to accept. With my line of work, I deal with risks while in the field; it isn't something new to me. After you walked away from me, my heart melted. Seeing your back turn away and not knowing if I would see you again ripped something from my soul. I decided you were worth the risk." Resting the photos down on his lap, his eyes finally reaching mine, the tears began trailing my cheeks.

Softly clearing the tears with his thumb, "Don't cry darling. I knew what I was getting myself into when I made the decision. Sleeping with a married woman is frowned upon in the military. While I love serving my country...I'm afraid losing you would hurt me more. Since we are being honest with each other, I've seen these photos and this same note before. They were left at the robbery of *ENVY*. On Sunday, while Kayla and you were at the spa, I spoke to my commanding officer and informed him of everything that was going on. I figured Casey had something to do with it but wasn't sure when or how to approach the situation. The cops also have a copy of everything." A sigh of relief escaped as my forehead lay on Tristan's shoulder, a small tinge of fear still evident at the thought that Tristan could still lose his career due to our relationship.

As if reading my mind, "Again, I made this decision Amber."

Biting my cheek, "What did he say?"

"He wasn't happy. He said with prior record of military service that I would receive some sort of reprimand if the command got word of what was going on. He stated that as long as the police were involved, that we would keep the matter private, for the time being. If the case ever went public, it would be something we would cross then," his fingers sliding a stray hair behind my ear, as the sparkle returned back to his eyes.

"So, you're not going to lose your job?" I asked, still needing some reassurance.

"Not yet, anyway," he responded.

More relief came over me as I reached over and hugged his neck.

Pulling away, "Well what do we do now? Casey is dangerous. I fear he is in town. The constant tension and feeling watched all make sense now, but why is he hiding? That's not like him."

"Sweetheart, he is the least of my worries. Casey doesn't know whom he is messing with. If he comes near you, he will regret the day he was born," he stated as a matter of fact. I knew he was right, but with him leaving, I needed more reassurance.

"But you're leaving. How will you protect..." pressing a finger to my lips to stop the worry, "Shh...Let me worry about that. Get dressed, we need to get going." Kissing my lips, he stood to leave the room, not allowing the conversation to continue any more.

"Wait..." I exclaimed, before he left the room, "I have something for you." Stopping, he turned around, a surprised look on his face.

"For me? A gift?" nodding my head to confirm. "It's nothing fancy, but when I saw it, it reminded me of you." Handing him the box, he returned to sit on the bed and stared at the black box in his hands.

"Amber, you don't have to get me gifts. That's my job to shower you with them," he said, still looking at the box in his hands.

"I know but I wanted to do this. Please open it," I begged. He finally opened the lid, finding the ring nestled inside, "I hope you like it. It reminded me of you when I saw it"

"Amber I love it, but..." I held up my hand returning the gesture to shush him.

"I know you can't wear it in the field, but I figured you could wear it with your dog tags or something," I said.

"Thank you, Amber. It's great," he said, leaning over kissing my cheek.

"I took a guess at the size, I hope it fits," I stated as he slid it on his right ring finger. It was a perfect fit.

Smiling at me, not saying a word, Tristan left the room. Standing, I rushed to finish getting myself ready. Hurrying to the bathroom, throwing loose curls in my hair, I pinned up a few strands with bobby pins and smeared on a little make-up. Returning back to my bed, I slipped into the most gorgeous gown. It slid down my arms and over my hips, clinging to each curve of my body with grace and elegance. It shimmered slightly in the dim light and flowed off the back with a small train. Looking in the mirror and twirling my body back and forth, I knew in that moment, this was one of the nicest gowns I probably would ever own. Walking over to my nightstand, I dabbed a little perfume on my neck. Taking a final look at myself, I stared with newfound confidence. Grabbing a clutch, I had lying in the closet, I threw in my keys and phone, exiting my room to meet Kayla and the men in the living area.

THE GALA

Arriving just before eight, the evening's gala was being held at the historic *Francis Marion Hotel* located at the heart of King Street. Exquisite details adorned the main lobby; from grand chandeliers, to lounge sofas spread throughout, no detail of comfort was left undone. The Grand Ballroom was no different. The room laid out with several tables, covered with a beautiful array of fresh flowers and linens, the center of the room opening to a wooden dance floor. Gowns and suits filled the room as all eyes fell upon Tristan and me upon entering.

Continued whispers of curiosity followed us as Tristan's hand held possessively at the small of my back, leading me through the room, making our way to the table to set our belongings down. Looking over my shoulder as the voices began dying down, Tristan's voice interrupted my thoughts of my own curiosity, "Do you want to dance?" reaching out his right hand, the ring sparkling in the dimly lit room. Nodding in acceptance, placing my hand in his, he led me to the dance floor.

The atmosphere in the room was romantic and quaint. Joining other couples on the dance floor, Tristan took the lead as we danced to *Wonderful Tonight* by Eric Clapton. Placing his free hand at the small of my back, he pulled me close, touching his nose to mine, "You smell exquisite! Perfume..." his nose now nestling at the base of my neck. Smiling away bashfully, my head laid gently upon his shoulder. My eyes fell upon a group of ladies, whispering and pointing at the sight of us dancing. Knowing Tristan was quite a catch, I was curious as to their fascination over us.

As he danced me in a small circle, he must have caught the group of ladies watching us. Pulling his shoulders back, my head lifting, he cupped my chin and leaned in to kiss me. His lips gentle and coaxing, wrapping my arms around his neck I invited him in further. After a few seconds of embracing, we pulled away as he nuzzled my nose. Not turning our heads, but extending our eyes over in their direction, we found their faces red and mouths on the floor, as the blond in the middle showed the most jealousy. Not able to stand it anymore, she clenched her fist and turned to return to her table.

Returning our attention back to each other, looking up at him, my hand rubbed the base of his hairline, "Who are they?"

"Ah, she's no one. She's jealous because she lost out on something she once had," his smile in a slight smirk, but I could see hurt registering in his eyes.

"Why?" searching for an answer I already knew.

"Because I'm with you," the shock on my face registered quickly.

Shaking off his response, still slightly befuddled, "Really, who is she?"

Letting out a defeated sigh at my incessant interrogation, "Cara Lester. We dated years ago. It didn't work, well at least not for me," my suspicions confirmed.

An ex was standing less than twenty feet from me. She was beautiful and charismatic in a southern way. Gorgeous blond curls, pinned in loose curls, her body slim as the cut of her dress hugged her petite form. She had a figure that every girl my age envied; one she would never have to worry about weight gain her whole life.

"May I cut in..." my thoughts interrupted as a woman tapped my bare shoulder. Glancing over my shoulder I found Rebecca looking stunning in a gold one-shoulder knee-length gown, her blonde locks pinned back in a loose twist. Her makeup was natural and her skin boasted a kiss of a tan. Pulling away from Tristan and turning his hand over to her, "Rebecca, you look beautiful. Of course, you can," Tristan's smile confirming my words of affirmation.

Before taking his hand, "Your dress is fabulous Amber. I knew it would fit you perfectly," her eyes stalking the lines of my body at the way the dress hugged my curves.

Tristan's secret exposed, turning a quirky grin his direction, "So you picked out the dress," his face a slight shade of red, trying to laugh off the fact he was caught. Excusing myself, "I need to use the ladies' room, anyway, you guys enjoy." Sashaying away towards the lobby, I knew this time was so important for the two of them with him leaving in a matter of days.

Before exiting, I needed to grab my clutch from the table. Retrieving it, I made my way out the ballroom towards the lady's room. The hotel did a fine job of preserving its original history, adorning and keeping with original architecture. Entering the lavished restroom, I made my way to the main wall lined with Victorian style mirrors and pedestal sinks. Adjusting my dress and correcting any lingering make-up smudges, I took out my lipstick to reapply. In the middle of application, Cara entered the bathroom. Maintaining my composure, heat flushed my face as nerves grew in my belly. Never one for confrontation, I needed to get out quick. Tightening the lid on my lipstick, Cara placed herself at the sink next to me; turning on the water to wash her hands, "He's just going to love you and leave you, you know." Shutting the water off and rubbing her eyebrow, removing any loose make-up, "He does that to every girl he dates. He's not one for commitment." Lifting herself back straight, turning to me, a smile plastered on her lips, "Just wanted you to know before you lost your heart, like I did."

My blood boiling at her abrasiveness, "I'll take my chances, thanks!" I scowled at her.

Reaching for a paper towel, "Suit yourself, but you guys remind me a lot of us in our early days. I hope your right," turning on her heel, leaving the bathroom, she tossed the towel before exiting.

Grabbing the sink to steady myself, her snarkiness wasn't wanted or needed at the moment. I knew she was trying to be the evil ex, causing issues between Tristan and me, but based on Tristan's actions over the past several days, I didn't feel like he was still hung up on some old flame. But when I truly thought about it, how did I know? I have my past; God knows he has his, whatever it may be. Could he really commit to someone, who couldn't even make her own marriage work? His response to our situation earlier said yes, but I needed to focus on the next couple of days. Only God knew if this would work. Everything was happening so fast, could it be too early to commit?

Taking one last look in the mirror, I straightened my shoulders, ready to conquer the world. Walking out of the bathroom and entering the main hall, I saw Tristan across the room lost in conversation with Cara; his eyes looking down at her with care in them. Questioning whether he was really over her, I couldn't stand the sight. Stepping forward, Cara lifted her hand to touch his cheek in a solemn gesture. Mr. Hyde was front and center as jealousy sprang in my gut; I decided it was time to go. Turning in the opposite direction, I walked out of the Francis Marion Hotel and headed back to my apartment.

JEALOUS MUCH

I knew once Tristan realized I had left, he would be there in a matter of minutes. I didn't care; I didn't need this emotional roller coaster right now. Mr. Hyde had taken full charge as I concluded I needed to end it, before I became too involved. I had enough going on with the threats from Casey, my divorce still pending, and Tristan leaving. I came to Charleston to get a clear head, not this. I knew what I needed to do.

Walking into my bedroom, I grabbed something and sat on the couch waiting for the dreadful knock that I knew would be coming.

Avoiding the knock and just coming in, Tristan was at my door within minutes. Entering the living room, he found me sitting on the couch. He was angry but concerned at the same time, "Amber, what the hell?" his breath trying it's best to catch up to his words, "Why did you leave?" bending over, resting his hands on his knees.

"Why do you think Tristan?" his eyes searching my angry face for the answer," Cara damn it!!! I walked out of the bathroom and found you two practically swooning over each other. I thought you two were done? You told me you guys were over years ago!"

His brow knitting together, tracing back the events of the evening, "Shit! Amber, it's not what it looks like. We were just talking."

"Talking? It didn't look like just talking Tristan. After all the hell of the last few days, the hell Casey is putting me through, and now I find you swooning with your ex, do you really think I am just going to sit around and be your pawn? It isn't happening," my words fuming; I didn't even realize what I was saying. He stood there quietly as my mouth spit embers at him, "How about this? How about I take you to a party, knowing my ex would be there. You go off to the bathroom and you find me standing with Casey? How would you have acted? Huh? Answer that one!" His hands now in fists at his side, as the words beat of his chest. He knew I was right and the thought really never crossed his mind if the situation was flipped.

"You're right," his voice eerily calm; not a true reflection of his body language, "I'm sorry. She's not important."

"That's all you can say Tristan? She isn't important?" Now I was standing and pacing back and forth in front of the couch, my hands flailing as my temper flared, "What the hell am I doing? I can't, I just can't do this Tristan." His face went soft as realization poured over him at what was coming next.

"Amber, please understand. You're it Amber. I screwed up! You're right, ok? If the roles were reversed, I would be pissed. I didn't know she was going to be there. She's a Charleston Elite! She goes to every party in Charleston and she happens to be dating one of the guys on the team. I didn't think about her being there. Please Amber, can we talk about this? Don't do what I know you are about to do! Not now, not before I need to leave," he was almost begging me not to end this, but it was what was needed. I couldn't handle the stress of this. We had just met and already our relationship was a roller coaster of emotions.

"That's just it, Tristan! You're leaving, you still talk with your ex, our relationship is all over the place, and I can't even make heads or tails of anything. A mad man who may or may not be my ex is chasing me, I'm in a new area, etc. etc. etc. There's just so much going on, that I came to Charleston to start over and clear the air and so far, all it has been is clouded with dark freaking clouds! I think it's time to break this off before we get to far into it, that it hurts too much to let go," my throat clenched at the finality of my words. Reaching behind me to the couch, I picked up Tristan's jersey and handed it to him. Once he took it, I reached behind my neck and unclasped the necklace that hung heavy.

Putting up his hand on top of mine to stop me, "No, keep it and the jersey. No matter what you say Amber we aren't done. You're it for me and I truly mean it. I hope you will see that. All I can do right now is give you the space you need to allow you to clear these clouds," the pain was so dark and heavy in his eyes, all I could do was look away, trying to seclude the tears that were threatening to escape.

"I'm sorry, Tristan it's the only way. I'm sorry. Please take them and go," shoving the items forward under the pressure of his hands.

Anger and pain flagged his face, as he reluctantly took the items back. Turning to leave, he stopped at the door, and walked back towards me. Removing the ring I had given him earlier, he lifted my hand, placing it in my palm. Folding my fingers, kissing my cheek, he turned and walked away, shutting the door that now stood between us.

Watching him walk away felt like the worst decision I had made. Forcing myself not to give in, I felt like I was betraying myself. He was the only man I had ever felt this connected to and here I was sending him away. Collapsing on the couch, I pushed my face into the pillow and allowed the tears to come as they may. My fist clenched around the ring and I pounded the couch with each angry thrust that entered my heart. My tears seemed to fall for ages, but finally drying up. I found myself blankly staring off as I clenched the pillow. Pulling my knees up on the couch, still in my gown, I fell asleep.

CARA

The door opening startled me awake as Kayla flipped on the light and found me lying on the couch, Keith standing behind her. Seeing my mascara stained face, she ran to my side, "Amber, what happened?" Her hands grabbing my face as she searched me over for any injuries.

Shifting up and sighing, not able to shed any more tears, "I'm fine. I ended things with Tristan. I just can't Kayla. I can't continue on this rollercoaster. It's too much too soon."

Standing with his hands in his pockets, breaking his silence, "Is this because of Cara?" Keith asked, somewhat shocking me.

"Partially. I saw them talking and he seemed quite smitten with her," stating sarcastically, rolling my eyes, almost disgusted at even saying what I was saying, "I could see there was still something there."

Shifting his weight to his other foot, "Did Tristan even tell you what happened between them?"

"Not really. He left the door open for assumption," I wasn't feeling confident in what Keith may be getting ready to tell me. I had a feeling I was about to realize a mistake I had made.

"I'm not one to share Tristan's business, but I think you need to hear this," taking a seat in the vintage wingback chair that bordered the sofa. Folding his hands together as his elbows rested on his knees, "Cara and Tristan met over 10 years ago in high school. They came from two different social classes, she the Charleston Elite, him from the laid back, go with the flow type. Shortly after high school, they began talking and eventually began dating. Their relationship and feelings for each other grew quickly and Tristan couldn't do much without Cara being at his side. They fell for each other quick and hard. Within a year of dating, Tristan was looking for more out of life. The firm was doing well and his mom and dad were pushing for him to make some decisions, so he decided he would do what most young men do and serve his country. Well this didn't sit well with Cara and she completely disagreed with his decision. She's very needy and couldn't stand the fact that she would have to be alone, so instead of breaking up with him, she cheated on him. It crushed him to the core. He loved her, on the verge of proposing to her and instead of spending the rest of their lives together, he walked in on her with another man in his apartment at the time."

I couldn't believe what I was hearing. Vomit rose in my throat as I realized my actions weren't that far off from Cara's, minus the cheating part. Part of me leaving Tristan was because I didn't think I can handle him leaving and here Cara had the same reaction.

It was never my intent to hurt Tristan but when I really sat and thought about my feelings, I was scared and confused by how fast things were moving between us. I gave up so fast on something that could be so good for me. I really questioned what I was doing. Keith continued, "The one thing I can tell you Amber is the way he was with her is nothing like he is with you. You are different. I've never seen him this way with anyone before. You have his heart."

Feeling lost at the information that Keith was giving me, "But why didn't he just tell me this to start with? He had the opportunity tonight at the party. If she hurt him that bad, then why even talk to her still? I don't know if he is even over her. The way he was looking at her tonight tells me he isn't."

"You have to understand that Cara was his first love. She isn't necessarily the one that got away, and yes, she did hurt him, but Tristan is a very giving and forgiving man. There are very few things he truly holds onto that hurt him. He most likely didn't tell you because he never really talks about it. She crushed him when it happened. He went into a slump and joined the Army shortly after. He got into it pretty deep and was away on missions all the time. After returning back from one of the missions, the Charleston Sharks recruited him and he started playing ball. This happened eight years ago and he's changed a lot since. You have to know, his lifestyle has brought girls in and out of his life, but none have mattered since you. Believe me Amber you are special to him. Try to talk to him," his voice was soft with concern as he revealed a side of Tristan that I didn't know.

"I don't know Keith. How can I talk to him, when he won't open up to me? He's vague. He's hiding something and he won't tell me what it is. Everyone has a past. I can get over the girls, fine; that's the lifestyle he's lived. I need to know what happened to him," coming up with every excuse to make myself feel better about my decision to end things.

Reaching over and grabbing my hand, "But why? Why is it so important to know? Besides, that is something he will need to tell you. It's not my place to tell you. Just prepare yourself if he decides to." Keith was right. Why was it so important for me to know? Maybe it was my journalistic side or maybe it was the missing piece of figuring out what tormented him. Standing, I walked into the kitchen for a glass of water. Out of the corner of my eye I caught Kayla whispering to Keith.

Yelling from the other room, "Good night Amber. I hope you get this all figured out. Just trust him. He's a good guy." I heard the door click and the lock snap as Keith exited our apartment.

Walking out with my glass of water, "Why did you send him away?"

Walking back to the couch and sitting, pulling a blanket across her shoulders, opening one side for me to join, "I figured you needed a quiet night. You've got an early morning and didn't need to listen to me all night." A slight giggle escaping. Walking to join her under the blanket, both of us still in our gowns, "It wouldn't be the first time." giggling back, though my heart was aching. It was nice to laugh for once. Leaning my head on her shoulder as she wrapped the long, fleeced blanket around my shoulder, "What do I do? Am I dumb for trying this out, seeing where it goes?"

Uncertainty in her voice, "I don't know. Did you tell him about Casey?"

Quietly answering, "Yes."

"And?" Looking for more than I was giving away.

I knew this was coming. I told her everything that had happened before the party. From the dress all the way to giving him the ring, nothing was left out. As I was closing my story down, I realized the ring was in my hand. Opening my fingers, the metal shimmered in the faded light from the kitchen.

"Amber, he really cares about you. He is risking his career for you. Men, who are just in it to get in your pants, wouldn't do that. You've told him everything and he is still here," she stated matter of fact.

I knew she was right. She always brought light to reality, "I know but that's what I don't understand. Why me? I'm not special. I'm just an ordinary girl, especially compared to Cara," I asked her, my insecurities evident.

"Casey has your head so screwed up. I should have killed him when I had the chance. Ugh!" shifting out of the blanket, facing me, grabbing my face between her hands, so I could clearly see her speak, "What's the real reason you won't let go Amber?" she asked, her question pointed. I had never thought of the question before. If I was honest, it was fear. I never had a true relationship. It was a scary venture.

"I don't know. There are a lot of things. One being the fact he won't open up to me," my excuses still plaguing reality.

"What do you mean? About what?" releasing my face, her hands now in her lap. I told her about the scars and how he won't let me touch him. How I've tried to make him feel like he makes me feel, but I feel like I can't accomplish that with him bottled up.

"If there are scars and he won't let you touch him, there are good reasons. Give him some time. You have only known him a few days. Knowing about Cara, he may be holding out to make sure this is just as real. He has been hurt in more ways than we know. He will open up in time and maybe he won't. You have to decide if you can live with never knowing. You both have been hurt and are both healing. Call him and just try to talk to him. What would it hurt?" Standing, she stretched on her tiptoes, "I'm going to bed." Kissing me on top of my head she left me with my thoughts.

Wrapping the blanket around my shoulders and sliding down on the couch, resting my head on the back cushion, I wasn't sure what I was going to do. Kayla was right, only I could decide. After staring at the faint, dark ceiling, I decided it was time to strip of this gown and retire.

Upon entering my room, walking to my bedside table, I laid Tristan's ring down. Changing out of my gown, I sat on the edge of my bed to send Tristan a text: *We need to talk, tomorrow.*

Turning my phone on vibrate, I pushed myself under the covers, falling back to sleep.

BREAKFAST

Waking the next morning, I sat up in bed, stretching my arms wide above my head. Reaching for my phone, I found there was a text from Tristan.

Yes, we do. Meet me at my condo at 8:30 for breakfast. I've already informed Mr. Klein that you will be late for work. He said it was no problem. There is a key card for you in your kitchen. You can thank Keith later.

A small smile traced my lips. I really didn't want to be late for work, but if he had already cleared it with Mr. Klein, I guess I could indulge him. The clock read *7:45*, leaving me enough time to brush my teeth, wash my face, and throw on my work clothes. Spraying back a few pieces of fallen hair from the night before, overall it looked good enough to wear to work. Grabbing Tristan's ring from the bedside table, and tossing it into my shoulder bag, I walked into the living room, and found the access card in the kitchen.

Making my way down the apartment steps and onto King Street, I didn't have that far of a walk to Tristan's and knew I had plenty of time. Pacing my walk, an uneasy feeling settled over me. The photos from yesterday flashing through my memory, questions of whether Casey was following me plagued my senses. If he was, why hadn't he showed his face or confronted me? Looking over my shoulder, I didn't recognize anyone in the crowd but Casey had to be in town, with the note that was left. What I didn't know is why was he here and doing this. Well I partially knew that answer, and that would be to win me back. But the lack of presence had me all confused. Was he really that hard up on me still? Of course, I knew he was still in need of me. The control was like a drug for him, an addiction he couldn't kick. He couldn't stand that I was the one that left, that I had taken all the control.

My pace quickened slightly and I finally made it to Tristan's condo. Entering the elevator, I inserted the access key. Resting against the back wall, I couldn't shake the uneasiness that had settled over me. Eventually reaching the top floor, entering Tristan's condo, Tristan wasn't around. Gliding over to the open windows, the sun was making her steady rise over the tops of the far buildings along the harbor. The early morning rays shimmered across the water, as the whiteness of the boats provided a blinding glare to nearby passers.

Interrupted by a voice from behind, "Ms. Slayton, please join us in the dining room," turning around I found one of Tristan's wait staff, "Mr. Ashton will be down in a few minutes."

"Thank you," I stated as he turned and left me in the room; noticing the arrangement of flowers on the coffee table had been changed out.

Making my way to the kitchen table, I found it neatly set and one of the waiters pulled out a chair for me. Another waiter brought me a dish of bacon, eggs, and toast. Filling my glass with orange juice, he asked if I needed anything else. Shaking my head, no, he turned to leave, as Tristan entered the room.

Nodding at his staff making his way to the seat across from me, "Good morning, gorgeous. I'm glad you came." He was wearing jeans and a white t-shirt, clean-shaven and was barefoot. His smell of baseball leather and soap filled the room. My nerves growing at just the sight of him, I needed to get this conversation over with.

As with any time I am nervous, I began rambling quickly without putting any thoughts into my words, "Tristan, I'm sorry. I didn't know Cara cheated on..." twisting my fingers in my lap, trying my best to calm myself down.

"Damn Keith and his big mouth!" his face slightly red from embarrassment, "I really need to quit telling him stuff."

"No, no. Keith is a very good friend," trying to reassure him, "There has been a lot he could have told me and hasn't."

"Well that is good to know. I'm sorry I didn't tell you the truth about Cara. I should have been the one to tell you and not Keith. It had really never crossed my mind to share what happened with you. That is my fault," he began explaining his actions for the prior evening's events. "When Cara touched my face, you must have left before you saw me remove her hand. It made me uncomfortable and I informed her that I was with you. Not her. She is the one that messed up and she hasn't been able to get over that fact."

Swallowing my pride, I knew I should have let him explain. I jumped to conclusions too quickly, "I'm sorry I didn't allow you to explain. We really need to work our indiscretions out Tristan. We will never work if we can't trust each other. I'm really trying my best. I'm just overwhelmed and scared," finally admitting the real reason behind my façade of running.

"I know Amber and I am really trying to allow you to work out your feelings when it comes to us. I'm not giving up on you and know this will take us some time. I know Casey messed with your head and still is, but there is something you need to know." shooting him a questioning look, "Did you ever press charges against Casey for the assault?"

I sighed, "No...but he was arrested on a DUI shortly after I left him. Why," raising my hands in a what's this about way.

"Then his prints would be in the system," almost answering his own thoughts. Anguish set over his face and I knew he was holding something back from me.

"What is it?" Prying him to get some answers. Literally sitting on the edge of my seat, my hands wrapping around the base of the chair and my knuckles white from holding so tight.

"I spoke to the police this morning about the robbery. They were able to lift some prints from the photographs, but they came back empty handed. The prints aren't in the system." My heart sank. They weren't Casey's prints, which means he isn't in town. He was having me followed, but by who? It was the only explanation for the photos that I could come up with.

Tristan saw the fear in my face, "If you'll let me, we'll get through this. You have to trust me. I promise I will never hurt you darling. You are too precious to me to lose again. I've almost lost you several times; I don't want to lose you again. I know this has been a whirlwind that neither of us thought would go so fast," stopping, forcing the words out, "But I can show you how much I care." Standing he walked over to the chair next to me and sat down. Holding his hand out in a way that requested my hand, I placed it in his. Lifting my hand for me to stand he led me to stand in front of him. Nudging for me to sit, I lifted my hips as I sat on the dark mahogany table, my feet swaying below me, my heels slipping on and off. Looking up at me, his eyes met mine and I could see nervousness throughout. I wasn't sure what he was preparing himself for, but I was a bundle of nerves with anticipation.

Breathing deeply, trying to regulate his breaths, he slowly took off his shirt, keeping my stare, never looking away. My breathing became heavy, my nerves intensified. Removing his shirt, the ripple of his abdomen exposed, he placed it on the table behind us. Grabbing my hand nervously, I noticed the tremor in his fingers as he opened my hand flat, placing the palm upon the scar on his left shoulder. It was five inches long and an inch wide, slightly puckered from where they had stitched it back together. His shoulders remained tense as he closed his eyes leading my hand to trace the length of the scar. My breath left my body and tears filled my eyes, as realization came that he was giving into one of his fears, something that made him so self-conscious.

Pulling my hand away, and covering my mouth, Tristan's eyes opened up to me. Seeing I was crying, he reached to wipe a tear that had fallen down my cheek. Stepping off the table, I straddled his lap, still holding his gaze as more tears fell. Trying to look away, I grabbed his chin, turning him back to face me. My eyes softened as we didn't say anything. I knew this was his way of opening up to me.

"Look at me, always at me." Choking out the words he had always said to me as I saw the tears in the swell of his eyes, knowing this hurt him more than anything. Reaching my hand out, looking to his eyes for permission, he nodded as I placed my hand on his chest. Tension growing under the tips, I gently moved my fingers along his chest, following the trails of scars that lined it, his hand tightening along my back but remaining silent. Each touch was torture, a reminder of what happened, but this was his way of sealing our relationship. Proving to me that he would give me anything, no matter how much it hurt.

Removing my hand and taking in a deep breath, "You don't have to do this Tristan. I can wait. I should never have pushed the issue. It wasn't my place…"

"Yes, I do. I need to. I need you to realize how important you are to me, to trust me. And it's something I need to overcome, a fear of my own. Just like I plan to make you feel like the most beautiful woman alive and help you rebuild what Casey tore away. This is a way you can do the same for me," he reassured.

"I do trust you Tristan, but we can take this slow." And with those words he pulled me close, sobbing in my neck as the emotional roller coaster he was fighting finally crumbled. Tristan exuberated masculinity and strength and here he was at his weakest.

Unsure of what to say or do, I sat there holding him. Something terrible had happened to him and I knew in time he would tell me when he was ready.

Quiet surrounded us and after several minutes, he lifted his head, reaching to wipe the tears from my face, "I'm sorry Amber."

Holding his cheeks in each hand, "It's ok. When you are ready to talk about it, I will be here to listen. I won't bring it up again."

His eyes perked up, "Will you? No more running?"

Smiling down, "No more running, and to show you how serious I am, I have something for you." Gathering my purse, I pulled out his ring. His eyes wide with relief, he grabbed the ring, placing it back on his finger. Reaching for my hand, he folded our fingers together, "I trust you Tristan, and I hope one day you will trust me enough to let me in. Thank you for this morning. It means a lot." I finalized, kissing his forehead.

Grabbing the back of my nape, "You mean more than you will ever know," pulling me into a tender kiss. Desire tickled in my stomach as his kiss turned to need. Wrapping my hands around Tristan's neck, pulling him in closer, he reached behind me, untucking my blouse, rubbing my back with gentle hands. The feel of his touch sending chills through me as goose bumps pricked at my skin. Placing my hand on his bare chest, him not flinching at the feel of it, I stopped him from going any further, "I have to get to work." Hanging his head with sadness, "Yes I know. I have several errands to run today also," some defeat evident, "I'll walk you to work."

Helping me off his lap, I straightened my appearance, "Thank you for breakfast." Pulling my purse under my arm, Tristan walked me towards the elevator. Pushing the button to call the elevator up, it arrived in a matter of seconds.

Entering the elevator together, scenes from the last time we were here flooded my memory as my skin flushed. Catching my change in color, a smile perched on his lips as if he was relishing in the same memories. Leaning in, "Your blushing..." a sly quirk curling larger at his lips. Standing straight, I remained quiet, still reveling in my memories. Reaching the bottom floor, Tristan led me out with my hand in his into the busy morning crowd.

Walking through the streets of Charleston together, we headed to my office, exchanging small talk. Enjoying the warmth of the early morning sun, "Would you tell me about your family? You haven't said much about them. I mean I've met Rebecca, but do you have any other siblings?" his composure somewhat shifting at my questions, "I noticed another girl in the picture above your fireplace. Who is she?"

Relaxing a little but somewhat tense as he recalled details of his family, "My mom, dad, and sister were killed by a drunk driver five years ago. Rebecca was with them when it happened and was the only survivor in the crash. I was on a mission when it happened. Police really aren't sure why the accident occurred, but the other guy was charged since he had been drinking," grief suddenly deep in his words.

Shocked, "Oh my Tristan, I'm sssoo..."

Interrupting me, "It's ok. It was a long time ago. Rebecca and I have grown closer since. She's my rock and we rely on each other when needed most. I'm lucky I still have her and now you.

Remember when you asked me the other night about washing other girl's hair?"

The question slightly off topic, "Yea."

"Rebecca is the only other girl. She became very depressed after the accident and let go of everything. I had to bring her back. She has made huge strides, and Dr. Fox has been a big help. She started *CADD: Charleston Against Drunk Drivers* after she got back on her feet. They do a lot of big fundraisers in the local area and provide educational opportunities to local schools and events. It's grown quite large through the years, but it's a great outlet for her to recover and deal with the grief." Listening to him talk about her made me realize how close of a bond they truly shared. They were all they had left and for years they relied on each other to get through the hard times. Shifting his free hand into his pocket, "As far as the driver of the vehicle, he received life in prison. It was really the closure we both needed with what happened to our family."

I wasn't sure what to say, so I just remained quiet as he continued on, "You would have loved my other sister. She was so witty and caring. My mom did a lot with charity work, and once Rebecca got back on her feet, she took over that part of the business. We took a small dive after the accident, but once we refocused our attention, things have been better."

It was hard hearing him talk about his family. He hadn't really asked about mine, but I was ok not divulging too much. In time I'm sure he would ask, and I would share about my deadbeat stepfather and mother who didn't give a damn.

"Well I would ask about yours, but it looks like that will have to wait," realizing we were at my office building. Leaning over, Tristan kissed me goodbye. Turning to walk away, he stated, "Pack an overnight bag and meet me at my place at 6:00 PM sharp."

Curious, "Oh? What do you have in mind?"

Turning and walking away backwards, smiling mischievously, "I've got a few things planned." And with a wink he was off.

THE OFFICE

Giddiness in my step from the morning, the receptionist greeted me as I entered my office, "Ms. Slayton, Mr. Klein wants to see you right away," my mood suddenly changed, as I knew this couldn't be good. He was mad I was late; I just knew it.

Knocking on his door. "Come in." Entering, he gestured for me to take a chair. He was boasting a white pressed shirt, with a lavender tie to accent, "Ms. Slayton, you have only been on the job a couple days and have already broken one of the rules. I simply asked for no personal e-mails. What concerns me more is the nature of this e-mail," caught off guard by the conversation. Recognizing my confusion, "You look confused. Do you recognize this e-mail?" handing me the white sheet of paper.

Reading over the print, dread raked my body and I felt all the color leave me:

> *Looks like you have been disobeying what you were told. You've received your last warning. ~C*

"By the looks of the e-mail, and your face, I'm guessing you don't know anything," his hands clasped together on the desk, as his back was straight against his chair...standard military stance of a retired officer.

"No sir, I mean, I…" trying my best to remain calm, but my nerves and frustrations began getting the better of me.

"Is there something I need to know Amber?" I began informing Mr. Klein of the last few days, only in reference to Casey and the pictures. Concern shown through his eyes with each detail I divulged, "Well Ms. Slayton looks like you need to inform the police. Watch yourself and if there is anything I can do to assist, please do not hesitate to ask. I know a lot of people, as does Tristan, we can help you sort through this," his statement firm and authoritative.

The gesture was well received, "Thank you Mr. Klein." I stood and made my way out of the office and proceeded to call the detective on the case. While I had him on the phone, he updated me on the latest findings and that they were still investigating all leads. Informing me that since e-mail was used, they would be able to trace the IP address to locate a potential location of the suspect. As I hung up with the officer, my phone buzzed letting me know I had a text. Picking it up, I saw it was from Casey.

Hey babe, left your boy toy yet? Ready to come home? We need to talk.

The message was unnerving. He always had a way of getting under my skin. I hadn't had a chance to change my number, but it was on my to do list at lunch. It was time to move on, for good. The thought crossed my mind that maybe Tristan received the same email but I decided to wait until later to ask. I hated that he was involved, but I wouldn't let that interfere with the last few days I had with him.

MARCO

L unchtime finally arrived and I signed off my computer, making my way down to Broad Street. I walked to the cell phone store around the corner as the sights and smells of the city surrounded me. Across the way was Joe's Hot Dog Stand with a crowd of lunchtime customers, a little bistro nestled itself between two tall buildings, and a deli offering the freshest cuts around sat next door. Turning the corner, I ran right into the arms of Marco, "Excuse me, I'm so sorry...Marco?"

"Amber..." his face softening after realizing who I was, "How's that headache?" The daylight allowed me a better observation than the other night. He was slightly taller than Tristan, his olive skin radiating against his baby blue gingham button down. He had the hint of stubble but his baby face probably didn't allow for any more.

Slightly smiling, "Better, thanks. Sorry about that night, I've got a lot going on."

Waving off my excuse, "No problem. Sorry I was such an ass. I thought we hit it off well, but I guess not so much. It's not a big deal. Off to lunch?"

"Yes, but I have some errands I need to run," pointing my thumb in the direction behind me in an effort to sway off an invite.

"Ahh I was just headed to a little bistro around the corner and was going to see if you wanted to join, but maybe next time?"

"Rain check?"

"Sure. Take it easy." waving me off as we went opposite directions.

"Huh, weird," I said aloud, trying to shake the uneasiness that had settled upon me realizing Charleston wasn't as big as I thought.

Making my way to the cell phone store, I was able to change my number. The friendly clerk took care of transferring my numbers, my pictures, and backing everything up for me, even providing me information on how to block numbers through my account if I needed to. Handing my phone back and finishing up, I headed back to the office.

Leaving the store and returning the same route I had taken here, I noticed Tristan talking with Cara at the bistro cafe across the street. Trying my best to remind myself to trust Tristan, I swallowed down my anger. Deciding to put my big girl panties on, and get over my fear of confrontation, I crossed the street, "Fancy meeting you guys here," leaning over, I kissed Tristan on the cheek. A look of surprise on his face, he was caught. "Well look at you Amber. You look nice. Tristan and I just ran into each other and I invited him to coffee." A smug smile playing on her lips, trying her best to make me jealous, but I was doing my best to remember what Tristan and I talked about earlier. I knew their relationship was over and I didn't know why he decided to have coffee with her, but I needed to show him that I did trust him.

"Really, just like that, huh?" slight resentment could be heard in my voice. Tristan growing tense, stood to avoid the confrontation growing, "Cara, I must go. Thanks for the coffee. Amber, may I speak with you," his hand gesturing me towards the sidewalk outside the bistro.

"No, we'll talk later, I must go. Sit, enjoy Cara, you are leaving. I would hate for any loose ends to be left undone." kissing him a little too long, I walked away, leaving him standing and watching me with my back turned. I could feel his eyes on me, and I knew the look was of shock. Overhearing, Cara continue on their conversation, and I invisibly patted myself on the back for keeping my cool.

Returning to the office, I finished up the article on the Day Spa and submitted it to Mr. Klein for review. He had already sent over my next piece, another quarter page article on the upcoming Fall Season. Wanting a more family-oriented article on the hottest thing this Fall, that was going to be a challenge, but I would make do. Giving me a two-week deadline, at the bottom of his e-mail he left a note.

Ms. Slayton,

I know your days are few with Tristan. Take the next few days off and enjoy them. Being a military man, this time is precious. See you next Monday.

Not believing what I was reading, I reread the note two more times. Replying with a thank you, I signed off for the rest of the day, needing to make the next few days memorable. It may very well be my last.

CASEY

Running home, I went to my room to pack a few belongings. Coming into the kitchen, I found Kayla standing at the sink, saddened. "Kayla, what's wrong?"

"Casey keeps calling me, Amber. He keeps telling me there is something we need to discuss. I have nothing to say to him." Somewhat taken back, I wondered why Casey would call her and not me. Well I did change my number, but that was only about an hour or so ago. It didn't make any sense, although the message sent earlier said something similar. I told Kayla about the text message, told her I didn't want him having my new number, so for her to call him and see what was up, not to let her guard down. She was angry with me.

Trying my best to reason with her, "Maybe it's about my case. The cops didn't match the print to Casey. He knows about Tristan, so maybe who ever this person is, is communicating to him also."

"Fine," reluctantly giving in. As much as I didn't want to call him, or have her, we knew we needed to. Dialing the number, he answered, "Kayla?"

With a bite in her tone, "Casey, what do you want asshole?"

Laughing her off in his usually cocky manner, "Well nice to talk to you too. You must have me on speaker, which means

Amber is there?"

Confirming his suspicions, "Yes, what do you want Casey?"

His tone quickly changed to one of concern, "Look Amber, someone is after you and I think I might know who?" Kayla and I both looked at each other, then back at the black iPhone screen, "How would you know, Casey?"

Speaking quickly as if someone was after him, "Look I informed the police when they called me for an interview. I can't say who it is, but they have a lead. Be careful Amber, as much as I know you don't want me back, I'm sorry..." Suddenly there was a shuffle coming over the phone, "Casey, are you there?" but there was only silence now coming from the phone. Kayla and I looked at each other, when a dark voice came on, "Don't worry Amber. You'll never have to see Casey again," the line disconnecting. Kayla dropped the phone, as screams tore from my throat, "CASEY!! CASEY!!!" My hands were on my face, my fingers digging into my cheeks.

"What the hell just happened?" Kayla remarked as she picked up the phone off the tiled floor, trying to dial Casey back, but no one answered.

Not realizing I was hyperventilating, "Kayla what is going on? What happened to Casey?"

Trying to keep her composure, "Amber, first calm down. We'll figure this out. Next, you need to call the cops. They need to know about this right away. This is serious now. Someone is out to get you and it isn't Casey." Trying my best to calm down, I knew she was right, but I needed to get to Tristan, he would know what to do. "Ok. Walk me to Tristan's house. I'll call the cops on the way. I'll be safer there anyway" Walking to my room, I packed up my bags. Kayla walked out of my closet, "Kayla, pack your stuff too. You need to stay with Keith or with Tristan and me. You're not safe here, not until we know what is going on." You could see that Kayla was as panicked, as was I. I don't know what happened to Casey but something told me I needed to fear for my life now.

DETECTIVE CAUDELL

Racing to Tristan's condo, we found it empty other than his wait staff. I had already called Detective Caudell who was on his way to Tristan's condo. Trying to call Tristan, he wouldn't pick up his phone. It too was going straight to voicemail, which left me unsettled. Looking at the clock it read a little after three, so it was still early.

Detective Caudell arrived a few minutes after we made it to the condo. Kayla met him downstairs, allowing him access to the top floor. Trying Tristan again, still going to voicemail, I left him a message to call me. I also followed it up with a text message. I did forget that I never gave him my new number, and in my message, let him know about it. I knew as soon as he heard the worry in my voice that he would call quickly.

Entering the condo, Detective Caudell sat us down and began taking notes as Kayla and I recounted the events of this afternoon. Reaching for his phone, he dialed a number.

Speaking into the receiver, "Hey James. I need you to go to 4205 Westwood Avenue and check on a Casey Slayton...Yea, ok sounds good," hanging up his phone, "He will call me with any details. Look ladies, it's good you are here, safe. Amber you are in real danger. The IP address was tracked to a local bistro right near your work. We watched the surveillance cameras and noticed you there today, did you see anything out of the ordinary?"

"No, nothing." thinking for a second, "Wait a second...Marco."

Pulling back in disbelief, Kayla giving me a baffled look, "Marco, like Marco from *ENVY* the other night?"

Turning to her "Yea, I ran into him today. He said he was headed to the same bistro as I left for lunch. Not sure if it helps."

The detective chimed in, "Anything will help at this point. Do you know his last name?"

I answered quickly, "Lucarelli, he's the new VP of Marketing for some local finance company. It was really strange walking into him today."

"We'll look into it. In the meantime, you need to stay together and off the street. Have you talked with Tristan today?" his question reminding me of the last time I saw him.

"Only at lunch. I've tried to call him, but can't reach him." So unsure of why he wasn't picking up. Fear gripped at the sudden possibility, my hand reaching my mouth, "Kayla, what if they got Tristan?" Finally saying my thoughts out loud.

Touching my shoulder, "Let's not jump to conclusions yet," doing her best to settle any of my fears, although I knew she was just as much a jumbled mess.

The detectives phone rang. Kayla's hand flew to mine for comfort. Grasping it tightly, we waited to hear what the person on the other end found, "Hey James, whatcha got?" Glancing over to me, his face not giving away any clues, "I see. Thank you, sir. I will be in touch soon." Hanging up, "I'm so sorry ladies," taking a deep breath, "but Casey is dead."

ALONE

Feeling my whole-body jerk with the jolt of being shoved, "Amber...Amber, are you ok?" concern and worry in Kayla's voice.

Rubbing my forehead, "What happened?" My eyes adjusting slowly, I found Kayla and the detective hovering over me. Feeling the plushness of the rug beneath my back, Kayla handed me a glass of water as I slowly shifted myself to a seated position. All I could recall were the haunting words the detective had relayed that Casey was dead. The shock of the news took over, as I began trying to piece together what happened.

"Oh Amber, don't cry. It will be ok," rubbing my shoulder in reassurance. I could see her tear stained face, doing her best to put on a brave front for me, "Tristan will be here soon and he will know what to do. I'm so sorry, Amber," her sobs growing heavier. The news, much less hearing the murder over the phone was horrifying. Someone was out to get me and I wasn't sure how to grasp this.

"What did they do to Casey?" I asked, directing my attention to the detective.

"It looks as though Casey was on the phone and the suspect approached him from behind, stabbing him in the back. He would have never seen it coming," Detective Caudell stating directly to the point, "So far there is no murder weapon or anything to lead us to a suspect. All we can do is wait for forensics to finish up and hopefully tell us the weapon used." My mind became foggy.

Gathering my thoughts, the best I could, reaching for Kayla's hand, "You need to call Keith. Maybe he knows where Tristan is. Maybe he can come until Tristan can get here." My heart breaking at the sudden realization that Casey was gone. I had left Indiana to escape him, to leave the pain of what he did, behind me and here I was in pain again that he would be absent forever.

No matter how much I hated him for what he did to me, he was still a part of me that would never go away. I gave him my life when we got married and that part will always be there. He was still my husband...a man I loved unconditionally until I could stand the hurt no longer. I never stopped loving him, but I knew life would not work for us with me staying.

Every word escaped me, staring blankly at the floor; my body began swaying on its own, "I need to be alone." Directing my words to Kayla, "There is a spare room upstairs. You can put your stuff there, until you can reach Keith. I'm going to take a bath." I was shutting down; the shock of the news, the uncertainty of Tristan's whereabouts, being hunted, it was like I was the plot to some suspense movie. I was walking on a tight rope that had gone slack and there was no way to tighten it.

Standing and placing his notebook in his pocket, Detective Caudell's voice registering remorse, "Ms. Slayton, I'll leave you ladies to it. If you hear of anything, please call us. We'll keep you posted of any details."

"I'll walk you out, sir," said Kayla, escorting him to the elevators, I stood making my way upstairs.

Finding Tristan's room, I dropped my overnight bag at the foot of the bed. My eyes had grown heavy from exhaustion and sadness. Walking into the bathroom, the floor to ceiling porcelain tile, and see through shower were designed with delicate detail. On the opposite end, a four-claw iron tub sat, waiting to be filled with the hottest bath water. Reaching over to the antiqued bronze knobs, I turned on the water as hot as I could stand and stripped down. Climbing in, my head finding the pillowed cushion, my body sinking further into the scalding water. My body was numb, feeling no pain from the outside world. The room was peaceful and quiet.

The quietness led my thoughts to recall the day's events; tears stung my eyes. I didn't understand what was going on; I had no answers. Having Tristan would help, but he wasn't returning any calls either. That didn't make my thoughts any less morbid. Tristan could be lying dead somewhere in a ditch. Who knew how far this psychopath would go? Was he only after me? After Kayla? What about everyone I ever loved? How far could he go?

My imagination ran wild with all the possibilities of what if scenarios. Plunging myself under the now tepid water, I held my breath as the weight of the water swallowed me. My hair floating around me, my eyes found the ceiling tiles of the bathroom.

Lifting myself out from under the water, I tried my best to relax back on the pillow. My arm dangling over the side, the cool air of the room rushed over my bare skin. This bath was to help me escape, when all the quiet did was fill me with doubt.

It was no use. Eventually the water cooled off and I finished. Finding a robe behind Tristan's bathroom door, I put it on, holding the plush cotton to my nose, smelling the vague scent of what was left of him. Walking into the bedroom, something on the pillow catching my eye, I walked over to find it was my laptop with a note.

My Darling,

I know I should have called, but I know you would ask too many questions. My commander called and I was called up early. I don't know when I will be back, but know that our unfinished business will be finished when I return. I installed Google Hangouts on your computer and will call when I can. Our memories of the last few days will help me during this time away. Your scent of strawberries and cream will remain with me as I go to battle. Please understand that I care deeply and don't want to hurt you.

I will call you soon.

TRISTAN

My heart sank leading my body to the floor, my head finding the carpet beneath. Kayla must have seen me lying there because next thing I know her eyes were meeting mine, as we were both now on the carpet. "What is it?" She asked, pushing my hair from my face. My stare blank and distant, my arms moved with robotic motion as they handed her the note. Curling my knees to my chest, Kayla read the note, "I'm so sorry Amber. We'll get through this together. We always do. Come on, let's get you into bed." Pulling me towards her and helping me up, I climbed on the bed grabbing one of Tristan's pillows. His smell lingered all around. Kayla curled up beside me, wrapping her arms tight around me.

Swallowing the knot in my throat, "Did you reach Keith?"

"Ya," her voice quiet, "He'll be here soon. He's at *ENVY* putting things in order. He said he would arrive as soon as he could."

"Ok," the knot giving way as the words choked out. My body consumed with exhaustion, sleep took over.

◆ ◆ ◆

Nightmares flashed frequently through the night as I tossed and turned, restless from the day's events. Finally giving up around three in the morning, turning, I found Tristan's side empty. Not sure where Kayla had disappeared to, I crawled out of bed and wandered down the hall. Hearing whispers coming from the guest bedroom, *"Shh, we'll wake up Amber,"* I heard Kayla tell Keith. A slight smile came across my lips, *Keith had made it.* The fact that he was safe was a little reassuring during this troubling time.

Walking back into Tristan's room, the moon illuminated a small path from the window. Following it, I stood there over-looking the lights sparkling across the harbor. A freight ship was making its way down the channel, while smaller sail ships anchor lights danced across the water. The peaceful night was calming, but anguish still consumed me; my husband murdered and my lover gone, my life torn to shreds in a matter of hours. I didn't know when I would hear from Tristan, committing my-self at that moment to refocus. I needed to bury myself in work, but remembered that the detectives didn't want us leaving the house. I wasn't sure how I was going to handle the coming days.

Hearing the creak of the door, Kayla walked in behind me, "Are you ok?" Slightly turning my head over my shoulder her direction, softly, "Yea, I'll be ok. It will take some time."

Walking closer, "I'm so sorry you are going through this. What are you going to do?" she asked.

Turning back to the window, "I guess I'm going to start plan-ning a funeral. Regardless of the fact I left him, he was still my husband. I know the detectives don't want me leaving town, but I have to do this."

Her arms wrapping around me in comfort, her head on my shoulder, "I'll help you find flights in the morning. Why don't you try to get some sleep?"

Leaning against her, "I tried, but couldn't. My mind has too many other things going on."

Not moving, "I know. Keith's over, I'll be in the next room if you need me," hugging me tight before letting go. Turning to walk away, "Hey Kayla..."

Stopping and facing me, "Yea?"

"Thanks," smiling she closed the door behind her.

Turning my attention back to the harbor, taking a deep breath, "God, I know I haven't prayed much, but if you hear me, protect me in these coming days. Guide me. Keep Tristan safe. I can't lose him too." Turning back to the bed, I crawled back under the sheets, laying my head down, closing my eyes; I finally drifted to sleep wondering what the coming days would bring.

THE NEXT DAY

Waking around ten, I forced myself out of bed. Making my way downstairs to find Kayla, Keith, and Rebecca in the dining room. They were discussing the local weather, all conversation abruptly halting when I made my presence known.

"Good morning Amber, did you sleep at all?" Rebecca asked, although my heavy eyes probably answered her question.

Yawning, rubbing away what Mr. Sandman had left, "Not really, but I'll be alright."

Pouting out her lip, she patted the seat next to her, offering me to sit. Taking her offer, I sat down, allowing the waiter to serve me my morning coffee. It's all I could bear, as seeing food right now, would make me feel worse than I already felt. My grief had turned to nausea as the night wore on, the events of the prior day making me sick to my stomach.

"Care for any breakfast," Kayla remarking. Shaking my head, the waiter was sent away. "You really should eat Amber; you need your strength." Not looking up at her, I knew she was right but I sat silently.

Kayla pushed on, "Amber, we spoke to the detectives this morning about your plans to go to Indiana. They don't advise it."

"Well they don't have a choice. I'm going, end of discussion," I spat harshly.

"We figured you would say that, so we already booked your tickets," Keith remarked. Glancing up, my eyes wide, "Really?"

"Yes," Kayla stated, "Keith and I are both going with you. Keith, not so much for me but for you. You don't need to go through this alone."

Looking at them both, "You guys really shouldn't," the tears swelling to the brim of my lids.

"We know, but we care about you. We will be there through it all. I don't plan to leave your side, so you might as well get used to me." Keith winked, "Tristan may be gone, but that doesn't ease up the responsibilities we have for each other when it comes to our ladies. Your safety and making sure you are ok is our number one priority. Tristan would want me to make sure you are well taken care of and this is part of that deal, ex-husband or not. He would do the same for me if the roles were reversed."

Holding all emotion back the best I could, "When do we leave?"

Looking at each other, then back at me, "This afternoon, around 4 PM. We will leave on Delta Flight 442 headed into South Bend Regional. After our layover in Chicago, we should be there about 11 tonight."

"How long are we staying?" asking more questions.

"As long as you need. I don't start school for another week, but if you need to stay longer, Keith said he doesn't mind staying," Kayla stated, Keith nodding in agreement.

"Shayla can manage *ENVY* while I am away, if we need to stay longer," Keith remarked.

"You guys don't know how much this means," my index finger catching the tears as they began dripping down my cheeks. Kayla moved to take a seat next to me, grabbing my hand, "We are just glad we can help. Keith and Rebecca plan to go to the apartment to grab your things. Rebecca already planned to pick you up a dress for the services, since I knew you didn't have anything appropriate. We'll get through this, we always have and we always will." Then the dreaded question hit me, my parents.

Nervously asking, "Where are we going to stay?" Kayla and Keith looked to each other.

Cautiously, Kayla answered, "I know your mom will want to see you Amber, but my parents said you could stay with them if needed."

Nodding my head, releasing a heavy sigh, "Ok, well I guess there's not much left to do." Standing from the table, carrying my cup, I made my way back up the stairs to Tristan's bedroom. I know it was rude to just walk away from them, but I assumed they would understand my need to be alone.

Setting my cup on the nightstand, walking over to the shades, pulling them shut, darkness blanketed the room. Crawling under the sheets, reaching over, I grabbed my laptop, deciding I needed to check my e-mail.

There was nothing new. I drew a quick email to send my new number to Tristan, not sure how much time he had online. I also sent one to Mr. Klein to inform him of what had happened, although I am sure Keith informed him, and that I would be out of the office for an undetermined amount of time. His reply came quickly and he informed me to take as much time as needed and that he would extend the deadlines on my assignments. He also stated that due to the circumstances, working from home was an option.

Searching the desktop, I saw Google Hangouts in my docking

area, and decided to login and try it out. Tristan had left the username and password. Searching around, I found my contacts, but Tristan wasn't available. Letting out a huff, I shut the lid, reaching over, grabbing my cup, I took one last sip of my now cold coffee. Scrunching my nose at the coldness, I set the cup back down, and shimmied myself under the covers. Wrapping my fingers together, laying them on my stomach, staring at the ceiling, I tried to relax. After tossing and turning for the next few minutes, I finally got comfortable and fell back to sleep.

INDIANA AFFAIRS

The following days quickly passed. Keith, Kayla, and I made our way to Indiana, greeted at the airport by her parents. I decided to stay with them, not wanting to face my stepfather. I didn't feel like reliving the reasons why I left and *I should be devoted to my husband* drama. Figuring I would have seen them at the funeral, they never showed up.

The funeral was a pleasant affair. Most of Casey's family was there and many of our old friends attended, offering their condolences. The subject of our separation was never brought up, which I was thankful for. The week also consisted of meeting with our family attorney to go over our will and sort out all the loose ends. The house we shared was put on the market, titles were transitioned into my name, etc. It was a tedious affair, but Keith and Kayla were both there to help me in the process. Toward the end of the week, the lawyer called to schedule one final meeting before I headed back to Charleston. He informed me that he had received notice of a life insurance policy that Casey had taken out when we first started dating. I was the sole beneficiary of the policy. It was enough money that if I didn't want to ever work again, I could probably get away with it by investing it. He gave me the contact information to an investor to help me start a portfolio, so I could make sure the money was handled properly.

Finally making our way back to Charleston and then the condo, Kayla told Keith to stay away for a few days, allowing me some time to relax, clear my head, and get my thoughts straight. The last two weeks had been nauseating, and every time I thought of what happened, it made me feel even sicker. Deciding to retire to my room, I resumed the same place I had the day we left for Indiana.

Days seemed to slip on. If I got out of bed, I carried my laptop everywhere with me in the hopes of hearing something from Tristan, but nothing. Kayla looked on merciless as I didn't sleep or eat. "Do you want me to get you something? You need to eat. You look frail." I knew she was right, but for the 100th time I told her no, I still felt so ill from everything, feeling the only thing that would make me better would be Tristan.

Deciding the bed was becoming uncomfortable and I could use some light, I made my way downstairs with my laptop. Grabbing the fleece blanket, Tristan kept under the coffee table, curling up on the couch, laying my head down, I laid the laptop on the coffee table. There was a buzz at the intercom. Walking over, Kayla pressed the button to ask who it was.

"It's Keith, can you come get me. Amber has my card." Within minutes they entered the living area. Standing to greet them, Keith kissed my cheek, "As much as I am happy to see you, you look awful Amber."

Trying to smile, "I know."

Doing his best to make me feel better, "It's ok, I won't tell. Well, I came with good news," my ears perking up.

"And?" impatient. It would be the first good news in weeks.

"Tristan is ok. My dad spoke to one of the guys in his unit and they were able to track down Tristan, well somewhat. All I know is that he made it to where he needs to be." Clasping my hand against my chest, relief poured over me. Exhaustion from the constant worry hit me and my knees buckled, "Whoa there, pretty girl, steady on your feet. Have you eaten?"

Shamefully admitting, "No."

"Good hell, Tristan would be pissed. Waiter…" hollering, the waiter entered the room. "Fix this lady a sandwich and make sure you continue three meals a day. If she doesn't eat, you call me," Keith directed.

"Yes sir," the waiter disappeared into the kitchen.

Kayla changing the subject back to Keith's news, "Well that is wonderful news. Any word on his return?"

"No not yet. If I hear, I will let you know." The waiter returned to the living area with a sandwich. Sitting, I looked over at Kayla, "Why don't you go show Keith what you did to the spare room." Sending her a glare that only she would recognize. "Are you sure you will be ok?" her way of trying to be motherly.

"I'll be fine. I'll see you in a few." Turning quickly, taking Keith's hand in hers she led him up the stairs, disappearing. Sitting down, I grabbed the sandwich, trying my best to swallow past the nausea. I wasn't successful as thoughts kept racing back to the past few weeks keeping me sick. Setting the sandwich down, I decided I would try to rest a little. Propping myself up, laying my head back, just as my eyes began to shut, a ping came from my computer.

Opening the lid, Google Hangouts popped up and I saw Tristan's piercing green eyes, the rest of him unrecognizable. A grizzly beard covered his chin and his hair wasn't as short as it was when he left. He was dirty, a sight I wasn't used to seeing.

"Darling…I've missed you," the pain evident in his voice.

"Tristan, are you ok?" I exclaimed, trying my best to hold back any emotion, "God these two weeks have been unbearable.

What happened?" Before he answered my questions, someone caught his attention. Looking over his shoulder and then back at me, panic registered in his eyes.

"Look darling, I only have a second to talk. Tell Keith that the rat is back in the hole. He will know what I am referencing. I have to go. I'll call when it's safe. Good bye gorgeous!" And just like that he was gone! I began crying, tears streaming down my face. Curling my knees to my chest, the waiter was back within a few minutes, "Finished ma'am?" Looking up, "No, just leave it."

"Yes ma'am. Do you need anything," asking before he returned to the kitchen.

"No, thank you." And he left the room. Seeing Tristan had settled some of the nerves. Forcing myself to eat, I knew Keith wouldn't be happy if I didn't. The sandwich touched my tongue and my stomach began gurgling almost thanking me for the food. Devouring the sandwich and chips, I gulped the water to wash it down. My stomach felt better and the nausea subsided some. The waiter returned within a few minutes, clearing my plate. Lying back on the couch, I was so unsure of our brief conversation. Tristan was in full mission mode and was leaving me with no answers, just like our whole relationship.

I had fallen asleep when I heard footsteps and giggles coming from up the stairs. Kayla and Keith were coming down, after their mini excursion to the spare room, when Kayla noticed my tear stained face, "What is it?"

Still lying in the same spot, "Tristan...he video messaged me."

Her concern still knitted across her brow, "What did he say, it's obviously not good."

Sitting up, "I didn't get a chance to talk. It lasted all of 10 seconds," looking up at Keith, "He said the rat is back in the hole. What does that mean?"

His already pale complexion grew paler, "Shit! This isn't good. Amber, he's in serious danger over there. Don't expect to hear from him for a while. Rat is our code word for someone he has been tracking for a while. If it is whom I think it is, pray he comes home safely," that was what I was afraid of. Not only was I trying to be killed, my boyfriend was also.

"Oh God," gasped Kayla as she brought her hands to cover her mouth, "That's not good. Amber, I'm so sorry," sitting next to me, rubbing her hand along my back, "Did you eat?"

Trying to sound a little perkier, "Yes, thank you Keith. I will try to eat better."

Keith's smile returning briefly, but disappearing again, "I'm glad to hear it. Look Amber, Tristan knows what he is doing and I know he would never do anything to put himself in serious jeopardy, but you can't sit here, waiting for him to call. He will call when he can. Everything will be ok. Hopefully his mission will be over soon. I hate to cut this short, but I need to head out. Call me if you need anything at all."

"Thanks Keith," we both stated, and Kayla led Keith down the elevator. Making myself more comfortable on the couch, laying my head back, I tried to make sense of everything going on. Keith was right, I needed to get back into a routine, try to focus my attention on work. My stomach growling, first I need more to eat.

Getting up, walking into the cooking area, I found the waiter who had served me earlier. Never being in the cooking area, I was surrounded by stainless steel appliances, and shiny ceramic tile. The prep area was immaculate; you could almost eat off it. "Yes ma'am," the waiter approaching me, "May I get you something?"

"Please Amber, we haven't been introduced," extending my hand out.

Taking it, "Yes, Amber. My name is Eric. Are you interested in anything to eat? You haven't had much since your return."

Dropping his hand, and folding my arms together, "Yes I know. May I have another sandwich? The last one hit the spot just right, but my stomach is telling me more."

Smiling, "Sure thing Amber. I'll bring it to you in a few minutes."

"Thank you." Turning back towards the living area, stopping for a moment, I called back, "actually bring it to the entertainment room."

"Sure thing," he hollered back.

Approaching the stairs, Kayla reentered, and I informed her I was headed to watch some TV in the entertainment room, I asked her if she wanted to join. She obliged, and followed me up.

Sitting on the sofa, within minutes Eric had brought my sandwich, as Kayla and I sat quietly enjoying the latest movie on *Lifetime Movie Network*.

MOM

Another two weeks had passed since Tristan's last call. Forcing myself, I found a routine with work, Mr. Klein requiring his assistant bring me assignments that I could do at home. He had our IT guy come by and help set up private e-mail, so the articles could be sent back and forth with ease. The assignments were few, but it was busy work and it was nice having a boss so understanding of my situation and doing everything he could to make sure I stayed safe. Per the detective's orders, I hadn't left the house in those two weeks and hadn't heard much from them, hoping no news was good news, though I doubted it.

Sitting on the bed, pulling up my personal e-mail, I hadn't checked it since the night everything had happened with Casey. I was curious if there was anything from my mom. The thought never really crossed my mind since I didn't want to speak to her, but I didn't know if she knew about Casey, especially since they never showed at the funeral. My stepfather loved Casey like the son he never had. They were close, almost scary at times how much they were alike. Opening my e-mail, the first and only message listed was from my mom:

Amber,

You have changed your number and I don't know any other way of reaching you. I am worried sick. CASEY IS DEAD! You need to call me and let me know you are ok.

Mom

The email was dated after the funeral. I don't know how she didn't know sooner, since it was on the news and in the local papers. Maybe my stepfather kept the information from her, but who really knows, especially if he hadn't been around, like he tends to do. He kept her so sheltered from things. Quickly replying back to her.

Mom,

I am aware of what happened to Casey. Although I left him, I am still his wife and beneficiary. I have things already taken care of. I am sorry to do this, but until you can support my wishes and my life, I will remain out of yours. You aren't going to hear from me, until I know you can fully support your daughter and not everyone else's thoughts on how I should run my life. Tell that sorry bastard you are married to goodbye and maybe we will talk.

Amber

Opening a word document, I began my next assignment; one I could do using the Internet. Within a few minutes, the ping of incoming e-mail sounded. Opening it up, I saw a reply from my mother.

Amber,

I understand your frustration and anger towards your stepfather. Your stepfather is a good man, despite his hardships. I have not seen him in weeks and do not know where he is. I'm glad to hear that you are ok. I will remain out of your life, as you wish.

Mom

This was so like her, to continue to stick up for him. My suspicions confirmed by her statement of my stepfather; it wasn't uncommon for him to leave and not come home. He had a serious drinking problem and would find the local whore and shack up with her for a while, or at least that is what all my friends would tell me. I never understood what my mother saw in the man, or why she stayed, but being controlled myself tells me he had a tight leash. Deciding it wasn't worth responding, I closed my e-mail and finished up my assignment for Mr. Klein.

Fumbling through the papers, I found the recent copy of *Low-country Magazine*. Sitting back on my bed, I flipped through the first couple pages. There it was, my review on the spa. They used the whole article, which turned into being a half page spread. "WOW! This is fantastic!" I said aloud, making my whole day, actually my whole month.

"What is?" hearing my voice, Kayla ask, walking into my bedroom. Showing her the article, she was impressed. Sitting beside me, the waiter came in and asked us if we needed anything.

Turning my hand up, Kayla asked for a cup of tea. Looking back to me she asked me how I was doing.

Nonchalantly, "Ok. I told my mom to leave my life."

"Do what! Good for you. Is she still with that bastard of a man?" Exclaiming at my forwardness.

Acting like I was surprised, "Yea, she said he's been gone for weeks. He's probably with Erica in the local motel, pissing his money away."

Rolling her eyes, "Probably. Hey, let's go do something and get out of this pad. I'll have Keith come with us to keep us company." Before I could answer, the condo buzzer rang. "I'll be right back." Kayla jumping up off the bed, running downstairs to see whom it was. Hollering, "Amber, it's the detective, I'll be right back."

Shuffling myself out of bed, in Tristan's robe, walking downstairs, I sat on the couch, waiting for Kayla to arrive with the detective.

Detective Caudell came in with his assistant. Detective Caudell sitting next to me, his assistant in the chair, Kayla remained standing after receiving her tea from the waiter.

"So, any good news?" I started.

Shaking his head yes, "We have a few leads on the case. The knife was found ditched about a mile from where Casey was killed. We were able to lift a print off it and tied it to a Roberto Marquez. Do you know him?" The name sounded familiar, but I couldn't place it.

Speaking up, "Hey that's the local loan shark in Indiana. What does he have to do with Casey?" Kayla queried. She knew of him from her ex-boyfriend who worked on the force up in Indiana.

He looked in Kayla's direction, "We're not sure yet. We are

still trying to tie the pieces together. Amber, do you have any unresolved family issues, or know of anyone who would want to hurt Casey, to get at you?"

The question had never crossed my mind. "No, sir. I've had stepfather issues growing up, but he loved Casey like his son," I answered.

Closing his notebook, "Well we don't have much else but once we get more information we'll be in touch," standing and extending his hand in my direction.

Shaking it and then shaking Kayla's, she guided her hand toward the elevator, "I will let you out." She escorted them back downstairs and within a couple minutes joined me back on the couch. "I wonder what Marquez has to do with all of this?" The same thought had crossed my mind. Changing the subject, "Now about going out. Interested?"

Raising my shoulders in excitement, "Sure, only if Keith goes. It wouldn't hurt to get out." I was beginning to feel claustrophobic from being inside all this time, though in the beginning that's all I wanted.

Taking a sip of her tea before answering, "I'm sure he will. He's running *ENVY* while Tristan's gone, so I know we'll end up there. Come on, let's get dressed."

Walking back to Tristan's room, I found a simple low-neck navy-blue shirt, and khaki pants. Wearing my tan leather heels, I tussled my hair half up, not wanting to look utterly sexy, since I had no one to dress up for. Satisfied with my look, I met Kayla at the elevator to head out for the evening.

ENVY

Greeting us in the lobby, dressed in khakis himself, he accompanied it with a black polo; business casual at best, since he was running the club. Holding out both arms to escort us through town, Keith always had a way of making us smile. Kayla and I took his arm exiting the condo. It was a cool crisp night pronouncing the arrival of fall. Tourist season had died down, but local colleges were back in session, which meant business would pick up.

Making our way to the old brick building, the bouncer let us in. Overhearing a guy from the crowd yell, "How do they get in?" I shot him a quick smile as we disappeared inside. The place was hopping, like it never stopped since the last time we came. Keith leaned over and told Kayla something I couldn't hear. Smiling and shooting him a flirtatious look, we headed to our normal VIP Lounge, finding Shayla waiting with our drink orders.

"You're a good lady," Keith exclaimed, impressed that we were already served.

"A little birdy told me you were coming." Keith shot her a surprised look as she sashayed away.

Shaking off her comment, "Ladies, a toast," lifting his drink, "To Tristan, may he be safe and return soon to join us on our new adventure." Our glasses clanging, each of us downing our drinks, "Wanna dance?" he exclaimed, obviously trying to keep things moving.

"You guys go on, I'm just going to sit here for a while," taking a seat in the booth, my eyes wandering to the mirrored wall that adorned Tristan's office. Memories flooding me to our first night at *ENVY*, the night it all began.

"Come on Amber, have a good time," pulling at my arm; doing her best to force me out of the booth, "Tristan would have wanted you to," her pleading almost unbearable. Finding success, she drug me to the dance floor.

The music was thumping and the room was packed. I needed to let myself go a little, enjoy the freedom. It had been so long since I had an evening out, this was my chance to let loose. Closing my eyes, my body moved to the beat. I couldn't help but remember Tristan's hands on my body the last time we were here. My skin tingled from the fading memories.

Kayla and Keith were dancing close, his nose in her neck, her hand wrapping around his from behind. Falling back into the present from my memories, someone moved in close from behind. My nerves went tense as the smell of old cologne invaded my nostrils. His breaths were heavy against my ear, my body freezing; knowing something was wrong. Loud enough for only me to hear, "Don't turn around."

Recognizing the voice, I couldn't pin point from where, the mystery man demanded, "Keep dancing," Not knowing what else to do, I began dancing the best I could. The music fading to the back of my mind, my body was moving out of beat from the current song.

After a moment or two, I began pleading, "Please don't hurt me. I can give you anything. Just tell me what you want and we will make it work."

His voice husky, "Hurt you…like what I did to Casey?" The blood drained from my face. Glancing over, Kayla must have seen the fear in my eyes and the paleness of my skin.

Nudging Keith, his brow furrowing at what was unfolding. Whispering something to Kayla, he disappeared in the crowd. Kayla walked back towards the VIP Lounge, leaving me alone. Swallowing the knot in my throat, all I could do was continue to do what the man was saying. Suddenly severe pain enveloped my body, followed by a loud blast. Screams echoed among the patrons, then dead silence.

HOSPITAL AGAIN

S lowly blinking my eyes, my eyes greeted the fluorescent lighting of the ceiling. My conscious state coming back around, I recognized the smell of staleness and latex. The echoing of the monitors rang in my ears. Moving my hands to the mattress to lift myself, pain swallowed me.

My hand met cold fingers, "You're awake." It was Kayla. My eyes fully adjusted and my suspicions were accurate; I was back at the hospital.

My throat dry, "water" I said hoarsely.

Grabbing the pitcher, she poured me some water. Placing the straw at my lips, I sipped, "Yea, what happened? All I remember is we were at *Envy*, dancing."

"You were stabbed Amber," her fingers squeezing mine, "Keith left me because he saw the knife. He approached the guy from behind, startling him. When he did, he stabbed you. Keith shot the suspect, killing him."

The events slowly replaying back in my mind, the dreadful words repeating themselves, "He killed Casey, Kayla. Who was he?"

"It was Marco, Amber," defeat in her voice.

"Wait, what? Marco, like tall, dark, and handsome who

danced with me just a couple months ago?" my face squished together.

"Yes Amber, him! I am just as shocked as you are. The cops haven't released any details to us. They've spoken to Keith briefly and shut down *ENVY* temporarily," a knock sounded at the door as Keith entered with Detective Caudell.

"Glad to see you're awake, Amber. You had us scared for a few days," Caudell stated. With the exhaustion of the last few weeks, I guess it wasn't a surprise that I had been out for so long.

"Any new details officer?" Kayla asked.

Looking at me directly, "I'm sorry, but I need to speak to Amber alone."

"Yes sir," they said, standing, "We'll be right outside," kissing my forehead before leaving the room.

Once the door clicked shut, "Amber we've discovered some new evidence that concerns us deeply. Marco Lucarelli, the man that stabbed you, was one of Roberto Marquez's henchmen from Indiana. He was hired to kill you."

My voice tired and shaky, "Oh...by whom?"

His stance stoic as he continued, "That we are still piecing together. We have a lead but wanted to ask you a couple of questions. Do you know a Richard Antinelli?"

Shaking my head, not able to recall anyone by that name, "No, it doesn't ring a bell."

"We searched Marco's bank accounts and found several large wire transfers from a Richard Antinelli's account into his. We are tracing the name and as soon as we know something, we will keep you posted," He stated, nothing new to me.

"I understand and thank you for everything," extending my hand to shake his.

Taking my hand, "You still aren't out of the woods yet. When word reaches this Richard character, he isn't going to be happy to find out that his employee is dead and you are still alive. Stay locked up until we know for sure. In the meantime, we will have police escorts put up to watch your house, Tristan's, and the hospital."

"Yes sir," I noted my understanding.

Releasing my hand, "Get some rest." Caudell left the room. Kayla coming back in followed by Keith.

Not wasting any time in her inquisitiveness, "What did he say?" I informed her of the information provided. She didn't know who Richard was either but at least it was a name.

Anger now clouded my being, clenching my fist, "Well we aren't leaving Tristan's apartment until this is solved. Think Mr. Klein will mind me still working from home," turning the question to Keith.

Grabbing my hand and squeezing, "He loves you like his daughter, so no he won't. He understands these situations," suddenly Keith's phone rang. Pulling it from his pocket, "Excuse me, I need to take this," exiting out of the room.

Finding her place beside me again, "I'm so sorry Amber. I pray they catch this man so we can go back to normal."

"Did someone let Tristan know?" I asked.

"Keith informed his commanding officer. Keith stated that he's thick in his mission and wasn't sure if they could get the message to him but would try," her hand squeezing mine, reassuringly.

Walking back in the room, "Babe, I need to run. I'll catch up with you later," kissing her cheek.

Her attention focusing on him, "Everything ok?"

"Yea, just need to run an errand," his hand pressing my hair down, kissing my forehead also, "You get some rest lady. We need you fully recovered."

"I will," smiling at him. Turning away, he hurried out the door, the doctor entering behind him.

Approaching my bedside, "Well Ms. Slayton, I'm glad to see you up," grabbing my chart. "All your vitals look good and it looks like you can go home tomorrow. How do you feel?"

Shifting slightly, "Like someone stabbed me."

Snickering, the doctor continued, "Well we were worried, you were touch and go. I would like a few minutes to speak to you privately." Turning his attention to Kayla, "Would you mind waiting outside."

Standing to leave, looking at me, "Sure. I'm going to go grab a snack. I'll be right back."

Leaving the room, Kayla closed the door to allow us some privacy. Grabbing the chair, he sat down, resting the chart on the bed beside me. "I'm glad you are feeling ok. We'll get you some meds for the pain, so you can sleep tonight. I wanted to speak to you about what happened the night you came in."

Pausing for a moment to find the right words, "The night you came in, there was a lot of blood, and we rushed you straight to the emergency room. On the table, the doctors were able to find the wound, and stop the bleeding from going any further. Once they were sure they had secured the wound, they found more bleeding."

Sitting up a little more, my focus remaining on the doctor, pausing, "What from?"

Clasping his hands together, "The bleeding was coming from your vaginal area. I'm sorry Ms. Slayton, you miscarried."

A knot forming in my throat, "I was pregnant? Are you sure?"

Confirming my question, "Yes. The baby was roughly 14 weeks along. I'm sorry."

Not able to comprehend what he was saying. There was no possible way, "14 weeks? I was pregnant, but that can't…"

"Were you on birth control?" asking to try and figure out how.

"Yes, practically forever," proving what he was saying just couldn't be.

His questions continuing, "Did you get sick or have to be put on any kind of medication?" Thinking back over the past few months, so much had happened, then recalling, "Yes, about 4 weeks before I left, I had to see the doctor for an injury that had gotten infected. He placed me on antibiotics."

His eyebrows raising in an ah ha motion, "You are aware that while on antibiotics, birth control is ineffective." Nodding my head, I should have known better, but I didn't know I would be leaving Casey, regardless of how bad things were getting. Casey had forced himself on me later that week.

"Pregnant?" the news really hadn't settled well with me. "Can I still have children?"

Squeezing my hand in affirmation, "Yes Ms. Slayton. The injury and blow of the attack was enough to cause the miscarriage but not enough to cause you the inability of having children. We will put you on some meds to help your system balance out. You will have some…" his words trailed off as the shock wore on about being pregnant. I was having Casey's baby, though part of me wasn't sad that I had lost it. Maybe it was the shock that prevented the emotions.

Focusing back to the doctor's words, "Your body needs to heal. The nurse will discharge you first thing in the morning. Do you have any questions?" Simply shaking my head no, he placed the chart back at the end of my bed, "Try to get some rest," he told me walking out.

Kayla came back in the room, noticing my demeanor, "Everything ok?"

"Yea," deciding not to tell her about the baby. I needed to process this and I wasn't sure I wanted everyone knowing, especially Tristan, with all that we had been through.

"What was that all about," pointing her thumb back at the door.

Shrugging my shoulders, acting as if nothing was wrong, "Nothing, just protocol I guess."

"I guess," her forehead high making her way back to the seat next to me.

Changing the subject, "There's a pretty hot guard standing outside your door."

Rolling my head to the side and sending a small scowl, "Kayla, you're with Keith."

Smiling, "Doesn't hurt to look. At least you know he's not some hairy old guy." Chuckling, it hurt to laugh but it was nice. Feeling a little easier knowing we were protected, "Are they going to charge Keith with murder?"

Sitting down in the chair, "No the cops aren't pressing charges, since he was trespassing on the property." I was relieved.

Trying to get caught up on anything I may have missed, "Any word from Tristan? It's been weeks."

"No, Keith hasn't mentioned anything. I'm sure he's ok," she replied. The nurse entered the room and put something in my IV. "This will make you comfortable. Ma'am visiting hours is over," looking over at Kayla.

"Well I am going to head out. The guard will stay over watch. I'll be here to take you home tomorrow." Kissing my forehead, she was out the door. It didn't take long for the drugs to kick in and the exhaustion to take back over.

CLAIRE

T he next day Kayla greeted me with the nurse, "Ready to go home?"

"Yes, I've spent too much time in this hospital," I responded, slightly sarcastically.

Giggling, she reached over to help me out of bed and into the wheelchair; the achiness of my wound radiated down my legs. Hissing, "We'll get you your meds when we get home," Kayla remarking, seeming quite peppy today. Sitting in the chair, Kayla pushed me towards the elevators. Making our way to the first floor, there was a waiting car to take us home. The morning sun was peaking its head under the overhang of the hospital, as the cool brisk wind shifted over us, the smell of baseball leather and soap washing through my senses.

Whispering in my ear, "Hey darling, how are you feeling," jerking to look behind me, I ignored the pain radiating up my side, finding the most striking green eyes that I have ever laid eyes on. There standing next to me was the man I so desperately needed for what seemed like ages. My emotions ransacked me as tears fell, not believing that he was actually home. He had shaved off his beard and was so clean compared to the last time I saw him. I was speechless. Reaching for him he bent down embracing me, wrapping my arms around his neck, not wanting to ever let go of him. Lifting me from the chair into his arms, he gently laid a kiss on my forehead. Wiping the tears from my eyes, he whispered, "It's ok darling, I'm home." I couldn't control the crying and the tears fell, as I held onto him, not letting go. Kissing my lips to reassure me everything was ok; he carried me over to the waiting car. Glancing over his shoulder, I saw Kayla standing with Keith. His arm proudly around her, she was crying; her hands clasped together.

Sitting me in the car, he shut the door as he scampered to the other door. Getting in, he helped me with my seat belt, and placed me into the crook of his arm. Giving the driver the orders to the apartment, my body relaxed against his. I finally felt safe with him home.

Waking up sore and rested after virtual exhaustion for over a month, I hadn't even realized I fell asleep after Tristan carried me to the car. Easing my way onto my side, I didn't find Tristan next to me. Rolling onto my back, with my arm over my eyes, thoughts raced that it was all a dream. The door opened and a silhouette of a man came into view. Tristan walked over to the bed, sitting next to me, he was only dressed in sweat pants, "You're up...How do you feel?"

"Better. Rested." I said, easing myself to a sitting position. Handing me a cup of water and my meds, I noticed he was wearing the ring I gave him. Swallowing them down, he grabbed the cup, placing it on the bedside table. Grabbing his hand, gently rubbing the ring I had given him over a month ago. Sitting quietly for a moment, he finally leaned in, cupping my chin, kissing my lips softly. "I'm so sorry Amber. I know this last month was hard for you."

"Let's not talk about that. You're finally home." Leaning towards him, slowly lifting my arms to his neck, I pulled him with me as I lay back on the bed. He shifted in beside me, his hand gently rubbing my back, as he looked down at me. Lifting my eyes to his, concern lingered. I had a feeling he knew something more than a stabbing happened, he did have control over my medication. I really didn't want to tell him, but felt he needed to know, to keep the trust between us. "I need to tell you something," almost embarrassed, I refused to look at him, "Tristan I miscarried Casey's baby." I could feel his arms tense as the words tangled in the air around us.

"I know," is all he said. I wasn't sure what to do, but lay still in his arms. Hearing the words finally admitted opened the wound that I had been trying to cover. Tears began soaking his shirt and his hand simply rubbed my arms. No words needed to be said, just comfort is what I needed and he knew that. He didn't ask for any explanation, he wasn't angry; he was caring and he was concerned and he did what he knew I needed in this moment. He let me cry and mourn the loss of a precious life.

Awaking several hours later, I found my bed empty again. Deciding I could use a shower, I shifted to a sitting position but found myself sitting in something damp on the cool sheets. Reaching for the light, flipping it on, I found blood. Confused at first, recollection of my miscarriage came to light. Lifting myself to stand, I went to grab a towel when Tristan entered the room and saw the blood, "Let's get you in the shower. I'll take care of this." Grabbing my arm, he helped me walk to the bathroom. Dressed in khakis and a long sleeve shirt, he rolled his sleeves up as he reached for the shower nozzle. "Will you help me?" embarrassed to ask.

"Of course." Walking me over to the toilet, I sat down, as Tristan removed his clothing. Helping me remove the bandages, we entered the glass shower together. Laying my head on his shoulder, his arms gently wrapped around me as the water pounded us from above, "I'm so happy you're home. The last month I've been to hell and back," lifting my head up under his chin, "Please tell me you don't have to go back?"

There was silence, then, "I have to Amber, I'm sorry." I could tell this was the last thing he wanted to tell me.

Sighing as silent tears fell. Lifting my head to face him, "Why did you come home if it wasn't done?" I asked.

"When I received word of everything going on, I spoke with my commander and informed him of the dilemma at home. It's not normal protocol to send soldiers home before orders are up, but they gave me a five-day break between travel. They have the mission under control until I can arrive back and finish it out."

With a heavy sigh, I laid my head on his chest, as the water continued cascading above us. I just got him home and he was getting ready to leave me again. "So, I have at least a few more days then?"

Not moving from his position, "I leave at 1700 tomorrow, but I have a way to make our time enjoyable," quickly recovering before I could say anything.

Curious, I looked up to him, "How?"

Looking down at me, "You'll see, but only if you are up for it."

Returning my head back to his chest, "I've been away from you for over a month, and I have one day left, anything."

Rubbing his fingers through my wet hair, "Great. We leave in an hour. Wear something warm. You will probably find something in the closet, as I put some clothes in there," he said, smiling coyly.

"Well I guess we need to finish up then." Reaching over I grabbed the shampoo, and with Tristan's assistance, we finished our shower. I couldn't do much to get ready, so I put my loose strands in a wet ponytail, twisting it into a sloppy bun. Wobbling to the closet, I found a Gap Navy blue long sleeve shirt and khaki capris, wearing my Sperry's to match.

Once ready, we made our way to the front lobby of his condo, a black Jaguar was waiting for us. Along the way, I kept nudging Tristan to tell me where we were headed, but he wasn't budging.

Excited like a little kid, "You're going to love it. I've wanted to do this since the first day I saw you." Intrigued, I eased into the car. Pulling from the curb, we made our way through the heart of downtown towards the Charleston Marina. There were several large boats, yachts, and a variety of different vessels. They were gorgeous, shimmering in the crisp coolness of the impeding fall night. "We're here," he exclaimed, making his way out of the car, around the back and opening my door. "This way my darling," bowing and extending his hand to the awaiting dock.

Giggling at his gesture, grabbing my hand we made our way down the dock and met Frank, the Marina Manager. "Mr. Ashton, so nice to see you. Claire is ready to go." My eyes shifted back and forth between Frank and Tristan.

Not glancing my way, "Thank you Frank. How is Charlotte," asking, obvious they were longtime friends.

Beaming at Tristan, "She is well, always a beauty. Took her out last week and she sailed as if she had never sailed before," his hand gliding across an imaginary horizon.

"Fantastic," exclaiming, "Oh, this is Amber. She's never seen Claire," realizing I was still standing there. I was still curious about this Claire.

Reaching out his hand, kissing my knuckles. "Nice to meet you madam. Ever been sailing?"

My eyebrows raising at the words, "No sir, but I'm guessing I am getting ready to."

Laughing his big belly laugh, "Yes ma'am. You'll enjoy Claire. She's quite the lady. Mr. Ashton takes good care of her." Leading us to a boat parked at the end of the harbor. It was beautiful. Claire's coat sparkled as the sunlight danced across her bow. "Wow, she's yours?" I asked looking over at Tristan.

His eyes softening, "Yes, would you like to go for a ride?" Frank grabbed the lines, prepping Claire to launch.

"Yes," I exclaimed excitedly. Helping me onto the boat, he showed me where to sit in the back. Frank finishing up with the dock ropes sent us off waving as we pulled out from the marina, yelling just out of ear shot, "Enjoy your evening," the noise of the engines roaring, drowning out anything else he had to say.

Tristan easing us back set us off towards the harbor. "I thought we were sailing?" I said jokingly.

"Oh, we will," he replied, a smile curling on his lips. "I'm just getting her warmed up and out of the marina. Once we get in the channel, we'll catch the wind and we'll be off. The water is perfect today. I'll need your help though, if you are up for it?"

Ignoring any pain that was evident, "I'll try my best. So, who's Claire?" not able to handle my curiosity anymore.

Laughing a hearty laugh, "The boat darling. That's her name."

My look, a little befuddled, I didn't know much about boats since we never did that growing up. "Oh, well how did you come up with that name," trying to stay on conversation.

Sadness hinted his features, "It is my sister's name. She was named after my mother's maiden name. When my parents and sister died in the car crash, I invested a lot of money from my inheritance. One of the things I purchased was this boat. I named her Claire, since it tied to two beautiful women. It suits her well."

Looking out over the water, "Well it's beautiful," remarking as I faced the dawning horizon of Charleston. Seeing the city line from the harbor was a sight. Known as the *Holy City* you could see the variety of church steeples that peered above the skyline. The views of *Waterfront Park* and *The Battery* were all in view as the sun was settling along the edge of the Earth.

Messing with some levers, "Ready darling?" Nodding my head, he killed the engine. "Ok grab the wheel. Keep her steady on course. Once I get the sails up, she's going to grab, don't let go." Memorizing his orders, he kissed my cheek and headed towards the front of the boat. He began pulling the sails up and suddenly I felt the wind catch as the main sail made its way to the top. Claire increased in speed, the wind pushing us out of the harbor and into the open sea. The feeling and power were exquisite. Watching Tristan, he masterfully tailored each step, allowing Claire's beauty to shine.

Making his way back to me, "Good job," taking back over the wheel.

"Where are we headed," I asked.

"There's a little island just a little south of here that I like to park right off. We'll spend the night there," his head nodding to the direction we were headed. "It has the most beautiful lighthouse. The sun casts such amazing colors upon its walls as it rises and sets. It's such an intricate part of Charleston's history and the beauty it bestows."

Shooting him a stare. "Spend the night?" I've never spent the night on a boat."

With a small smirk, his face turned in my direction, "The night sky is gorgeous. There are no lights, no sounds of the city, just you and the stars and the crashing waves underneath," remarking as his memories took him back to a forgotten time he once enjoyed.

"Sounds romantic," I expressed as I put my arms through Tristan's, laying my head on his shoulder as we made our way through the open sea.

SAILING

On the water for about an hour, Tristan had moved from bow to stern, as he calls it, working every line to keep Claire on her steady course. The evening sky was beautiful as dusk brushed the crest of the ocean waves. With Tristan at the helm, I walked up behind him, wrapping my arms around his waist and laid my head on his back, "So where will we be sleeping?" I asked.

Not answering me right away, placing his hand over mine, he flipped a latch to hold the wheel in place with his free hand and turned to face me. His hands finding my waist turned me so my back was against the wheel. Leaning against me, his eyes looked down into mine and the waning sun sparkled a mixture of iridescent green. No words needed to be spoken in this moment. It was just us and the sea around, a moment we needed in our months of ups and downs.

Placing his hand around the nape of my neck he pulled me close, brushing his lips on mine. It was tender and sweet, not rushing or pushing, but simply embracing the serenity of it all. Pushing firmer, his kiss went from soft to passion with a hint of nervousness. Something was amiss but I didn't care. Kissing him back, our moment shared with the passing birds and trailing winds as Claire continued her voyage south.

Breaking away, his forehead against mine, "We're here,"

reaching behind me to unlock the wheel. Looking around, I could see the end tip of an island. "Why don't you go down and check out Claire, while I tidy things up here? I need to bring down her sails," showing me where to go as he headed to prep the boat for anchoring.

Walking below, I found the room downstairs encased in dark mahogany. There was a small kitchen and a gorgeous king size bed. The sea was calm and you could barely feel the boat rock. It was a small piece of heaven.

A rush of hunger hit the pit of my stomach; I began scouring the cabinets looking for something to eat. Finding some chicken in the fridge and spices in the cabinets, I started piecing together a tasty meal for dinner. Tristan peeking his head through the small entry way that led to the stairs. "What are you cooking? It smells heavenly," he said walking down and entering the cabin.

Standing at the tiny little prep area, he somehow managed to squeeze behind me, his nose reaching over my shoulder to take in the scent of my meal. "I'm starving," stating as I continued cooking, "so I decided to cook us dinner."

"A home cooked meal sounds perfect," pressing his nose into my hair, slowly kissing my neck, keeping his hands gentle on my waist. Nudging my elbow into his stomach, I playfully pushed him away, "Desert food gets old after a while," a subtle reminder of where he had been.

Quickly changing the subject, "You don't want dinner to burn..." trying to keep from losing concentration.

Groaning in defeat, I playfully looked over my shoulder as he walked off towards the bedroom area. Taking off his shirt, easing himself up on the king size bed, he laid down on one of the fluffy pillows. Glancing back at the meal cooking, I turned back to find Tristan fast asleep, as if he hadn't slept in months.

THE EVENING

inishing up the meal, not wanting to wake Tristan, I found how to set up the dining room table and had everything set out. Crawling up beside him on the bed, easing on my side, I admired his face. He was so peaceful when he slept. I had never seen him sleep before.

Solemnness overtaking me, the vague memory reminding me he's leaving again, and soon. This might be the last time I get to watch him sleep. My eyes admired his body, as they moved from his strong chiseled face, down the hardness of his body, I couldn't help but notice the scars. Taking my hand, ever so gently, I began rubbing the outline of each. As my hand reached the first scar, Tristan bolted in a sudden rush, grabbing my hand with full force, pushing me down on my back. Opening his eyes, all I could see was rage filled within them.

"Tristan let go," I hollered, realizing he wasn't aware of what was happening. His weight on top of me, the pain from my wound radiated through me with the pressure. For the first time in months, fear raked my body, the same way it had any time Casey was near.

"TRISTAN," I screamed, finally snapping him out of his unconscious state. Seeing my hand in his, now almost blue from the pressure of his grasp, "TRISTAN LET GO OF ME," screaming again, this time he freed me. Raising his hands to his mouth.

"Amber, I'm so...I didn't mean to..."

Pulling my hand to my chest, rubbing the color back into it, "It's ok," my heart racing, practically beating out of my chest. The pain from my wound still tore through my body from Tristan's weight.

"Did I hurt you? Amber I'm so sorry," lifting his body off the top of me. Huddling onto the other side of the bed, his knees pulled into his chest; Tristan placed his palms into his hands. Ignoring the pain in my hand, I calmed my breathing, reminding myself that this wasn't him.

Shifting over, pulling his hands down, I placed my hands on his cheeks, slowly rubbing my thumbs across it. Lifting his chin, searching for his eyes to reach mine, no anger present, just sadness. "It's ok," reassuring him, leaning in and kissing him softly.

"Amber, maybe I'm not the one for you. My fear is I will hurt you. I already have," his voice full of hurt and despair. Stating softly, "You don't need this in your life, not with everything going on at home," removing his eyes from mine in shame.

Reassuring him, "Tristan, you accepted me for me. I'm not giving up on you. This is the first time this has happened. Have you spoken to Dr. Fox?"

His eyes still cast downwards, "Not in months"

Shifting myself into view, "Maybe you should see her before you head back tomorrow. It might help."

His stare blank, "I can't see her until my mission is over. It won't help."

Easing into a question I longed an answer for, "Does your reaction have to do with your scars?" needing some guidance.

Not giving much, "Yes."

"Ok. I promised I wouldn't pry, but it may help if I knew

more," trying my best at feeding my need for answers. I had gone months with not knowing, I was hoping he could shed some light on a snippet of his past.

Shaking his head, "Not yet. It's too soon. I promise you, I will tell you when I know it's right." Looking over towards the dining room table, he saw dinner sitting cold. "Why didn't you wake me up when it was done?"

Looking at the table myself, "You were sleeping. I've never seen you sleep, so I wanted to let you rest. I guess I know why I have never seen you sleep," I said sheepishly, trying to lighten the mood.

His scowl deepened, "It's not funny Amber, I could have seriously hurt you."

Changing the subject, "I'm fine. Are you hungry?"

Leaning his head on his shoulder and glancing my way, "Yes. I'm sorry dinner's cold."

"It's ok. I'm with you and that's all that matters," Grabbing my hand, kissing it, we made our way over to what was possibly our last meal together.

Finishing up, Tristan cleared the table once our plates were cleaned. Trying to assist him, he refused, informing me that since I cooked, he would take care of the rest. Walking over to the bed, I laid my head on the pillow, watching Tristan as he moved elegantly through the small area of the cabin. With the gentle sway of the boat, I began to relax, drifting off to sleep.

STARRY NIGHT

"**M**y darling, wake up" Tristan said softly brushing his knuckles across my cheek, gently coaxing me out of my peacefulness. "I want to show you something, come with me," reaching for my hand. Still in a comatose state, I made my way out of bed and up the stairs, out of the cabin. It was dark and all you could see was the starry clear sky above us. Turning the small corner, Tristan led me down a candle lit walkway towards the front of the boat, where there was a blanket laid out on the sunning deck, candles surrounding it. "Please sit," Tristan said motioning towards the blanket. Instead of sitting, I decided to lie down and observe the starry skies above us. It was beautiful. As I lay there observing Orion, The Big Dipper, Pisces and a few other constellations I knew, I couldn't grasp the beauty upon me. I had lived in the city my whole life and nothing was more breathtaking.

Tristan lay down beside me, reaching over; he pulled a blanket over top of us. Shifting on his side, he just watched me as I took in each twinkling star. "It's beautiful Tristan, so peaceful," I concluded.

"As are you darling," reaching over, easing my chin to face him, rubbing my cheek, I could see love in his dark green eyes, as they twinkled against the candlelight. Lost in his trance, he gently pulled me towards him, kissing my lips for just a second and resting his head on my forehead, "I love you." Three words, so sweet and perfect for a moment like this. Pulling my head away, my eyes meeting his. He was nervous and waiting.

Embracing him with kisses, "I love you too." Kissing him deeply, passion filling the moment between us. Pushing his shoulder, rolling him onto his back, I gently shifted on top of him, losing myself in his eyes. His hands found the bareness of my back from under my shirt, the feeling so comforting and soothing.

The wind softly blew my hair, Tristan lifted his hand to push the wild strand behind my ear, gently rubbing my cheek, looking deep into me, "I couldn't imagine this night any other way," Kissing him softly, sharing the peacefulness of the moment with the stars.

Slowly rolling myself back onto the blanket, Tristan placed his arm under my neck for support, his other arm around my waist, as we laid quietly for the rest of the evening.

LAST MOMENTS

Waking to a morning of reds and oranges, I found the blanket next to me empty. Stretching my arms, not as painful as yesterday, I was curious to know where Tristan had disappeared. Hearing footsteps approaching from behind, "Good morning, darling. Sleep well?" Tristan asked as he sat down behind me, legs straddling me from behind, handing me a cup of coffee.

"Yes, the best in over a month, and probably for a while," kissing my cheek, as I reached down and pulled the blanket over us. A colorful array of oranges and reds danced across the eastern sky, bouncing off the crests of each passing wave. I had missed the setting of the sun last night, but the rising was a perfect ending to a wonderful night. "Isn't it beautiful," I said. Tristan just looked over and smiled and I knew what he was thinking, he didn't have to say it. Wrapping his arms tighter around my waist, pulling me close against him, I lay my head against his chest, my comfort spot.

"What do you want to do today?" he asked.

"I could stay here all day," replying.

Kissing the back of my head, "As much as I would love to sit and devour your scent, we must return." Sadness creeping its ugly head at the sound of those words, but I wouldn't let it ruin the moment.

My heart heavy at having to end this perfect venture, "I know. Let's make the most of it. Whatever you want to do, we'll do it," I said.

"Ok then, get dressed. I've got a few ideas." Removing his arms, he stood and headed to the back of the boat to prep her to sail. Standing, I cleaned up the blanket and made my way down to the cabin, finding my bag. I pulled out my pull over sweat-shirt and jeans and put back on my Sperry's. Walking back up-stairs, I heard the sound of the motor running. "Are we going to drop her sails today?"

Focusing on the dials of the boat, "No, unfortunately winds aren't right today. We'll just cruise in on her," he replied as he walked towards the front of the boat to lift the anchor. Watch-ing him work, my eyes made its way around the beautiful land-scape that displayed before us. I had never seen such beauty. In the distance you could see the shrimp trawlers heading to get their daily catch, the dolphins jumping along the wake of the boats, seagulls flying overhead for a chance to catch their daily meal, a true testament of Charleston's beauty. And on the other side sat the beautiful lighthouse Tristan had spoke of the night before.

Heading back towards the marina, we met Frank at the dock. Tying Claire up, he helped us off. "Beautiful night last night. Hope you had no trouble out of Claire." Frank stated.

"No sir, she was a beauty, like always. Thanks for everything, Frank, make sure she shines for me," Tristan remarked, patting his back.

"As always sir." Frank replied, as we walked up the dock, hand in hand.

Making it to the Marina entrance, the black Jaguar was wait-ing to pick us up. Entering the car, the driver went to pull away,

I asked, "Where are we headed?"

"You'll see," he replied, a slight smile perched at the edge of his lips. "Hungry?"

"Yes, famished." I replied.

"Good, I know a great little place," motioning to the driver that we were ready.

Driving through the streets downtown, vendors had already opened their shops and patrons were slowly making their way down from their rooms. The driver eased his way through each turn, finally coming to stop in front of another historic building on King. Recognizing it from my few walks sightseeing in the city, the building didn't look like much from the outside. "We're here," stating as he exited the car, rounding the back, and opening my door for me.

Stepping out of the car, I saw the sign on the door read, *Halls Chophouse.* Tristan opened the door for me, leading me inside and the host greeted us, "Mr. Ashton, we didn't know you were back in town. How may we assist you?" he asked. The restaurant was quaint with a romantic feel. The area small, but upscale, the staff professional and courteous. Glancing around, Tristan and the host continued in conversation. "Luke, I'd like you to meet Amber. She just moved here a few months ago and we were hoping for some of your famous Gospel Brunch."

Acknowledging me and turning back to Tristan, "Well we would be delighted. Anything for our best client." Gospel Brunch? But it wasn't even Sunday. Looking around, I noticed the place was empty. "Right this way, sir." The host led us to our table, bringing out the Brunch Menus for us to review.

Handing me the menu, "Since we normally don't serve Brunch during the week, I will be your server today. The chef has fired up the grill and I'll be happy to take your order when you are ready."

Glancing over the menu, I saw so many different choices; I wasn't sure how I would narrow it down. There was She Crab Soup, Omelets, Eggs Benedict, French Toast, Biscuits and Gravy, everything imaginable. My mouth watered at all the choices. Continuing my glance over the menu, Luke brought us some water and asked if we had any special drink requests, Tristan ordering us two Mimosas. Within a few minutes he brought us our drinks, and we placed our order, the She Crab Soup to start, followed by Shrimp and Grits, hearing rumors that Charleston was the place for both, Tristan ordering the same. Taking our menus, he turned away, leaving us to the quietness.

Raising his glass in a toast. "To us, may these last couple days be the start of what's to come," touching our glasses in celebration, we each sipped our Mimosas.

Finishing up brunch, we spent the remainder of the day, walking through the streets of Charleston. It was a warmer than normal day for this time of year; a slight overcast in the air, with an occasional peak of sun. We window-shopped, checked out the latest vendors on Market and met Kayla, Keith, and Rebecca for a late lunch at *Fleet's Landing*. The day was a perfect ending to a hellish few months.

Making our way back to his condo, standing silent in the elevator, we both knew that our time together was dwindling down. Grabbing my hand, lifting it and kissing my knuckles, he peered out of the corner of his eye, sadness looming. Reaching with my free hand, I grabbed his arm and gently squeezed as I rested my head on his shoulder. Savoring the last remaining seconds alone, we reached his condo. Walking through the door, Tristan's cell phone rang. Pulling it form his pocket, "Hello," he quipped.

"Yes sir…Yes sir…Right away, Sir…" based on the responses, I knew this was the call. Hanging up the phone, turning to face me, "It's time." Those were all the words that needed to be spoken. My stomach was in my throat as we spent the next several minutes helping Tristan get his gear together. Words weren't really spoken in these moments, mostly directions from Tristan on what needed to be packed. Emotions were running high between both of us as we tried to manage the black sheep in the room.

Throwing his duffle over his shoulder, grabbing my hand, we made our way back downstairs. Walking him over to the elevator, he sat down his duffle and pressed the down button, then turned to face me. Lifting his hand to my cheek, he leaned in kissing me, trying to hide that this was good-bye. Pulling me in to his chest, my arms glided around to his back, my cheek nestled across his chest, hearing his rapidly beating heart. The ping signaled the elevator doors opening, and he broke away from my arms. Rubbing his fingers along my cheek one last time, there were still no words spoken, just silence and longing looks as we silently read each other's thoughts in this moment. Stepping into the elevator, turning to face me, he finally broke his silence, "I love you…wait for me," his final words as the elevator doors shut.

ALONE AGAIN

S taring at the stainless-steel reflection of myself trying to process the finality of the last few moments, the quietness of the condo overwhelmed me and my knees finally gave way. Dropping to the floor, the tears fell as I placed one hand to my face, the other on the coldness of the elevator door. Bending over, curling myself into a ball, I sobbed. Walking into the living room, Eric saw me lying on the floor. Hurrying over, "Ms. Slayton, are you ok? What is wrong?" Helping me sit up, all I could do was lean over and cry on his shoulder. Unsure of where to place his hands, he simply put them on my shoulders as the sobs wet his freshly pressed work shirt.

He sat there quietly, brushing my hair smooth, like a father does with his crying child. Calming down after several minutes, I looked up to find a reassuring small smile from Eric. No need for words, he helped me to my feet and walked me upstairs, "Can you take me to the entertainment room, please?"

"You got it," he said, as he steadied my stride, helping me find the couch in the now darkened room. The sun had set, forecasting my mood as the day's events finally came to an end.

"Thank you," I stated as Eric grabbed for the throw lying in the basket at the end of the couch, "May I get you anything to eat?"

Covering me with the blanket, "Not right now, but thank you," I stated as I nestled deep within the covers.

"Yes ma'am," he said, with a turn on his heel he exited the room. Grabbing the remote, I turned on the TV to the local news. The news reporter snipped a clip showing Rebecca, the caption reading, "CADD Charity Ball a Success." My heart warmed for her, knowing she had pulled off a successful function that related to something so dear to her past. Just as the article was finishing, Kayla walked in with Keith. Seeing my puffy eyes, she strolled over, nestling beside me, her arm finding her comfort spot to console me. Keith knew, without even asking, the tears had been for Tristan's unannounced departure, "It will all work out Amber. He's good at his job and this mission is his biggest."

Just staring at the TV, "I know. It's hard adjusting to this life. How did you do it? Growing up I mean?"

Looking over I found him dressed in jeans with a vintage green V-neck t-shirt. His hands in his pockets, "You adjust. You create a routine and live each day. You pray every night and every morning that they return home safely. You find your trust in Christ and know that no matter what Christ's plan is in place in this. You have to have faith."

Yea that was something far from my thought in the last few years, though I found myself praying more lately. We never really went to church, growing up; actually, I don't recall the last time I had gone. Maybe Keith was right, maybe it was time to revisit this unknown area. Maybe I could find the strength needed to get through this journey.

"I see your point. Maybe I will give it a shot." I replied, his freckles coming together as the smile on his face broadened. Looking at his watch, "Well I need to head over to *ENVY* and make sure all is well over there. I'll catch you girls later." Both of us nodding, he kissed Kayla on the cheek before exiting the room.

Turning to Kayla, I laid my head on her shoulder and took a deep breath, praying a silent prayer, a peace overcoming me.

A NEW DAY

The morning light cascaded through the open windows of the entertainment room, my eyes slowly fluttered open as the dawning of the new day appeared. I saw Kayla still curled up on the other end of the couch. "It's a new day," I said to myself. It was time to finally do what I came to Charleston to do, start a new life. I had a great job, a great boyfriend, so all I needed to do was take control of the area that seemed to be lost and that was everything inside of me. I decided, no more tears, no more hurt. It was ok to mourn for myself, but I had done too much of that lately. It was time to hide Mr. Hyde once and for all.

Pushing Kayla's feet to the floor to wake her, "Get dressed, we're going out today."

Her half-asleep grunts filling the room, "What's with you today? Got a little pep in your step, I see," sitting up and rubbing the sleep from her eyes.

"It's time to restart," I hollered as I headed to Tristan's closet to retrieve something to wear. Finally settling on something suitable, I headed to the shower to wash away the grime of the past few days. My wound was fast healing and changing my bandages was pretty easy these days. Removing the bandage, I walked into the shower.

Once done, I blow dried my hair, styling it to my satisfaction.

I applied a little makeup, thinking to myself that this is what I needed. I needed to start taking care of myself. While I wasn't a believer, Keith was right. I needed to have faith that Tristan would be ok. I knew he couldn't call me all the time; he did keep his end of the deal and called when he could. As a journalist, the inquisitive side of me was natural, but I needed to remember that he had a job to do and I just needed to come to grips that I most likely would never know anything related to Tristan's career.

Finally done with making myself feel clean and beautiful, I snapped a photo with my phone and emailed it to Tristan's e-mail. He needed to see that I wasn't moping around and that I was continuing on my days, though he wasn't here to enjoy them. The file flickered sent and tucking my phone in my back pocket, Kayla walked in carrying a cup of coffee for me. She was dressed for the day also, and noticing my peppier step, stated, "What's with you? You seem happy!"

Still managing myself in the reflection of the mirror, "I am. Keith helped me realize last night, that no matter what, everything will be ok. I need to get back on track and focus on my life, whether Tristan can be here or not. Since it's the weekend, we're going out. Keith can tag along for security detail if he would like to."

Kayla seemed a little befuddled, "But what about what the cops said?" I was kind of shocked that she was being so serious when she was normally the carefree one.

Capping the lid on my lipstick, "What about it? Staying inside all day isn't going to help me recover from the past month," snapping quickly, "I left my husband, he was killed, I became a widow, lost a baby, lost a..." and before I could finish, my hand rushed to my mouth, realizing the cat was out of the bag.

Kayla's mouth growing wide as shock crossed her face upon my confession, "Baby? What are you talking about Amber?" I had spilt the beans, not even thinking. It was time to come clean.

Sucking in deep, "While in the hospital this last time, the doctor told me that I had miscarried. The stabbing had caused it," a slight sadness looming in my throat as I broke the silence to Kayla.

Touching my shoulder, she looked at me in the mirror, "Amber, I am so sorry. Why didn't you tell me?"

Touching her hand, "I didn't tell you because I felt that it wasn't the right time with everything going on. I didn't need to add any more stress to myself or anyone else. I really wasn't sure how to process it," I expressed.

"Was the baby Casey's," her question causing a knot to swell in my throat.

Swallowing it down, "Yes. It's almost as if the chapter is finally closing on me. I wasn't ready for a baby, really didn't need to have one with Casey, but I am saddened to know that motherhood was so close for me to only be lost by a tragedy."

Hugging me, her arms heavy with sadness. While I hated what Casey had done to me, it was finally clear that a baby could have been my step to help make things right, but I will never know what could have been. Not allowing myself to get sad again, I gently pushed Kayla way, wiping the slight moisture from my eyes. Looking at Kayla, she repeated my actions, we giggled some, "Did you tell Tristan?"

"Yes. He was the only one who knew. I think he already knew since he handled my meds. He was very sweet about the whole thing. Oh, also, I have something to share," trying my best to clear up the cloud that hovered, "He told me he loved me."

Stepping away to look at my face, her mouth practically on the floor, "What? Amber that is awesome! I am so happy you found someone so good for you. I have a secret too," she exclaimed, my eyes looking to hers, finding joy, "Keith told me too!"

"Aw, so exciting!" Giving each other a quick hug, we giggled like two schoolgirls just asked to the high school prom. "I guess they are two peas in a pod," Kayla shaking her head in agreement.

Tossing the last of my beauty treatment down, "Come on, let's go." Leaving the room, embracing the day ahead of us.

ANOTHER THREAT

We met Keith at the corner of Market and East Bay, greeting us with warm smiles and hugs. Kayla had called him on the way to see if he would be our security guard slash escort through our excursion downtown. She enlightened him on my newfound mood and he agreed that embracing it was the right thing to do. I needed to get out of that apartment, it had too many memories and the last thing I needed was to continue my depressive state. It wasn't good for anyone around me.

We walked through the streets of downtown, starting with the Market down Market Street. It never gets old walking through the historic building, finding different vendors each time. My love of people watching also quenched, as the onslaught of tourists is ever changing. Lunch fast approached and we decided to try out a little Italian place called *Bocci's*. Recommended by many locals, we had heard that everything on the menu was exquisite. After a magnificent feast, we returned to the sites of the City, settling on a carriage ride to rest our weary feet from the uneven paved cobblestone roads of Charleston. While gorgeous, they could do a number on your toes if you weren't careful. The horses were beautiful as they pulled the elegant carriages, the local historian telling of stories past.

"Isn't this great?" Kayla was exclaiming as the charming, picturesque scenery of Old Charleston passed us.

Taking a deep breath of fresh air, "It is and so worth seeing the City this way." Ending our journey through town, we decided it was time to retire for dinner. We figured Rebecca would be waiting at the condo for us, as on most weekends she is. I wanted to congratulate her on her recent campaign.

Entering the condo, we found a small box labeled, "Amber," but no return address. Not wanting to think the worst, my gut settled on thinking it was odd and turning to Keith, his face registering the same. Removing his cell phone from his pocket, he dialed our detective. The bomb squad and detective arrived within minutes. Once there, they moved us to a safer location. As with most suspicious packages, they had to evacuate the building and barricaded off the street to pedestrians. Once the all clear signal was received, the squad leader proceeded to inspect the box and its contents. A miniature explosive device was inside, but hadn't been detonated. The squad leader disengaged the bomb.

"Amber, looks like whomever is after you have seemed to locate you. I have made the decision to place a watch outside this condo until we can find whoever placed this device here. We are currently pulling the surveillance to see if its ones of the few leads, we have. Because the case crosses state lines, we have had to involve the FBI at this point. According to them, these individuals are tied into a large organized crime ring out of Indiana. We haven't found Marquez or Antinelli yet, but they have been under investigation for some time for money laundering and illegal gambling. Do you know if any of your family has any debts unpaid and you happen to be the one, they are targeting as bait to get them to pay?"

I hadn't really thought about any of this. All of this was news to me, "No, sir. My stepfather has a terrible drinking habit and Casey would disappear at times for short stints but gambling and money laundering had never been present."

Jotting down some notes, "Well if you happen to hear or re-call anything of the sort, you know where to find me. We'll get you back inside here shortly," shaking my hand, he turned to head towards the other officers present at the scene.

"There go our dinner plans," Keith moaned as we continued to wait to enter into our building. Rebecca and the condo's staff had met up with us outside. Small chatter was present among the patrons as we waited for the all clear from the officers. As a precaution the officers wanted to search the remaining condos, as well as Tristan's to make sure there weren't additional de-vices present. After about an hour of waiting, the all clear was given and we were allowed to reenter.

THE SUSPECTS
KEEP COMING

Keith's woes were soon forgotten as he gobbled up the delicious course that Rebecca had made before our mass evacuation of the condo. "That was delicious Rebecca, as always," Keith remarked, hesitating to lick his plate clean.

Giggling, I remembered, "Rebecca, congrats on the success of your latest campaign. It seems like it was wonderful?"

Beaming with excitement, "Yes! It was quite exquisite! I would have invited you but I knew Tristan was home and didn't want to intrude on your time," she stated solemnly. I hadn't even thought about the lack of invitation with everything going on. The days seemed to blend together over the last few weeks; it had almost become a blur. "Oh no issues at all. I really appreciate the consideration."

Reacting as if a light bulb clicked, "Speaking of functions, the CADD will be putting on their annual Masquerade Ball on New Year's Eve. You should come. It will be a lot of fun, maybe get you out of the condo some." I could tell she was trying to cheer me up, but going without Tristan didn't seem like fun at all. "If it makes you feel better, I will most likely be dateless. You could be my date." She further stated, "Like a girl's night. What do you think?" It did sound like fun and shopping for a dress might help clear my head. Plus, it could be an additional piece for the paper. Allow us to get exclusive coverage of one of the City's biggest events of the year.

"Sure, why not?" I replied.

Clasping her hands together, "Oh it will be so much fun Amber. I can't wait to see Keith in a tux!" Kayla remarking from the background, "We don't have too much time to narrow down a dress so why not go shopping next week?" she asked.

"Sure," the sadness still peeking in my throat. It did sound like fun, but without Tristan there, how much fun could it possibly be? Shaking off the negative thoughts, the last thing I needed was to charter that territory again.

Finishing up dinner, Kayla and Keith left, as Rebecca cleared the kitchen area with the staff. Deciding to retire to my room, I checked my e-mails to see if there was anything new from Tristan.

Opening my laptop, the familiar ping registered, displaying a new email message from my mom:

> *I know you asked us to stay out of your life, but I am still your mom. I am worried about you. We haven't heard much from you since Casey died and wanted to make sure everything was ok? Your stepfather hasn't been around much. He seems to have taken the death pretty hard. If you find it in your heart to reply, I just want to know you're safe.*

> *Mom*

My skin crawled at the thought of my stepfather mourning

over Casey. I never understood their closeness or my mother's obsession with staying with my stepfather. I sent a quick reply to let her know I was fine. I didn't want to speak of the case or anything but within seconds another reply came from her:

Thank you for letting us know. Also, some FBI detectives were by here. Do you know why? I am guessing it involves Casey's death but the FBI seems a little extensive don't you think? They said your stepfather is a possible suspect. I just don't see how. He's a good man. If you know anything Amber, please fill me in.

Mom

My stepfather was a suspect? It didn't make any sense and Detective Caudell hadn't mentioned that piece of information. And her statement about him being a good man was just all wrong. Good men don't beat their wives much less control them. I wrote a quick note back stating she knew as much as I did and hoped that would settle her inquisition. I would make a note to follow up with Detective Caudell in the morning.

As I began shutting my laptop another ping came across my laptop. Rolling my eyes and sighing, I reluctantly opened the lid back. To my surprise, it was Tristan, not my mom. My heart fluttering in my chest, I had communication finally:

My Darling,

It's amazing to see you smile. While it's only been a short time, I know your heart has been so hurt. That beautiful smile reminds me of happier times, although few. This mission has been rough for me knowing the state you are in, so to see you smile is reassuring. I hope you send me more, as your face pushes me to finish my mission and allow me to get home sooner. I promise I am almost done here and we can finally be together.

I love you.

Tristan

It was relief to see those words on my screen. A smile reached my eyes as I read the note over and over. I hugged my laptop trying to feel closer to Tristan but it didn't help much. Replying back, I filled him in on the latest events but not wanting him to worry too much. I also let him know about Rebecca and my date to the Masquerade Ball in a couple months. *I can do this. As long as I have some communication, I will be ok;* I thought to myself as I wrote the notes on the keyboard. I had read that communication could stagger overseas, depending on where the soldiers were located. Since I hadn't received a Hangouts call, my guess was that he was in a remote location with very little connectivity. Closing my laptop, I laid it against Tristan's pillow.

Getting up I found my nightclothes and decided it was time to retire for the evening hours. Once again, my day in Charleston was eventful, though startling. Deciding I wouldn't let it get to me, I finished readying myself for bed. Crawling under the sheets, I tapped the laptop as my way of saying goodnight to my beloved and I closed my eyes for the evening.

THE MASQUERADE BALL

The months seemed to pass ever so quickly and before I knew it, it was the night of the Masquerade Ball. Tristan and I had held steady conversations via email and occasionally I was able to see his scruffy, dirty persona over the Internet. He was unrecognizable at times, but Keith stated that he had to live as a different person due to his mission. It did make sense, but it wasn't my Tristan.

The case had settled down some. The detectives and FBI were working hard on their leads and keeping me abreast of the latest on the case. While no arrests had been made yet, it seemed as if the suspects were keeping a low profile and were quite hard to track down. They were guessing they caught wind of the investigation and went underground until things quieted down. It was nice to have a slightly normal life again, although I still had a daily detail with me.

Kayla and I had spent weeks finding the perfect dress and decided to create our own masquerade masks. It was a fun project to complete. My mask complemented my dress with its sequined outlines and black composition, feathers adorning the center. My dress was exquisite; a floor length black, off the shoulder gown, adorned with an ornate sequined pattern throughout. Seeing my dress, Rebecca decided to complement it with a silver number to match.

The day was here, as I sat in Mystique Spa getting primped and pampered; Rebecca was on one side and Kayla on the other as we were teased, tossed, painted, and brushed. Once the girls were finished, our nails were lavish and our hair flawless.

We left the spa knowing we would be some of the most beautiful women at the event.

Making it back to the condo we dressed in our finest gowns. Grabbing my matching clutch, I walked over to the mirror to place my mask over my face. Revealing my reflection, I saw a girl I never recognized, one with hope and admiration. One who was strong and happy for the first time in a long time. Although Tristan wasn't here to enjoy this night, Rebecca and Kayla made sure to keep my days busy and happy.

I met the girl's in the living area, as Keith made his way up the elevator. Upon entering and seeing Kayla, she stole his breath as he raced over to adorn her with affection. Giggling, "Stop babe, you're going to mess up my makeup."

Stopping reluctantly per her request, "Well I'll be, you ladies are quite fascinating this evening." And he was right. We were all quite exquisite.

Exiting the condo, we were met with a limo that carried us to the once familiar *Francis Marion Hotel*. The hotel was so beautiful, like I remembered. The chauffer exited the limo, opening the door to a red carpet that lined the entrance of the hotel. Local photographers and news crews lined the carpet, reaching out to Rebecca for an exclusive interview on tonight's events. Removing herself from our party, Keith interlocked Kayla and my arms escorting us inside to what was this year's biggest party. Looking over my shoulder, Rebecca radiating at the attention from the media, she was in her comfort zone.

The room was beautifully decorated. Acrobat dancers dancing in the corners along silk hanging from the ceiling, large floral and feather displays adorned the tables, along with expensive crystal china, guests were dressed to impress; truly an exemplary party. Local musicians played, as people danced, while servers set food out for guests to sample. Finding my seat, Keith and Kayla decided to take advantage of the music for a slower dance together. Observing their moves, I had never seen Kayla happier. My heart fluttered for her, sadness looming as I wondered how life would be if Tristan had been home. The written communications over the months had really brought us closer together but it just wasn't the same as him being here.

Leaning on my hand and daydreaming of what could be, a stranger lurking in the crowd caught my attention. He was dressed in a classic black tux, accentuated with a black tie, clean and pressed. His mask covering most of his face, his eyes and mouth the only thing to be seen. It was hard to make out any features from this distance, but he stood assuredly and poised. His stare penetrating me, lifting my head I looked around behind me but saw no one but couple's engaging in private conversations.

Returning my attention back to the stranger, he had disappeared. Shrugging off the uneasiness, a waiter passed carrying glasses of wine. Acknowledging him, he handed me a glass, and I easily downed the liquid. Thinking a masquerade ball would be a good idea, I wasn't so sure now. Not being able to see anyone's faces made the event a little uneasy, but trying to make the most of it, I let the feelings pass. My detail was right outside, comfort settled over me, knowing there was protection.

Keith and Kayla returned to the table and sat down. Whispering sweet nothings to each other, Keith broke away; tapping my hand playfully, "Cheer up."

Smiling, "I'm ok. I'm having a good time."

"You don't look like it," cocking his one eyebrow up in disbelief.

"Seriously, this is great," trying to settle his intuition.

"I have an idea," jumping up, grabbing my hand, "Dance with me."

"Yes," Kayla exclaimed, "Go dance with Keith. Take your mind off things for a little while." Giving in, I took Keith's hand as he led me to the dance floor. Taking the lead in a simple waltz across the floor, I couldn't help but notice his freckles showing under his mask. Kayla helped to match Keith's mask to her silver dress. His eyes sparkling as we danced to the slow beat of the live band. "Amber, I know these last few months have been hard, but I wanted to tell you that I am very proud of how you have taken this transition." My eyes met his; his compliments continuing, "The military life is hard, but I can promise you, the moment they make it home, it's the best feeling in the world."

As his words finished, I felt a small brush on my shoulder, "May I cut in?" A slightly familiar voice spoke from behind, Keith's eyes smiling at the stranger making the request.

"Of course," Keith replied, twirling me around into the unknown stranger's arms. Nervously grasping the stranger, looking up I found eyes that shimmered and sparkled in the dimly lit room, familiar eyes, green eyes. The mask was familiar, as I recognized it to be the lurking stranger from across the room. Nervous, *it's not possible,* I thought to myself. My thoughts raced as the stranger began leading our dance in the middle of the ballroom. A slight breeze rippling through the room pushed the smell of leather and soap my direction and I knew. Reaching up I lifted the mask off to reveal Tristan dancing in my arms. My heart racing at his sudden appearance, I didn't hesitate pulling him in and kissing those lips that I had missed for so long. Releasing my kiss, he kissed my forehead; no words spoken. Just holding each other, we continued to dance until the song finished.

As the guests clapped to the live band, Tristan walked me back to the table. Still in complete awe, I hadn't found my voice to say anything. Approaching the table, Keith stood to shake his hand and Kayla embraced him with a hug. Our crew was back together. Fast approaching the table, apologies being spoken, Rebecca finally appeared. Stopping as she reached the table, she realized her brother was standing in front of her. Her hands reaching her mouth, she became speechless at his surprise appearance and they embraced in a hug. Pulling him back, she looked him over and hugged him again.

Stepping back, she gently slapped his chest, "You jerk! You know I don't like surprises," the first words pretty much spoken among the crowd.

Laughing it off, "I'm happy to be home. I have good news," all our attention now on him, "I'm home for good. My mission's over," relief and cheers pouring over us. We were so excited, we hugged and embraced, knowing Tristan wasn't going to be leaving us again. Wrapping his arms around my waist, finally speaking to me, "I love you Amber. I promised you it would all be ok and now I am home." Kissing him, we were interrupted by Rebecca at the podium.

"First off, I want to thank each of you for coming tonight. CADD wouldn't be the success it was, if it weren't for all of your support. Secondly, I just received the best surprise tonight. As many of you know, my brother, the second founder of CADD, has been deployed in Afghanistan. Well he arrived home safely tonight," the room erupting in applause. Tristan waving off the gestures and thanking people who tapped his shoulder welcoming him home.

Rebecca continuing, "And third, I would like to invite one of our board chairs up here, Keith Mitchell, for some quick words," each of us looking at each other, curious as to what Keith had to say. Tristan whispering in my ear, "Watch," a Cheshire cat smile piercing his lips.

"First, thank you so much for attending this evening. As one of the board members, seeing this wonderful crowd fills my heart, knowing that we are combating a problem that seems to be growing in our state. When Rebecca started this foundation, I knew it was so dear to her heart, I felt that one of the ways I could help was to be on the board to make sure this foundation ran the way it needed to. However, that's not why I stand up here. A few months ago, I met the love of my life. This beautiful blond had moved in the same apartment building and I fell head over heels the moment I saw her. She is everything I could ever want and seeing how she has been with two of my closest friends, I knew I had a keeper. So tonight, I raise a toast to the beautiful Kayla Marks and want to ask her, if she would spend the rest of her life with me? Kayla will you marry me?" Sudden applause erupted and my face turned shocked over to Kayla. She was crying like a baby, her sobs coming hard.

Tapping the table to get her attention, she finally walked up to the stage, as Keith came down to the floor on one knee. Only being able to shake her head yes, she accepted his ring, grabbing his face, pulling him into a passionate kiss. Guests continued their congratulations and Tristan hugged my waist as we watched our best friends start the beginning of their lives together. "Maybe one day that will be us?" Tristan remarked, hugging his arms tight around my waist. Reassuring him, by rubbing his arms, and kissing him on his cheek, I knew it would be. *We just need to make it through our last battle together.*

CHAOS ENSUES

The evening couldn't have gone any better. Tristan was home and Kayla and Keith were engaged. It was the perfect way to start the New Year. Dancing in the ball room, the lead singer announcing, "Folks its one minute to midnight. So, grab your loved one, get on the dance floor, as we bring in the New Year together." Already having my loved one in my arms, the singer began counting down to the start of a fresh year; a new life together, new beginnings once again. *5, 4, 3...* the guests counted, finally reaching to one, as the champagne popped and kisses and hugs were embraced. Tristan wrapping me in his arms kissed me with strong passion and momentum.

My hand caressing the base of his hairline, our eyes locked together, the room moved in slow motion. Nothing could take away this moment from us. His eyes deep into mine, Tristan's expression changed drastically as yelling and crashing tables filled the room. Women were screaming as gun shots rang out in the room around us. Grabbing my arm, he hurled me out of the room and down the stairs out a back door. Looking back on my way out, my police detail had a man on the ground, his knee in his back, placing handcuffs around his wrists. The crowd of people stampeded out of the ballroom and into the streets. Tristan called on his cell for his car that sped around the corner to meet us. Before reaching us, a darkened vehicle drove past, shots ringing out from the window in our direction. Jumping on top of me, Tristan pushed me to the ground covering me with his heavy weight. The car sped off, the driver of Tristan's security detail jumped out, gun in hand, but unable to fire due to the crowds of people around.

The commotion in the street was chaotic as people scrambled to safety. Barely being able to peer under Tristan's heavy body, I saw his detail scattering around us, trying to keep any other predators away. Trying to lift myself up, Tristan heavy on top of me, I yelled, "Tristan, get up. I can't breathe," but there was no movement from him. Trying to lift myself again, I felt the warmth of moisture seeping through my dress covering my skin. I was able to shift my hand to visibility when I saw the red tint of my fingers. Screaming, "TRISTAN...NO... DON'T...HELP ME..." scrambling to claw my way out from under him, Tristan's security detail quickly ran over, rolling him off of me.

"We need an ambulance now," his detail screamed into the phone, another beginning CPR on him. My body free from Tristan's weight, I slid onto my knees finding Tristan's hand, squeezing it. Leaning down into his ear, pushing his hand to my chest, "Don't do this now. Don't leave me," my heart racing in a panic and tears flooding my cheeks. I knew Tristan was a fighter, but I prayed that this would not be the way he would go. Pushing me away, Tristan's detail continued CPR until the ambulance arrived. Silently praying, I curled my knees to my chest, *God don't take him now, not when I just got him back. He's my everything. Please God, if you exist, let him live.*

Rounding the corner, Keith rushed over at the sight of his friend on the ground; Kayla rushing to my side, consoling me as I sobbed into her dress and Tristan's blood staining it. "Not now Kayla, not again," I cried beating my fist into her chest. Rubbing my head all she could do was tell me it would all be ok. The ambulance arrived, the paramedics taking over CPR. Tristan was still unresponsive to the manual rescue efforts being performed on the scene. All I could do was stare at my beloved lying there, helpless; looking frail and worn.

Loading him onto the gurney, the paramedics notified us that they would transport him to Roper Hospital, just up the road. Keith said he would ride along and Tristan's detail informed us that they would transport us to the Emergency Room. Arriving at the hospital, we sat in the waiting room until Dr. Timble walked in, recognizing us from our prior visits, "He's ok." You could hear the sighs of relief from everyone waiting in the room, Dr. Timble continued, "He took a shot to the arm and chest but he's a fighter. He is in critical but stable condition. He will be in surgery a little longer to remove the bullets and once he is done, he will be moved into recovery."

"When can we visit," Keith asked.

Shifting his hands to his pockets, "Probably not until tomorrow. He will most likely be here for a couple days and we will move him into a room, once he has woken in recovery."

With a stern tone to his voice, "We aren't going anywhere until we can see him," Keith remarked, crossing his arms, putting his foot down to the doctor. It seemed as if Dr. Timble was used to this conversation from him; he didn't try to fight him. Nodding his head, "I figured you would say that Keith. Like I've told you before, I suggest you try and get comfortable. You may be here a little while."

"Thank you doctor," we all replied in unison; Keith picked up his phone out of his pocket and exited the room.

"Are you ok," Kayla turning her attention to me. My legs curled into my chest in the tiny waiting room chair, my stare blank against the ceramic tile floor. I was in shock, not even having a chance to really register what had happened. Looking down, the bloodstained dress reminded me of the events that had transpired this evening.

Shaking uncontrollably, "I'm ok. He saved me Kayla."

"I know," her hands rubbing my bare back.

Keith returning with a bag in his hands, tossing it to Kayla, "Here are some clothes for you guys to change into. There's a bathroom right around the corner."

Exiting together we found the bathroom, stripping out of the memories that had unfolded this evening. Holding my gown in my hands, the blood had all but dried among the darkness of my dress, slight hues making themselves present among the stitching of the dress. Flashbacks to the happiness of early evening seemed so distant from what transpired.

Shoving the dress into the bag, I quickly changed my clothes and exited the restroom before Kayla finished making herself presentable. Along the corridor, I came across a room labeled *Chapel.* Feeling compelled, I decided to enter finding a dimly lit, peaceful sanctuary. Walking to the front row, there was no one but my thoughts and me. Sitting among the pews, I sat solemnly reflecting on my life up until now. So much had happened, I felt I could seriously write a book. My life was nothing but a ride of bad luck. A joyful evening turning to sorrow, and the last few months I had lost so much.

As if there was an imaginary push, my knees fell to the pew and my hands came together, I began to pray. Tears rolling down my cheeks, my silent prayers went up, trusting that whomever I was praying to would hear them and allow some good to happen.

As soon as my spoken word of "Amen" was said, the door swung open and Keith entered, "He's in a room. He's asking for you." My heart fluttered with hope.

Silently replying, "Thank you," to the imaginary being that answered.

Walking several corridors, the fluorescent lights illuminating the numerous hallways until we finally reached room 707. Peeking through the window, Tristan was hooked up to several machines, allowing the nurses to keep track of his status. Lying there asleep, I almost didn't want to walk in. His face looked so old, his body tired; it was the first time I was able to truly see him since he made it home. He looked peaceful lying there. The door creaking as it opened, his eyes fluttered open. Lifting his head to see me better, he smiled as I walked in the room.

"Sorry," I remarked.

"It's ok. I'm just glad you're safe Amber," his words weak, as his eyes fluttered between opened and closed.

"Shh! You don't need to talk. I'm ok. We're ok," touching my hand to his forehead, sliding it down, my knuckles brushing his cheek.

Clearing his throat, I could tell the pain meds were keeping him from being coherent. Kissing his forehead, "Go back to sleep, I'm not going anywhere tonight" and for once he did as he was told. Sitting myself in the chair, I found one of the extra flat pillows and curled myself into the tight little seat. Dozing off, I heard Tristan whisper, "I love you Amber."

TYING UP LOOSE ENDS

In the days that followed, Tristan slowly recovered from his wounds. Though stubborn as a mule, he followed my orders and allowed me to take care of him for once. The time together of his recovery was exactly what we needed to reconnect back to physically being present with one another. Though it wasn't the ideal situation, it seemed perfect.

We found out from the detective that the man they arrested was Marquez, the man who killed Casey. Though it was hard to break him, after making a plea deal with the FBI, and being ordered into Witness Protection, he provided police the lead they needed to arrest Antinelli. They found him hiding out in my stepfather's garage, so my stepfather was arrested as a co-conspirator. Come to find out my stepfather had been gambling away the money from the garage and had put me up as collateral.

Once they investigated my stepfather, he came clean as to why he had done such a heinous thing and the only thing he could say was that he was jealous of how I always came between him and his closest relationships. It was also discovered that was why Casey and him were so close, as Casey was one of his betting partners. His lawyer was trying to get him a plea deal on insanity, since the criminal psychiatrist had diagnosed him as bipolar and schizophrenic.

After the arrest, my mother emailed me, finally apologizing for all the years of hurt that she had caused me, never believing me about how bad of a man my stepfather was. We have been working on an amends and I finally gave her my phone number. She even came for a visit and was really pleased with how far I had come since leaving Casey. She even apologized for never supporting my decision and told me she was trying to work on being a supportive mother. She finally went into therapy for my father's death and to recover from the years of abuse she had suffered at the hands of my stepfather.

For Tristan and me, we are taking one day at a time, growing together. We moved in together shortly after the hospital stay and once he was recovered, he went back to work at *ENVY* and the architecture firm. Rebecca and Keith had held up the business end of things until he was fully recovered. Life was progressing like it needed to.

It was officially spring in Charleston, one of the prettiest seasons around. Everything was beginning to bloom and Kayla was in the backroom officially getting her hair and makeup done for the biggest day of her life. Walking in with her dress, stopping myself, I couldn't help but smile at the radiant bride, beaming at herself in the mirror as she put her earrings in her ears. Hanging her dress and removing it from its bag, Kayla walked over and hugged my shoulders. Leaning my head back, "I'm so happy for you Kayla. You are absolutely stunning," I remarked.

Her mom walking in, "Ok darling, it's time to get your dress on," helping her into her gown. Future thoughts of becoming Ms. Ashton popped into my head. I never thought I would ever plan another wedding, but with Tristan by my side, I knew it was a possibility. We had even talked about getting married one day and kids in our future. To help me cope with the loss of my baby and to overcome the abuse, Tristan had made sure I began seeing Dr. Fox. It had really helped me begin to recover.

As Kayla put the finishing touches on her dress, her father walked in admiring his only daughter and the beauty she possessed. She truly was the prettiest bride. Sneaking out for a minute to check on Keith, I found Tristan along the way, "You look radiant, darling," clasping my hands in his, leaning in and kissing my cheek. He knew better than to touch my dress.

"Why thank you. You look dashing yourself," I remarked, observing his simple khaki pants, pressed white shirt, with suspenders and patriotic bow tie.

Pulling at his tie, a grin on his face, "I know," acting nonchalantly.

Smiling off his charisma, "Where's Keith?" I asked. Pointing me to the opposite room, I left Tristan and entered to find Keith sitting on the bed, taking in the quiet. Closing the door behind me, "You ready?" I asked, sitting next to him, taking his hand.

"Yes," he remarked quietly.

Turning my head to try and find his eyes, "Nervous?"

His eyes remaining on the floor, "Yes."

Putting my arm around his shoulder and gently squeezing, "Don't be. She's the girl of your dreams, the mother of your future children; you can't picture your life without her. She's Kayla, no different than the girl you knew yesterday, only today you get to keep her forever," doing my best to ease his nervousness.

Finally meeting my eyes and smiling, leaning in and kissing my cheek, "Thanks Amber." Taking a deep breath and rubbing his sweaty palms on the pants of his tux, "Guess its time," as he blew out the breath he had been holding in.

My cheeks high on my face, "Yep. Ready to go?"

Standing, we interlocked arms, walking out to Keith's future.

The wedding was beautiful. Taking place along the pristine marshes of Charleston's waterways, Kayla accented her wedding with beautiful hues of lavenders, blues and pinks. The reception sat among Charleston's Boone Hall Plantation, The Boathouse being the perfect setting for Keith's and her southern affair.

No detail was left undone and as the evening sunset along the grassy marsh, the chirps and sizzles of the evening life began their sing sang song. The candlelit reception was filled with music, as guests danced to the latest trends.

Tristan and I sat among the guests, admiring our friends in their wedded bliss. His arm around me, whispering, "Can we talk outside?" Glancing over, I could see nervousness looming.

Knitting my brows together, "Sure."

His fingers lacing with mine, we walked outside the boathouse and along the paths of the Oak Tree lined walkways, illuminated with hanging lights, as the Spanish moss tickled the tops of our heads. Finding a park bench and offering me a seat, I sat down, Tristan sitting close beside me.

Leaning forward and resting his elbows on his knees, his eyes looking at the marsh in front of him, a small laugh bellowed, "Funny, the last time we were on a park bench, things didn't go so well."

"You're right. Are we about to have a repeat," my elbow pushing against his.

"I hope not. You don't have any more secret husbands that I need to know about, do you," eyeing me suspiciously.

My arm linking through his, my fingers lacing into his, finding his face, "Nope, not that I know of."

"Good," a quick smile replaced with a firm line. With a deep breath, "There's something I've been wanting to tell you for a long time and I needed to make sure it was the right time before I shared this with you." Now sitting quietly, I wasn't really sure where he was going with this conversation. Gently squeezing his hand for reassurance, "About three years ago, during one of my missions before I joined the Sharks, I was in a deep mission in the mountains of Afghanistan. I was deep undercover with the enemy when my cover was broken by an inside traitor of the organization. The leader of this group found out and placed me in captivity."

I wasn't sure where this was going, but I had a feeling this wasn't going to be a story I really wanted to hear. Continuing on, "In my training in the Army, we are taught to resist when in captivity and I never thought I would ever have to use this training in my career. While being held captive, this leader beat me, tortured me, I had become a Prisoner of War. As one of his tactics, he used a knife to cut just deep enough in my skin to leave the deep scars you see on my body." My fingers finding my eyes, wiping away the tears forming at the hurt I was hearing for the first time. Lifting his thumb, he helped wipe away a stray one, as he sniffed his nose...the story getting to him also.

I couldn't imagine the bravery it was taking for him to share this with me. With the little I was hearing, I now came to realize why he never told me before. Pausing for a moment, swallowing hard, "My last mission in the Army was to capture the man who took me prisoner, the one who had caused all my scars. Many people don't know that I was taken as a Prisoner of War."

"How long were you a prisoner," finally speaking up.

"6 months," his eyes straight forward, "I sat in cold, damp

rooms, not being allowed to go to the bathroom, barely having food to eat. They did everything they could to break my will," tears now streaming down his cheeks, his body visibly shaking from recalling the horrid details.

Shifting and leaning back against the bench, his arms crossing, you could hear the staggered breathing as he forced himself to push forward into his story, "Towards the end of my time as a POW, the Army put in a rescue operation. It was a nighttime rescue, but the leader received word and escaped the compound before they could capture him. They found me barely alive in one of the compound rooms. During my captivity, I made a vow that I would come out of this alive. I had to. Rebecca needed me and I had so much to look forward to here at home. I wasn't about to let these people destroy every part of me. When I recovered in the hospital, I committed to myself that my last mission would be to capture the man who tortured me. So, on this latest mission, I did just that, I caught him and I spared his life."

Jolting back at what he had said, "Wait, you spared his life? Why? Why let him go when he caused you so much pain?"

Finally looking at me, clarity evident in his green eyes, "You see I couldn't bring myself to cause him the same harm he caused me, although I have been trained to do that my entire career. It's what he expected and what he wanted. I didn't go in alone and plus my orders were to keep him alive. They arrested him and are putting him on trial, but first they are trying to gain as much intel as possible." Taking my hand in his, "I'm sorry I couldn't tell you sooner. No one knows the full story, except you and some of my higher ups in the Army, of course. I trust you Amber and I hope you can see why I couldn't tell you soon..." Grabbing his cheeks in my hands, I kissed him to stop him, providing the reassurance that he needed. Taking my one hand from his cheek and rubbing my knuckles, "Thank you," his forehead against mine, his eyes closed, his shoulders finally relaxing.

Lifting his chin, he opened his eyes to meet mine. Providing a reassuring smile, my heart still breaking inside, "I hope I didn't put a damper on today. I know it's supposed to be a happy day, but today marks a new beginning for many, and I needed to close that chapter."

"I understand," I said, "How about we go back and dance?" not trying to change the topic but more or less trying to lighten the mood. I now fully understood why he had kept this from me for so long. It was so much to take in and he couldn't share it without closure. I am guessing most don't get to have closure in situations like this. Tristan was different; he was a determined man. If anyone could get the closure needed, he could.

Giving me his dashing grin, "You got it," kissing my cheek. Standing, reaching for my hand, my fingers lacing in his, my other hand finding the strength of his arm. Looking up to him one last time, we headed back to finish celebrating with Kayla and Keith.

The End or Is It...

THERE IS HELP
OUT THERE...

If you or someone you know is a victim of domestic violence, there is help for you out there. Please call 1-800-799-SAFE or visit www.thehotline.org for more information.

Every state also has local shelters and help. Simply visit Google and search domestic violence hotlines.

Just remember, your life is precious and there is help for you out there.

AUTHOR'S NOTE

Dear Readers,

This book was written from the depths of my soul. You see I was a victim of domestic violence years ago. I had married a man who I wanted to spend the rest of my life with, only to become a victim of abuse. I didn't hide what was going on from family and friends and knew, in my heart, it would only escalate if I stayed.

It wasn't long after the hateful words and the physical abuse started that I decided to leave. It was psychological warfare for me. I had been under control of this person for so long, my body tore at the idea of even going back. Promises were made, but deep down I knew they would only be broken. My family put their foot down and said if I went back, they would not help me leave again. I knew I couldn't do it again without their support.

It wasn't long after these promises that the ugliness arose again and I knew I made the right decision. Shortly after leaving I met my soul mate that helped me overcome what I had gone through and be the person I am today.

Years later I still battled my subconscious. It was about 12 years to be exact and the idea for this book came to me. I began writing and couldn't stop. While I didn't encounter some of the abuse Amber did, a lot of what she went through I relate to and

I know many others do too. This book allowed me to heal a part of me that was broken for so long.

So in closing, I hope that if you are in a similar situation that you find the courage to leave, to seek help, or to find your voice. Domestic violence is not a joke and I want you to realize there is help for you out there. For those that did leave, remember you are a survivor; you are not a victim. Don't let anyone ever make you feel like you are a victim. I am proud of you for finding your voice and for standing up for what is right.

Love to all,

Lisa

ACKNOWLEDGEMENTS

This book wouldn't be possible without the love and support of my amazing husband. What started as a journey of self-healing from a similar abusive past, this book was an outlet for me to begin healing from one of the hardest times in my life. As the years carried on, and the book became even deeper to me, my wonderful husband encouraged me to publish the book. My hope is that someone reading this book will find the courage to leave an abusive relationship. There is help for you out there.

Next, I want to thank my amazing editors. This book has come so far from the start and without the amazing help of Melissa Habrat, I wouldn't have made it any further without her encouragement and knowledge in how to pursue further writing this. She really provided me the encouragement and motivation to keep writing. Her words provided me the confidence I needed to push through when I felt I couldn't.

After years of setting it aside due to mom life, I finally picked the pieces back up. Finalizing the book, I realized I needed an extensive review and edit. Lori Hill, an amazing schoolteacher, took the time out of her crazy schedule to provide me the edits necessary to make this book the best it can be. Through countless hours and meetings, celebrations are definitely in order for the completion of the first of many books to come.

And finally, I want to thank every one who has supported me

through the years. Whether it was healing, encouragement, con-versation, love, friendship, laughter or just a shoulder to cry on, the wisdom and lessons I have learned are invaluable to the life I currently live. Above all, I wouldn't be here without my Lord and Savior allowing this to be a part of my life's path.

Made in the USA
Columbia, SC
20 June 2019